A

CANDLELIGHT REGENCY SPECIAL

CANDLELIGHT ROMANCES

UNEXPECTED HOLIDAY

Libby Mansfield

A CANDLELIGHT REGENCY SPECIAL

Published by
Dell Publishing Co., Inc.
1 Dag Hammarskjold Plaza
New York, New York 10017

Copyright © 1978 by Paula Schwartz

Dell ® TM 681510, Dell Publishing Co., Inc.
ISBN: 0-440-19208-8
Printed in the United States of America
First printing—April 1978

CHAPTER ONE

The sound of a blow, followed by a sharp cry and the thump-ker-thump of a body rolling down the stairs, did not seem to disturb the two young men seated before the comfortable fire in the library of Carbery Hall, dispiritedly sipping their after-dinner brandies. The imperturbable gentlemen, Reginald Windle, Viscount Farnham and his friend James Everard, the someday-to-be Earl of Gyllford, were the guests of Geoffrey Carbery, an inattentive and irksome host who was, as usual, not to be found in their company.

"Did you hear thomething?" Reggie asked, his lisp emphasized by the effect of the brandy which was also beginning to show in the heightened color of his rather chubby cheeks. Though turned out most fashionably in an evening coat cut for him by Mr. Brummell's own tailor, Reggie was a stone-and-a-half too heavy to be considered a Dandy. However, his generous nature and his ever-ready propensity to share with his friends the enormous fortune with which his father had endowed him made him an extremely popular member of that set. Even his inability to disguise his lisp did nothing to diminish his popularity.

Opposite him, deep in a tall, winged chair, his friend Jamie nodded disinterestedly. James Everard, on whose boyishly handsome face no trace of brandy yet showed, was a well-built young man of twenty-two. His curly auburn hair and shapely legs would have been decided assets had he aspired to Dandyism, but he cared only for sports. He was held in high es-

teem among the Corinthians for his prowess in boxing and his skill as a horseman. He had little interest
in fashion. As Reggie had pointed out to him earlier
in the evening, his clothes looked positively careless.
His neckcloth was tied in a quite commonplace fold,
his shirtpoints were slightly wilted, and his breeches
revealed the merest suggestion of a crease at the hip-
line. But such were the depths of despond into which
the two friends had fallen that neither was much
disturbed by these solecisms. "Sounds like someone
falling," Jamie murmured in answer to Reggie's question.

"Do you think we ought to have a look?" Reggie suggested mildly.

Jamie sighed and put down his glass. "Might as
well," he said, getting up and stretching. "There's
nothing better to do."

Reggie took a last sip of brandy as Jamie crossed
the room and opened the door. "Good heavens!" he
exclaimed at the sight that met his eyes.

"It's Geoff!" gasped Reggie, just behind him in the
doorway.

There at the foot of the stairway lay their friend,
Geoffrey Carbery, rubbing his head and blinking his
eyes dazedly. Above him, halfway up the stairs, stood
Miss Evalyn Pennington, the governess of his young
sister and brother, and the cause of his shameful neglect of his guests. When Jamie and Reggie had accepted his invitation to visit Carbery Hall for some
good shooting while the autumn weather prevailed,
they had expected a busy, active fortnight. But Geoff
had taken one look at the governess and had been a
useless host from then on. If he wasn't following her
about on her walks with her charges, he was extolling
her charms to his bored and unsympathetic friends.
To no avail did Jamie point out to Geoff that his
mother would never permit an alliance with a governess; to deaf ears did Reggie repeat the observation
that Miss Pennington showed him not the slightest in-

terest or encouragement. Geoffrey was deeply immersed in his first love and, as Jamie remarked to Reggie—with all the authority of complete lack of experience or interest—calf love was not an affliction known to respond to reason or restraint.

"Geoff, are you hurt?" Jamie asked. "Miss Pennington, is he hurt?"

"That is precisely what I intend to ascertain," Miss Pennington answered coolly. She tucked the heavy volume she was carrying under her left arm, smoothed back a stray wisp of dusky hair with her right hand, and then came calmly down the stairs. "Will you be good enough to give me your assistance?" she asked, handing her book to the wide-eyed Reggie and kneeling down beside the fallen youth. Lifting Geoff's head onto her lap, she looked up at Jamie. "A brandy should do very well, I think," she said. Jamie shook himself into action, raced into the library, and hurried out with his own half-finished drink. He knelt beside his friend and forced the glass between Geoff's lips. At the first swallow, Geoff shuddered and lifted his head.

"What happened?" he asked foggily.

"I hit you with the Atlas," the calm Miss Pennington replied, "and you tumbled down the stairs. I think you have a slight bruise, here behind your left ear, but I'm convinced it is of little consequence. Do get up, sir, and permit me to return to the nursery."

But by this time, Geoffrey had noted with appreciation the position in which he was luxuriating and was reluctant to surrender it. "May I lie here for a minute or two, please," he pleaded, "until I feel a little more the thing?"

"Now don't be childish. Here are your friends, waiting to support you into the library where you will be much more comfortable stretched out on the sofa near the fire," Miss Pennington answered reasonably.

Jamie, filled with a combination of relief and disgust at his friend's words, began to put the pieces together. "Geoff, you devil's brat, don't tell me you accosted poor Miss Pennington right there on the stairs!"

"Well . . ." Geoff shifted in her lap uncomfortably.

"If that don't beat all!" Reggie exclaimed, shocked.

"Get up, you lobcock!" Jamie sputtered. "I wish she hadn't banged your head with that Atlas, so I could have done it properly, with my fists!"

Geoffrey groaned in anguish. "I didn't mean to . . . to . . . But after all, Evalyn, you never let me . . . You won't even listen to anything I have to say to you. . . !"

Miss Pennington sighed. This was not the first household in which she had been employed where a gentleman had been tempted to behave improperly. She was not aware that her dark curls framed a face which, while its features might be considered unexceptional, was made lovely by the serene expression of her mouth and the sparkling brightness of her grey eyes, nor that she carried her slim, shapely body with supple grace. The fact that several men, young and not-so-young, had allowed their attraction to her to find expression in improper advances was puzzling to her, for she was convinced that her behavior gave them not a jot of encouragement. In the past, the directness of her immediate rebuffs had sufficed to quell such amorous advances. This time, however, the smitten Geoffrey would not be discouraged. Even after she was brought to the necessity of defending herself with the Atlas, he still was persisting in his attempts to declare himself. She looked down at his head resting on her lap. "I know what you have to say to me," she said firmly, "and I've told you over and over that it is a subject which needs no further discussion. Now, if you wish to prevent further embarrassment to yourself and to me, please let Mr. Everard and Lord Reginald help you up and take you to—"

A scream from the top of the stairs interrupted her. They all looked up to find Lady Carbery staring down at them aghast. "Geoffrey! Geoffrey, my darling boy, what is it? What has happened to you?" she cried as she hurried down the stairs. Reg and Jamie hastily lifted Geoff to his feet. Miss Pennington rose gracefully and brushed out her skirts.

"It's nothing at all, Mamma," Geoffrey muttered uncomfortably, "nothing at all. A little fall. I was a bit dazed, that's all."

Lady Carbery's right eyebrow lifted suspiciously as she looked from one to the other. She was only partially relieved by the assurance that her eldest son had suffered no physical hurt. The presence of Miss Pennington in the midst of all this hugger-mugger made her large bosom swell with indignation. "Miss Pennington," she said in coldly ominous tones, "will you kindly explain your presence here, surrounded by all these . . . er . . . by my son and his guests?"

"I was just excusing myself, ma'am," Miss Pennington replied with her usual aplomb. "I was on my way to return this Atlas to the library. I had entertained little Algie with a bedtime tale of Samarkand, and he wanted to see where it was."

"Never mind fobbing *me* off with bedtime stories, Miss! I distinctly saw you sitting on the floor with my son's head in your lap!"

"Oh, now, I say!" Jamie couldn't help remonstrating.

Lady Carbery looked at him quellingly. Guest or no guest, James Everard would not be permitted to interfere in her management of her household. Jamie met her eye, lowered his, and choked back any further comment.

"No need to rip up at Miss Pennington, Mamma," Geoff put in heroically. "All she did was try to help me after I fell."

"I see," said Lady Carbery coldly. The inappropriateness of chastizing Miss Pennington in front of her son and his guests belatedly occurred to her. "Very well. We'll say no more on this matter now. However, Miss Pennington, after you have replaced the Atlas and seen to the children, please come to me in my dressing room." And with these dire words, she majestically turned and mounted the stairs.

Jamie looked at Miss Pennington sympathetically. "I'm afraid Geoff has placed you in a fix," he said.

"Please don't concern yourself about me, sir," Miss Pennington said politely. "Lord Reginald, if you would be so kind as to replace that book, I'll return to my duties." With a bow, she turned and made her way up the stairs, the graceful carriage of her head and the unhurried swing of her step giving no hint of inner agitation.

But later, the three gentlemen, seated around the library fire, could not rid themselves of their feelings of oppression and guilt. "Mamma is sure to give her notice. I've really done it this time," Geoff muttered dejectedly.

"I'll say you have," Jamie growled. "If ever I've met a worse gudgeon than you! To accost a girl living in your own home . . . ! It really beats all!"

"I know. But having her so near, and not being able to get her to listen to me—"

"Pleathe! Let'th not hear any more about your thuffering. We've heard nothing elthe for dayth on end!" said the aggrieved Reggie.

"Right!" Jamie seconded. "It's Miss Pennington we're concerned about, not you. What will the poor girl do if your mother turns her off?"

"I don't know. She's been in service ever since her father died and left her penniless. I suppose she'll have to look for another post. If only she'd consent to marry me . . ."

Jamie and Reggie groaned simultaneously. "Will you stop talking fustian?" Jamie exclaimed impatiently. "Your mother would never permit it."

"That doesn't matter. I'm of age."

Jamie looked at him with scorn. "Huh! You couldn't oppose your mother if you was eighty."

"And anyway," added Reggie, "Mith Pennington don't want any part of you."

"Just so," Jamie agreed, "so let's hear no more on that score. I was wondering . . . how is she to get another post? Won't she need a letter from your mother? A letter of commendation or some such thing?"

"A letter of commendation? Oh, my lord!" groaned Geoff. "If I know my mother, she'll turn her off without so much as a kind word."

"You don't mean it!" Reggie gasped, much shocked.

"Why would your mother turn her off without a recommendation? Miss Pennington didn't do anything at all reprehensible. It was you—"

"I know . . . I know. But mother thinks that Evalyn has been . . . has been . . ."

"Has been what?"

A flush suffused Geoff's bony cheeks. "Has been . . . er . . . setting her cap at me."

"If that don't take the cake!" Jamie said with disgust. "As if a beautiful creature like Miss Pennington would chase a scrawny, squint-eyed fool like you!"

"Well," Reggie put in reasonably, "you know what motherth are."

"No, I don't, not having had one since I was a baby. But never mind that. What, tell me, is Miss Pennington to do if she is turned off without a good recommendation?"

Geoff dropped his aching head into his hands. "I'm dashed if I know," he groaned.

Reggie got up and paced about helplessly. "Maybe one of uth could write a recommendation," he ventured.

Jamie glared at him. "That would be just the thing for a woman who wanted a nice, respectable governess for her brats—a recommendation from a bachelor!"

"Oh, I thee what you mean. Thorry."

Jamie sipped his brandy thoughtfully. "If only my Aunt Clarissa was here. She'd know what to—" His eyes lit up with sudden inspiration.

"What ith it, Jamie? Have you thought of thomething?" Reggie asked hopefully.

"Wait. Let me think. I may have a plan." The

others watched in respectful silence while Jamie sat immobile. Then he looked up. "How does this sound? I'll write to my Aunt Clarissa immediately, asking her and my father to invite Miss Pennington to spend the holidays with us. Then, as soon as the invitation arrives, I'll take Miss Pennington home to Gyllford with me. When Aunt Clarissa gets to know her, I'll warrant she'll take it on herself to get Miss Pennington suitably placed."

"Oh, capital!" exclaimed Reggie, clapping Jamie on the back. "That would be the very thing! And athk your aunt to have Lord Gyllford invite me too, while you're about it."

Geoff jumped up eagerly. "And me, too, Jamie. Perhaps if I were to see Evalyn outside my own home, she might change her mind about me."

Reggie and Jamie stared at Geoff in disbelief. "You!" Jamie said scornfully. "You, my boy, can whistle for it! You ain't going to be invited. We don't want you anywhere near that girl."

"Oh, I see how it is," Geoff muttered querulously. "You want her for yourself!"

"Who, me?" asked Jamie in surprise. "Don't be a harebrain. You know I ain't in the petticoat line. Besides, she's much too clever a female for my taste."

"Well, Reggie, then."

In response to that accusation, Reggie simply snorted. His shyness in the presence of females was too notorious to need mentioning.

"If neither of you is interested in her, why are you going to this bother? Why should you be concerned about her?"

Reggie shrugged. "Can't help it. Can't abide theeing anyone in trouble."

"It's only gentlemanly, after all," Jamie explained reasonably. "It wouldn't be at all the thing merely to ignore the poor chit's distress. Especially when the trouble was caused by our own friend and host."

"Very noble, I'm sure," Geoff said with chagrin. "But I don't see why I can't come too."

"Because she'd never agree to come if you made one of the party. Your crackbrained behavior has seen to that."

"And anyway," Reggie put in, "you'd do much better to stay here—at home with your Mamma."

Geoff gave Reggie a dagger look and returned sulkily to his chair. "Your aunt and your father might disappoint you," he said with sour satisfaction. "They may not wish to invite a perfectly strange female to spend the holidays with them. Did you ever think of that?"

Reggie and Jamie exchanged glances. For once, Geoff had scored a home thrust. Inviting a female to his home was not a thing Jamie had ever done.

"What do you think, Jamie?" asked Reggie in concern.

"Don't worry about Father and Aunt Clarissa," Jamie answered with an assurance he was far from feeling. "They'll come through. I know they will."

CHAPTER TWO

The Rutherford ball was in full swing. The dance floor was crowded with elegantly dressed couples, the card rooms were filling with smoke, the buffet tables were thickly surrounded, and the staircases were thronged with latecomers pushing their way up and early leavers inching their way down. It was obvious already that the Rutherfords were hosting the greatest squeeze of the season.

Philip Everard, the fourth Earl of Gyllford, stood in the immense hallway with his sister, Lady Steele, and surveyed the crush with dismay. "What a mob!" he muttered. "You should have warned me, Clarissa."

"If I had, you'd never have agreed to escort me," she retorted, handing her wrap to a waiting footman. "Now, come along like a dear boy, and don't glower."

"Might I not see you seated and take my leave? I'm sure Gervaise will be delighted to see you home," Philip suggested tentatively.

"Of all the shabby—! And after you promised faithfully that *this once* you would see the evening through! I gave my word to Letitia Rutherford that you would be here, so let's hear no more about scuttling off."

Philip grunted disconsolately. "I do not 'scuttle,'" he said under his breath as he cleared a path for his sister up the stairway with absentminded efficiency. It would have been hard for a stranger to guess that this ill-matched pair had descended from the same parents. Lord Gyllford, tall and spare, his dark hair slightly greying, seemed nevertheless to be younger than his forty-four years. Those observers who knew him even slightly could sense that only his good breeding and his sense of appropriate behavior for men of middle age kept his youthful energy in check. His sister, Clarissa Steele, reached only as high as his shoulder, a plump and placid matron who, though several years his junior, seemed older than he.

They were both widowed. Lord Gyllford had lost his wife after only six years of contented wedlock. Even his sister was not fully aware of the depth of that wound. Something deep within him had walled itself off, and a determination was born in him, somewhere below the surface of his mind, to avoid the possibility of suffering that pain again. None of the many lures set out for him by eligible ladies and designing Mammas had caused the slightest diminution of his determination not to remarry. When, a few years later, Clarissa's kind and good-natured husband,

Henry Steele, had succumbed to pneumonia, Philip had invited his sister to return to Gyllford, her childhood home, and run it for him. Happily for him and his son, the rapidly growing Jamie, Clarissa's cheerful warmth had made the absence of a wife and mother less painful, and the years had passed in adequate contentment, marred only by a nagging guilt at the back of Philip's mind that perhaps Clarissa had bypassed her opportunities for remarriage to make a home for him.

This sense of guilt caused him to leave his beloved Gyllford for a month each year to allow his sister to enjoy the excitement of London society. He himself found the entire stay a crushing bore. His active mind could find no satisfaction in the fripperies and pastimes of the London season. At Gyllford Manor he kept enormously busy with the management of his estate and with his writing, his secret vice and joy. He had had two books on political theory of a somewhat radical nature published under a *nom de plume* and was proud that not one of his acquaintance had ever guessed he had authored them. He was now busily at work on a third book, and the necessity of escorting Clarissa to London was a most unfortunate interruption.

Well, he was in for it tonight, he thought, and may as well make the best of it. Perhaps Gervaise and some of the political circle could get together in one of the card rooms . . .

"Philip?" Clarissa's voice cut in. "I insist that you stand up with some of the young ladies for the country dances."

Had the woman been reading his mind? Philip turned and frowned down at her with mock severity. "My dear Clarissa," he said, "I love you dearly and am eternally at your service, but I draw the line at gallanting young ladies on the dance floor. At my age, I think I may be considered exempt." And with that quelling statement, he guided his sister to the door of the ballroom and greeted his hosts with smiling composure. Lady Steele sighed, adjusted her turban, and did likewise.

On the other side of the room, Sally Trevelyan noted their entrance. So adept was she at social intercourse that none of the several young men surrounding her had any notion that she had been watching the door for the past half-hour. Miss Trevelyan had long since acquired the ability to seem to give her attention to several men at once while her mind wandered where it willed. She had been a reigning beauty for several seasons. Her spectacular loveliness, the sophistication and elegance of her manners, and her considerable fortune, made her the toast of the polite world. Each season, wagers were laid at White's on the likelihood of her succumbing to matrimony, but each season she remained unwed. Sought after as she was, Sally surprised everyone by resisting all suitors. But she loved to create surprises. She enjoyed being the center of attention. She enjoyed knowing her name was on everyone's lips. Why marry while she could attract hordes of admirers? Why marry while each season provided at least a dozen suitors for her hand? Sally flicked a green-eyed glance at the doorway where Philip Everard was being embraced by a simpering Lady Rutherford. Philip was the exception in Sally's mind, the one matrimonial prize she would have liked to win. But Philip had never asked her.

Sally turned to her entourage and dismissed them, saying lightly, "Ah, I see my friend, Mrs. Lanyon. Be off, will you? I wish to be private with her." She crossed the room alone, enjoying the stir her appearance made. Her blond hair was curled in the spectacular new style, *à la grecque,* and her shimmering green gown clung closely to her limbs as she walked. She knew the ladies on the sidelines were watching and gossiping. They suspected that she damped her dresses to make them cling. Well, let them suspect, she thought, tossing her curls arrogantly. They would do it too, had they the figures for it.

She dropped down in a chair next to Mrs. Lanyon with a sigh of relief. Alvina Lanyon was a young matron known to be fast, but the friendship suited Sally well, though she knew that the association was doing no good for her reputation. Alvina had a cool, calculating mind, much like Sally's own, and their intimacy was satisfying to both of them. Alvina was the only woman with whom Sally could be herself.

Alvina looked at Sally knowingly, glanced up at her current *cicisbeo* who was bending over her, and dispatched him for a glass of champagne. "Did you see who just came in?" Sally asked without preamble.

Alvina nodded. "He's finally made an appearance. I saw him carried off by our hostess," she murmured lazily.

"But now he seems to have disappeared. I wonder where he's gone."

"Into one of the card rooms, I should imagine."

"Yes, to talk the evening away with his cronies, blast the man!" Sally said.

Alvina laughed. "I don't see why you bother about him. The man is past forty, and if you ask me, he's rather frightening. Though I'll admit he's devilishly handsome."

"Don't be a fool. Philip has a brilliant mind, a great deal of address, a sharp wit when he bothers to show it, and a fortune that even I couldn't dissipate. There isn't a female in this room who wouldn't set her cap for him."

"I suppose you're right. But of what use is it to get yourself into a sulk? The Earl of Gyllford is obviously not interested in you—or in any romantic involvements. Forget him."

"No," Sally said, her lip curling in an unbecoming line of arrogance. "I don't intend to give up so easily."

Alvina looked at Sally in surprise. "You've not lost your heart to him, have you?"

"I don't know," Sally said thoughtfully. "I'm not at all sure what I feel." She had often asked herself that question. She knew that he attracted her, that she had set her cap for him and, to her chagrin, he had not responded. The more she had tried to attach him, the thicker had become the wall of cool reserve behind which he'd barricaded himself. Perhaps her feeling for Philip was merely the result of pique at her failure to attract him. But whatever the cause, she was determined to bring him to his knees, and she didn't care a jot if her feeling for him would outlast his capitulation. Her green eyes grew hard and feline as her mind jumped from scheme to scheme. "It would not be so difficult if I had some time alone with him," she said.

"Well, you're not likely to do it this season," Alvina said, leaning back. "I overheard Lady Steele inviting Martha Covington to Gyllford Manor for the Christmas holidays. That probably means they are planning to return to the country next week. You've missed your chance this year."

Sally turned her cat-like eyes on her friend speculatively. "Returning to the country, are they? Well, well, how delightful."

Alvina looked at her friend suspiciously. "What schemes are you concocting now, my dear?" she asked.

"Nothing so very shocking," Sally answered with a mysterious smile. "I was just thinking that a couple of weeks in the country might be the very thing I need. The very thing."

Lord Gyllford's London establishment, Gyllford House, was always quiet on the day following a large ball, for callers were turned aside to permit Lady Steele to remain in bed until well into the afternoon. Lord Gyllford invariably took advantage of the opportunity which the unwonted peacefulness permitted him to closet himself in his study and work at his writing. The day following the Rutherford ball was just such a day. Not until the rays of the December sun became too feeble to light his page did Philip realize that it was time to put his writing aside and join his sister for tea. With a sigh, he thrust the papers into a drawer and leaned back in his chair, stretching and yawning. At that moment, the door opened and Clarissa bustled in, arresting Philip's stretch in mid-air.

"Aha!" she said accusingly, "I've caught you at last."

"Caught me?" her brother asked innocently.

"Yes, my dear, you are caught in the act."

"In what act?"

"In the act of doing nothing. Yawning over an empty desk! It's just as I suspected. You don't do any work in here at all. It's your cowardly plot to hide away from human companionship before tea time."

Philip unfolded his tall frame from his chair and strode over to his sister. Putting his arm affectionately about her shoulders, he smiled down at her. "And why would I want to avoid the company of a woman of your great charm and wit?" he asked lightly.

"And beauty, too, my dear, don't forget that!" declared Clarissa, slipping her arm about his waist as they strolled across the hall toward the sitting room, where a well-laden tea table awaited them.

"How could I forget your beauty, when your face is smiling up at me so prettily? Philip rejoined, looking down at his sister's plump and pleasant countenance. "Of course," he added, "that ridiculous widow's cap which you insist on wearing hides too much of your greatest asset."

"Never you mind about my assets. It's only proper that a widow look like one." Clarissa patted the offending cap lightly and settled herself behind the teapot.

"In that case, I shall find myself obliged to do something to change your widowed state. The world should certainly be permitted to see more of your lovely hair."

"If that's a new way you've found of hinting that I

should accept Gervaise, I don't mind telling you that I shall be much obliged if you'd refrain from embarking on an old and long settled subject of dispute."

"What? Give up fighting Gervaise's battle? The poor man would never forgive me. You're a heartless, wanton female to allow Gervaise to waste away in loveless, lonely melancholy."

Clarissa laughed. "Waste away! He can afford to waste away—three stone at least! And as for lonely melancholy, he spends more time at Gyllford than he does at home."

"Exactly so. Perhaps if you'd marry him, I would see a bit less of him."

"I've never been given a better reason for getting married," retorted Clarissa. "It seems you are determined to get rid of me, either by hiding from me in your horrid study or packing me off to marry Gervaise."

"I may be guilty of the second, but acquit me, please, of the first offense. I've really been working all afternoon. I had just finished when you came bursting in. By the way, shall Gervaise be with us at Gyllford for the holidays?"

"Yes, indeed. There's no putting him off you know. And last evening I invited the Covingtons to come with their entire brood. And . . ." she paused guiltily.

Philip cocked a quizzical eyebrow at her. "And . . . ?"

"And . . . I've asked Sally Trevelyan, too."

"Sally Trevelyan?" asked Philip in surprise. "Why on earth—?"

"I don't know, Philip. She went out of her way to be pleasant to me last evening—you know, she can be quite delightful when she tries—and when she mentioned that she would be quite alone for the holidays, my heart went out to her."

Philip shook his head. "You're much too tenderhearted, my dear. But, Clarissa, I must warn you—if you have any ideas in that direction—that matchmaking is a dangerous business, especially involving me. After all these years, I hope you know that I'm not hanging out for a wife."

Clarissa threw up her hands. "Heavens, Philip, don't eat me. Weren't you doing the same to me not a moment ago? Besides, Sally knows by now that you're a hardened case. She won't be so foolish as to set her cap at you again."

"Well, then, her holiday will be a sad bore, with no one to flirt with. Let's hope Jamie brings home a few friends, so that Sally and the Covingtons' girl may have some game to snare."

"Good heavens!" Clarissa gasped. "I forgot to tell you about Jamie! That's why I burst in on you in the study. We've had a note from him."

"Good. What has that scapegrace son of mine to say?"

"You'll never believe it! He wants you to invite a friend of his for the holidays. A young lady!"

"A young lady? You don't mean it! Jamie?"

"That's what he writes." Clarissa pulled a letter from her pocket and handed it to her brother. Philip scanned it quickly.

"It sounds quite mysterious. 'A young lady of my acquaintance.' What are we to make of that?"

"I've no idea, I'm sure. And what sort of young lady would ask to be invited?" Clarissa mused, a bit troubled.

"Do you mean you think she's not quite proper? I hardly think—" Philip read the letter again. "No, I'm quite sure you've misinterpreted. *He* is doing the asking, not she. This Miss Pennington knows nothing about it as yet, I'll wager."

Clarissa took the letter and read it once more. "You may be right. Well, then, shall we invite her?"

"Certainly. I can't wait to see what manner of female has attracted my scamp of a son. I can't believe that Jamie is taken with a girl."

"Why not, Philip? He's twenty-two. He's certain to get, as he calls it, leg-shackled sooner or later."

Philip frowned. "Leg-shackled? There's no question of that, surely?"

"No?" teased Clarissa. "Why not? You'd been married for two years by the time you were his age."

"That's true enough. Jamie was born when I was twenty-two. But times were different then. We were more serious at that age. More responsible."

"Perhaps," said Clarissa with a knowing smile, "but boys do grow up, even now. Oh, dear . . . Philip! You may be a grandfather before long."

"A grandfather?" Philip looked at his sister in dismay. "A *grandfather!* Good God!"

CHAPTER THREE

Evalyn Pennington folded her last garment into a well-worn portmanteau, put the two halves together, and cinched the straps. The work was not laborious; her possessions were meagre, making the traveling bag quite easy to lift and carry. She placed the bag near the door and took a last look at the small, neat room which had been her home for two years. She felt no twinge of sentimentality on leaving it, for it had not been a happy home. Although comfortable and warm (for Lady Carbery had never begrudged her a fire or clean linens), she had never been made to feel part of the family. Lady Carbery had an unyielding and unaffectionate nature, and she made sure that everyone understood that Evalyn was nothing more than a servant at Carbery Hall. Even the children were imbued with that awareness, thus making her position as their mentor and guide all the more difficult.

Among the servants, however, she was a person apart. Her gentle voice and serene disposition endeared her to all of them, but, aware of her superior birth and education, they could not help but treat her with diffidence and constraint. She was a lady, no matter how Lady Carbery tried to demean her, and the servants instinctively knew better than to make her one of their own.

In the five years since she had entered service, Evalyn had never given any outward indication of her loneliness. She had been reared by her father, Captain Pennington of the —th Foot. Back in '77, at the age of twenty-five, he'd been wounded at Saratoga, had returned to England, retired on a modest pension, married, and set up his small establishment in the quiet of the Devon countryside. For many years, Captain and Mrs. Pennington had yearned to have a child, but by the time one was conceived, they had quite given up hope. Evalyn's mother was past thirty at the time of her birth, and she died shortly after the new-born Evalyn was placed in her arms. Captain Pennington was then forty years old, and although he loved his daughter dearly and gave her the best care and education that his means could provide, he could not change the reserve which his military life had imposed upon his disposition. His wound had left him partially crippled and often in pain, but he had never complained nor asked for sympathy. In fact, any sign of pity from his loved ones or the servants would make him irritable in the extreme. Thus Evalyn grew to maturity without the nourishment of female tenderness, and without acquaintance with feminine tears and vapors. With the spartan behavior of her father as her only model, Evalyn learned to control her emotions, to eschew tears, and to disdain self-pity.

Had she not been her father's daughter, Evalyn might well have given way to self-pity now. Her interview with Lady Carbery had been insulting and humiliating. Lady Carbery's hints that Evalyn had set her cap for the scrawny and unprepossessing Geoffrey would have been laughable if the remarks were not followed by a prompt dismissal from her post, without so much as a notice to recommend her to another employer. The only things which stood between her and destitution were the meagre savings in her reticule and the address of a distant cousin whom she had never met. Her plan, conceived in desperation, was to use her savings to buy passage to London, there to find her cousin and beg for bed and board until she could find a new position. With one last glance around the unloved room, she tied her cloak at the neck, raised her hood, picked up the portmanteau and left the room.

Her goodbyes to the household staff having already been said, she was glad the stairs and hallway were deserted. She quietly let herself out the front door and closed it behind her. To her surprise, she found Lord Reginald and James Everard standing on the stone steps leading down to the avenue, almost as if they had been lying in wait for her.

"Good morning, Miss Pennington," said Jamie with a slight bow.

Evalyn answered with a hurried curtsey. "Excuse me, sirs, but I must ask you to let me by. The London stage leaves from the inn in less than an hour, and it is almost a mile's walk from here."

"You're not planning to go to London?" asked Reggie in chagrin.

"Why, yes, sir."

"Did you find a position already, Miss Pennington?" Jamie asked. "Please excuse me for appearing to pry into your affairs, but I have been . . . that is, we both have been concerned about you."

"That is most kind in you, but there's no need for concern. I'm going to visit a cousin for a time, until I can find a new position."

"But, Mith Pennington, will you be able to? I mean, with no letter of commendation . . . ?" Reggie asked worriedly.

Evalyn smiled as bravely as she could. "I'm sure something will turn up. Perhaps my cousin has some connections."

"*Perhaps?* Don't you know?" Jamie asked, puzzled.

"Well, I am not yet acquainted with her. But please, sirs, I must hurry along. Do excuse me, and thank you for your concern."

Jamie and Reggie stared nonplussed as Miss Pennington started off down the avenue. Then Jamie ran after her and took the portmanteau from her hand. "May we not escort you to the inn? Reggie and I have a matter which we'd like to discuss with you."

Evalyn hesitated. If Lady Carbery were observing her departure from an upstairs window, Evalyn's acceptance of the escort of two young gentlemen would certainly add fuel to the fire of her ladyship's suspicions. Well, thought Evalyn, let her think the worst! Lady Carbery had done her all the harm she could. Evalyn put her chin up defiantly, nodded her acquiescence to Jamie, and walked off down the avenue with an escort at each side.

It was Reggie who launched into an explanation. "We jutht wanted to apologize for the dithguthting conduct of our friend," he said, "and . . . and . . ." Here his courage faltered.

"It was the most shocking bad taste," Jamie went on, "to say nothing of the disastrous results it has had—making you lose your post through no fault of your own."

"Yes," agreed Miss Pennington, "but since you both have expressed your sympathy several times already, I don't see—?"

Before she could finish, Jamie held out to her a sealed missive which Evalyn saw with surprise was addressed to her. She opened it, and her eyes flew over the words. Lord Gyllford and his sister sent their warmest regards and cordially invited her to spend the Christmas holidays at Gyllford Manor. What did it mean? "I don't understand," she said, looking from Jamie to Reggie questioningly. "I've never had the pleasure of meeting your father and his sister."

"I asked them to invite you," Jamie explained. "You see, it seemed to us that you would find it difficult to acquire a new post without a letter of commendation."

"Yes, that's true, but I still don't see—"

"My Aunt Clarissa could help you. She has so many friends in Devonshire. Surely one of them must have need of a governess."

"But would she recommend me for such a post without knowing me?" Miss Pennington asked reasonably. "She could scarcely, in good conscience, do such a thing, especially with the knowledge that Lady Carbery has turned me off."

"But that's the beauty of my idea!" Jamie explained eagerly. "She's bound to get to know you if you're our house guest for the holidays. And then I'm sure she won't feel any hesitation in recommending you."

The lane they were following took a turning into the wind. The many capes of Reggie's greatcoat flapped briskly, Jamie turned up his collar and pushed his hands deep into his pockets, but Evalyn didn't even notice the sudden chill. Mr. Everard's kind invitation had thrown her mind in a turmoil. She could not deny the attractiveness of his plan. The possibility of two weeks as a guest in a comfortable home, a Christmas holiday in which she would be treated with civility, even kindness, and the prospect of being assisted to find a new post, all these were infinitely more desirable than the prospect of begging for board from an unknown relative, and searching for employment without aid. But the proposal was too good to be true. She could not accept. There were too many obstacles.

She stopped and turned to Jamie. "Your generosity and concern quite overwhelm me, sir. I can't think why you should have taken this trouble about me. But you must see that I cannot accept."

"No, ma'am, I can't say that I see that at all, can you, Reg?"

"No, indeed," said Reggie earnestly," it theemth like an exthellent plan to me."

"But surely you both realize that it would be highly improper for me to travel alone in Mr. Everard's company," Miss Pennington explained shyly.

"Oh, but I'll be going along too," Reggie said with pride in having settled a ticklish problem with dispatch.

"Don't be an idiot, Reg," Jamie muttered. "You would scarcely be viewed as a proper chaperone for a young lady. Miss Pennington's right. We need another female with us."

The three of them walked on in silence. Just as the inn came into view, Reggie chortled. "I have it!" he exclaimed. "We'll hire an abigail."

"An abigail?" asked Jamie, his eyes lighting up. "You mean some village girl?"

"There mutht be thome girl at the inn who would be thuitable. What do you think, Mith Pennington?"

"I think you are most generous, but I couldn't dream of allowing you to undertake such an expense in my behalf."

"Nonsense," Jamie put in firmly. "On that score I will not allow you to voice an objection. Reg has so much of the 'ready' in his pockets that he'll not even notice the expenditure. The problem is solved, and you must now agree to come with us to Gyllford."

Evalyn couldn't help but laugh at Jamie's readiness to spend Lord Reginald's money. Her laughter broke the strain and changed their moods completely. They refused to take seriously any one of the number of objections she tried to put forth. Their good spirits couldn't help but affect her own. The deep dejection which her plight had put upon her seemed miraculously to evaporate. A Christmas holiday at Gyllford!

The thought of it lightened her heart and lifted her hopes. It was too tempting a prospect to refuse.

Still laughing, they swept her into the inn. Over her much-weakened objections, they looked for a girl to hire to be her abigail. The ridiculousness of the thought that she, a governess, would arrive at Gyllford with her own abigail made her laugh again. Within a very few minutes, the innkeeper's red-cheeked, excited niece had been engaged, and had run off to pack her belongings. Then Reggie, in his grandest manner, demanded a private dining room in which Miss Pennington was to wait for them while they returned to Carbery Hall to take their leave.

Alone and breathless, Evalyn went to the window of the dining room. It overlooked the inn yard, where, in the midst of much noisy bustle, the London stage was being readied for departure. The passengers were squeezing aboard, the luggage was being tied to the top, the ostlers were running about checking the horses. Evalyn felt a twinge of misgiving. If she had a proper sense of conduct and decorum, she would now be aboard that coach, crowded in among the passengers, heading for a bleak and unknown future. Instead, she was soon to be heading in quite another direction, in a private, luxurious coach, with her own abigail in attendance, and a full fortnight of holiday before her. Undoubtedly her character was not as strong as she had supposed. She was sadly wanting in rectitude. But her awareness of this weakness in her character did nothing to dispel a sense of happy anticipation such as she had never felt before. As she watched the London stage lumber off, there was not a glimmer of regret in her shining eyes.

Jamie and Reg walked back to Carbery Hall to pack their belongings and make their farewells. They were quite satisfied with themselves; they had done a good deed, and they had succeeded in spite of some ticklish problems. "I think we sailed rather neatly over some rough waters," Jamie boasted as they walked briskly down the lane toward Carbery Hall.

"Yeth," agreed Reggie, "but I don't think it will be all clear thailing ahead."

"Why not? My Aunt Clarissa will handle things from here on," Jamie assured him airily.

But Reggie shook his head. "Your father and your aunt are bound to wonder why you brought her," he said thoughtfully. "Mith Pennington'th a mighty pretty thing. I'd wager anything you like that they'll think you're enamored of the girl."

Jamie hooted. "What? Me? You're addlebrained. They know me better than that! If you're making yourself uneasy over such nonsense, you're crazier than a coot!"

CHAPTER FOUR

A *grandfather!* The word had burst upon Philip with the effect of a gunshot. Now, two weeks later, back at home at Gyllford, it still had a way of jumping into his mind. He stood at his shaving mirror and stared at his reflection. The hair at his temples had already turned more grey than black. When had it happened? How was it possible he had not noticed it before? Those grey hairs had encroached upon his head as the years had encroached upon his youth, in stealthy stages, bit by bit. He remembered how he had laughed at the first pale hair that had appeared among the dark, as if that grim reminder of the impending future were a joke of nature. The reality of aging had seemed

so far in the future that the warning had appeared
ludicrous. But now, before he had had a chance to
accustom himself to the realization, he had become
quite grey, and his youth had disappeared.

A grandfather. Philip shook his head and grinned
at himself ruefully. He was not usually given to such
mawkish, feminine musings. Besides, Jamie wasn't
even married yet! Forty-four years of life did not make
one ancient, not by any means. What he needed was a
good breakfast, a brisk walk on the grounds of his beloved Gyllford, and a couple of hours at his desk,
wrestling with the logic of his antagonist, Burke, to
put him in a more sensible frame of mind. But the
lift that the thought of his writing always gave him
was soon dispelled by the realization that his house
was filling with guests. Gervaise and Sally were already in residence, and the whole Covington family
was expected to arrive this afternoon. The duties of a
host would keep him from his desk all day. He sighed
and, his depression returning, he went reluctantly
down to breakfast.

Clarissa and Sally were already settled at the table
in the breakfast room, drinking their second cups of
chocolate. Gervaise was lingering over the sideboard,
loading his plate from the generous buffet with cold
meats, smoked fish and coddled eggs. The sight of his
cheerful countenance did a little to lift Philip's
spirit. Gervaise's very appearance occasioned smiles.
He always tried valiantly to dress as befitted a man of
style and substance, but his girth and his indolent
nature were constantly at war with his clothing, and
winning. Without warning, a button would come loose
here, a seam would split there. His much-harried valet
would send him forth tailored and pressed to perfec-
tion, but Gervaise would return to the dressing room
before long, looking sadly rumpled and shabby. Now,
just minutes after leaving his dressing room, his waistcoat buttons already gave the appearance of being

strained beyond their strength. Philip was sure the middle one would pop off before Gervaise's breakfast was completely consumed. All unconcerned, Gervaise's eyes twinkled and his round cheeks creased in a welcoming smile for Philip.

"There you are, my boy," he greeted warmly. "We've been wondering if you had overslept this morning."

"I must apologize to you all. I had no idea you would all be so prompt. I dawdled in front of my mirror, I'm afraid."

"Not you, Philip, surely. I've never known you to do so before," Clarissa said in amused surprise.

"That is because you never told me how grey I'm growing, my dear. I noticed it this morning with quite a shock."

"Nonsense!" Sally laughed. "It makes you look quite attractively distinguished."

Philip bowed his thanks and turned to the sideboard. Was Sally still determined to pursue a useless flirtation with him? Bother the holidays, he thought, bother the guests and bother this whole interruption of his pleasant life's routine! His day was quite cut up.

Sally Trevelyan looked at him musingly. If he had calculated a manner meant to attract her, he couldn't have found a better. As he turned back to the breakfast table with his plate of beef and eggs, she motioned him to the seat beside her. Philip seemed not to notice; he took a seat beside his sister. Sally smiled to herself. Let the man struggle. She had two lovely weeks before her—there was plenty of time.

The Covingtons arrived at mid-afternoon. Hutton, the Gyllfords' imperturbable butler, announced the arrival of the carriage to Lady Steele and managed to throw open the front door, descend the steps and take a magisterial stance at the bottom before the coach had come to a complete stop—and all without hurrying his usual dignified gait. Clarissa and Philip followed soon after, making an impressive welcoming party for the new arrivals.

The six-year-old twins spilled from the carriage first, racing past their hosts and up into the hall with all the abandon that five long hours of suppressed energy can stimulate in little boys. They were followed out of the carriage by their sister Marianne, a seventeen-year-old miss with bouncy curls and warm blue eyes now shining with the excitement caused by this prolonged escape from the schoolroom. Next came her father, Edward Covington, his usual worried, anxious expression covered over with a smile of relief that the journey had ended without mishap. Twenty years of marriage to the good-natured Martha had etched a number of worried creases into his forehead and a sense of nervous fearfulness into his spirit. Marriage to Martha was a series of crises and disasters for which, he had to admit, she was neither to blame nor able to resist generating.

Martha was helped out of the carriage, and she eagerly hugged and kissed Clarissa and Philip with effusive warmth. Then she turned to the footmen who were attempting to unload the great number of boxes and trunks which the Covingtons found necessary for their survival away from home. "Be careful with that one, please," she urged, "for it contains all the children's gifts for Christmas morning. And that one has the wine, does it not, Edward? Clarissa, we've brought you some of that excellent Madeira Edward discovered on the Continent last year. Oh, and that one goes to Marianne's room, if you please."

Keeping up a steady stream of warnings and instructions, Martha moved with the rest of the party to the front hallway. This large, high-ceilinged room had become a sea of activity. Old friends were greeting each other with kisses. Children were being tossed in the air. Wraps were being removed and carted off up the stairs. Footmen were weaving their way through the press loaded with boxes and trunks. Suddenly, one of the twins, having had enough of the petting and patting of his elders, darted across the stone floor without heed and collided with a footman who was staggering toward the stairway under the burden of a large trunk which he carried on his back. The impact caused the man to stumble, the trunk fell to the floor with a tremendous crash, and burst wide open.

The entire assemblage gasped and turned to stare at the wreckage. Martha's corsets, stays and undergarments, and the pots of rouge she had hidden among them, all lay exposed to public view. Martha, aghast, responded as she always did in times of crisis—she swooned. Clarissa and Edward bent over her, administering vinaigrette and soothing murmurs. The guilty twin burst into tears. The servant stammered his apologies. Lord Gyllford tried to still the hubbub by urging all the other guests into the library where a fire and refreshments were waiting.

In the midst of this confusion, the front door opened to admit Jamie and his party. The little group, rosy-cheeked and in excellent spirits after an invigorating ride through the English winter countryside, stood stock still surveying the chaos, their smiles fading into puzzled concern.

Lord Gyllford came forward to greet them. "Don't look so appalled," he said, smiling reassuringly at his son. "We've had a bit of an accident with a trunk, but it will all be set right in a few minutes. How do you do, Reggie? It's good to have you with us."

"Sir, I'd like you to meet Miss Evalyn Pennington. Miss Pennington, this is my father."

Philip turned, looked down into Miss Pennington's upturned face and felt an unfamiliar lurch somewhere deep in his chest. The serene grey eyes smiling up at him were set in a face whose sweetness of expression struck him with complete surprise. Could this calm, composed, and lovely creature possibly be the choice of his immature, scatterbrained son? He felt quite breathless with shock as, for one frozen moment while he stared at her, the world around him ceased to exist.

Miss Pennington bowed. "How do you do, my lord," she said quietly. "It was most kind in you to invite me. We seem to have arrived inopportunely, I'm afraid."

Philip recovered himself at once. "Not at all," he said, a reassuring smile lighting his face. "This is quite normal behavior in our household."

Clarissa bustled up in time to hear his words. "Philip, what a dreadful thing to say! How do you do, Miss Pennington? Please forgive this confusion. If you'll bear with us until Mrs. Covington is recovered, we'll be able to see to your comforts as we should. Reggie, my dear, how good to see you! And Jamie, love, it's good to have you home."

With a quick kiss for Jamie and a hug for Reggie, Clarissa turned to go back to the side of the still swooning Martha. A small, involuntary sigh escaped her at the sight before her——the maids hastily gathering up armfuls of lingerie and running up the stairs with them; Gervaise and Sally bending over the prostrate Martha; Edward Covington shaking his head and muttering, "I knew it, I knew something had to happen," under his breath; and the twins, as boisterously as if nothing had happened, chasing each other up and down the staircase.

"I beg your pardon, ma'am," came a soft, calm voice behind her, "but may I be of assistance? I would be glad to take the little boys and settle them in."

Clarissa looked at Miss Pennington with an expression of gratitude and relief. "Oh my, that would be most helpful, and most kind in you. . . ."

"But my dear," Lord Gyllford objected, "it would be unforgivable of us to put a guest to work, like a governess, as soon as she puts her foot in the door. We could not so impose on her."

"If you please, my lord, I would not feel in the least imposed upon. I *am* a governess, after all, and

I'd be grateful to be permitted to make myself useful." And without waiting for an answer, Miss Pennington handed her cloak and gloves to a waiting servant and gracefully crossed the floor. Philip and Clarissa stared after her as she spoke a few words to a young woman they took to be her abigail. Then the astounding Miss Pennington took each of the twins firmly in hand and in seconds had disappeared with them around the bend of the stairway.

"Governess? Did she say governess?" Clarissa asked Jamie in surprise.

Jamie grinned down at his puzzled aunt. "Yes, she did. Wonderful, ain't she? Don't worry about it. I'll explain later."

Jamie and Reggie moved into the hall, greeting the others. Martha soon revived, and by slow degrees the whole party made its way to the library, where hot soup and mulled brandy did much to restore order and good spirits. But Philip gave scant attention to the laughter and banter around him. He was staring at his son. Jamie must possess depths beyond his ken. He had brought home a young woman who, although obviously beneath him in station and wealth, seemed vastly superior in character. Certainly she was not at all the sort of young woman whom Philip would have thought likely to attract a young buck so newly on the town. Philip had to admit that the sight of Jamie's choice had completely surprised him. In the past, he had prided himself on the aplomb with which he had withstood the shocks, disappointments and worries of fatherhood. But this time . . . well, this time Jamie had shaken him profoundly.

CHAPTER FIVE

When guests were lodged at Gyllford Manor, the two hours before dinner became the quietest time of day. The ladies were closeted with their abigails, who carefully dressed their hair; the gentlemen either stole a little time for a nap, or discussed with their valets the costume for the evening. Philip availed himself of the temporary lull in the day's activities to visit his son for a *tête à tête*. He found Jamie standing in front of his mirror doing violence to the third neckcloth with which his valet had provided him. Wellstock, the meek and modest manservant who had served Lord Gyllford for years, was always happy when Jamie was at home. Since Lord Gyllford rarely requested his assistance, it was only when young Everard was on the premises that Wellstock could employ his considerable talents as a sartorial expert to the full. Now he hovered about his charge, his face not quite masking the mixed emotions he was experiencing—delight to be assisting a gentleman of fashion again, and dismay at the sight of Jamie mangling his beautifully ironed neckcloths. On Wellstock's arm hung three more freshly pressed cloths which, he was certain, were destined for a similarly tragic fate. Lord Gyllford surveyed the scene with amusement. "I see you have not yet learned to make a simple fold," he remarked to his son.

Jamie sighed and cast the crushed linen into Wellstock's waiting hand. "I seem to be all thumbs when it comes to tying these cursed things," he grumbled, placing number four around his neck.

"Never mind. I'll show you an easy fold I've developed," Philip reassured him. He smiled at Wellstock's ill-disguised expression of offense. "I know I won't do as well as you, Wellstock, but I think you may safely leave him in my care."

The valet reluctantly took the hint and bowed himself out of the room. Philip, standing behind his son, tied the cloth in a few dexterous movements. "There. That should do."

"It's excellent, father! A capital fold! What do you call it?"

"Call it?" Philip's eyes twinkled. "Well, let's see. Since it's so simple that even you can learn it, why not call it *the Incapable?*"

Jamie grinned back at his father. "Never mind," he said. "I'll call it something modish, like *the Arabesque* or *the Windfall*. That ought to impress Reggie and the other Dandies of my acquaintance." He gave the neck-cloth an affectionate pat and turned away from the mirror. "Please sit down, sir. I suppose you've sent Wellstock away because you want to scold me about something. What have I done now?"

"Scold you? What makes you think that?"

"Isn't that what fathers always do when they arrange to speak to their sons privately?"

"Is scolding the only private communication possible between a father and son? What a lowering thought! No, I had no such intention when I sought you out." Philip looked at his son keenly. "Is there something on your conscience that requires a scold?"

"I was afraid you might be put out about Miss Pennington. Do you mind that I brought her here?"

"Mind? Of course not. Why should I?"

"I don't know. Reggie thought you might not like being saddled with a strange female for the holidays. And a governess to boot."

"I admit to being surprised. She's not the sort of person I would have expected you to bring home. But she seems a most well-bred and charming young lady, and we're glad to have her with us."

"I knew it!" Jamie exclaimed in relief. "That's what I told Reg. I assured him that once you and Aunt Clarissa got to know her, there'd be no problem."

"Problem?"

"Yes. Having a governess as a guest. Reggie thought it might be awkward."

"I hope you told Reggie that your aunt and I are not such snobs."

"Oh, he didn't think that!" Jamie said hastily. "He only thought that you might not want to concern yourselves—"

"How foolish of Reggie. Surely you both must realize that anything that concerns you concerns us. A fine parent I should be if I failed to be interested in all your concerns."

"I knew you'd feel that way. But I must admit it's a relief to hear you say it. Evalyn—that is, Miss Pennington—deserves a bit of a holiday, you see. Lady Carbery is a real dragon to work for. She treated Evalyn as if she were a . . . a . . . cook maid! Never gave her a kind word. And then, with Geoff accosting the poor girl wherever she went, well, you can imagine what a dreadful time she's had."

"It would certainly seem so," said Philip, trying unsuccessfully to picture Jamie's involvement in that scene of domestic contretemps.

"Not that Miss Pennington ever complained," Jamie went on earnestly. "Not she. She always handled everything with the most remarkable coolness. You should have seen her give Geoff a leveler. Knocked him down the stairs with an Atlas!"

"You don't mean it! That gentle little thing?"

"Word of a gentleman! Knocked him right on his keester. And then came down the stairs as calm as you please and brought him to. And when Lady Carbery appeared, Evalyn was not in the least flustered. Carried it off as if she were serving tea, by God! Really, she's the most redoubtable girl."

Philip couldn't help smiling. What Jamie's description of his beloved lacked in romantic terminology was certainly compensated for in enthusiasm. Oh, well, he thought, literature is full of cases of unlikely matches. Cupid is said to be blindfolded when he shoots his darts. If his son chose to give his heart to a *redoubtable* girl, Philip had no objection. Jamie could have chosen much less wisely.

"Do you think Aunt Clarissa will like her?" Jamie asked.

"Of course she will. I think she likes her already. The way your Miss Pennington took over the twins this afternoon made a wonderful impression on both of us."

"Good. Then Aunt Clarissa won't have any objections to making the arrangements after the holidays?"

"What!" exclaimed Philip, shocked. "After the holidays? As soon as that?" Surely his son could not be contemplating such a hasty marriage. "There's no cause . . . er . . . there couldn't be any special reason for . . . er . . . urgency, could there?"

Jamie looked puzzled. "Urgency? No, of course not. We just thought that after the holidays might be a good time."

"Do you mean that you and Miss Pennington have already discussed a date?"

Jamie had an uncomfortable feeling for a moment that he had missed something in this conversation. "Well, no," he explained patiently, "I haven't said much to Miss Pennington yet. I wanted to discuss it with you and Aunt Clarissa first."

"You haven't yet asked Miss Pennington?" Philip was at a loss. Just how far had this affair gone? "I'm afraid, Jamie, that I'm a little confused. Do you and Miss Pennington have . . . an understanding?"

Jamie was shrugging himself into his coat. Now that

he knew his actions had the approval of the family, he was finding the subject of Miss Pennington a bit of a bore. "An understanding? Well, yes, I guess you could say that. She understands why she's here, of course. I told her she was sure to win your approval—and Aunt Clarissa's too—in a week or two."

"But surely you didn't think we could make satisfactory arrangements in so short a time!"

"Well, as to that, it certainly doesn't matter to me how long it takes. We could leave it for Aunt Clarissa and Miss Pennington to decide, couldn't we?"

Philip stared at his son in amazement. Jamie had very easily been persuaded to delay his plans. The switch from loverlike impatience to reasonable indifference was most confusing. The younger generation was quite difficult to understand. Philip sighed and rose. "Well, I'll tell your aunt to give the matter some thought. Miss Pennington seems to be a sensible young lady. Between the two of them, I'm sure they'll know what's to be done."

"That's what I told Reg. Leave it to my aunt, I told him. We won't have to trouble our heads about a thing."

Philip blinked. "What has Reg to do—? No, never mind. I'd better go talk to your aunt before the guests assemble for dinner." And Philip retreated hastily out the door.

A few minutes later, Jamie sat watching Reggie make a final inspection of his attire. Lord Reginald was resplendent in a coat of blue superfine covering a waistcoat of yellow satin embroidered with flower baskets in which each flower was a tiny jewel.

"How do I look?" Reggie asked, turning slowly before the critical eyes of his friend.

"That waistcoat—well, I don't know. Don't you think it's a bit overpowering?"

"Overpowering? How can you think that? You know nothing about thtyle."

"Then why did you ask me? Anyway, I didn't come in here to inspect your waistcoat. I just want to let you know that the Pennington matter is settled. I've told my father the whole story, and he says Aunt Clarissa will take care of everything."

"Oh, capital! I mutht thay, Jamie, it'th very kind of your father and your aunt. I don't think my mother would go to tho much trouble for a mere nobody."

"My father doesn't like to think of people as nobodies. Y'know, I sometimes think my father is a radical thinker. Anyway, we've done our part, and now we can forget it. Let's go downstairs. I want to get another look at that little Marianne Covington. She's grown up to be quite a taking little thing. Did you notice?"

"No, I didn't," responded Reggie flatly, "and I hope, Jamie, that you're not going to turn out ath big a bore ath Geoff."

Meanwhile, Philip was apprising Clarissa of his chat with Jamie. "The long and short of it is," he told her, "that Jamie wants to marry Miss Pennington as soon as the holidays are over."

"As soon as that?" gasped Clarissa. "You can't be serious."

"That's what he told me. But he's perfectly willing to wait as long as you and Miss Pennington think necessary."

"How strange! Does he want us to announce the engagement right away?"

"I didn't think to ask him that. He says they have an understanding. Believe me, Clarissa, that's more than I have. His attitude is completely confusing to me."

Clarissa looked at her brother tenderly. The idea of his having a married son was just too new to him. He needed time to become accustomed to it. "Don't worry, dear," she said consolingly, "we needn't do anything at all until after the holidays. By that time, we shall have grown accustomed to seeing them together, and the whole matter will seem much less shocking. Give it a little time."

"I suppose you're right," Philip agreed.

"We'll go on as usual. There's no need to announce anything until we get to know Miss Pennington better. We won't make any definite plans until after the new year, when all the guests have gone. That seems reasonable, doesn't it?"

"Quite reasonable."

They left Clarissa's room and headed for the stairway. It would not do to be absent while the guests assembled. "At least we may thank our stars that she's such a fine, sensible, imposing girl. Quite lovely, in fact," Clarissa remarked cheerfully.

"Not lovely," Philip said with a sudden grin, *"re-doubtable."*

CHAPTER SIX

Evalyn sighed with pleasure as Nancy, her one-day abigail, brushed her hair to a soft glow. Everything in the room glowed. There was a cheerful fire in the grate that lit the hangings of the large four-poster bed with a golden light. The paneling of the walls gleamed. The panes of the tall windows sparkled with reflected firelight. Evalyn had never slept in a room so large and beautiful.

Nancy seemed to read her mind. "Ain't this place fine, Miss Evalyn? Did ever you see a prettier bedchamber?"

"Never. It's almost too lovely to be true. I keep

thinking I'll wake up and find myself back at Carbery Hall."

"Me, too. Not at Carbery Hall, o' course, but back at the inn. Me uncle sure knows how to keep a girl hopping. Being here's like a dream. Even me room downstairs is elegant. You should see the pitcher they give me for me washstand, Miss Evalyn. Shining white it is, with blue flowers all over it. I'm almost afeared to use it, it's so fine. And the walls is painted white, and there's blue curtains and a blue spread. And it's all fer me alone! Y'know, Miss Evalyn, it's the first time in me life I've had a bedchamber all to meself!"

"Perhaps you shouldn't become too attached to it, Nancy. After all, you were only hired to accompany me on the coach. You'll probably be sent home tomorrow," Evalyn explained gently.

"I know, Miss Evalyn," said the unquenchable Nancy, "but tonight it's all mine!"

Evalyn smiled at the young girl's unflagging good spirits. Her own were not so consistent. One glance at the worn blue poplin dress, more appropriate for the schoolroom than the dining room, was enough to dampen her joy in her surroundings.

"Must you wear your hair pinned up so, Miss Evalyn?" Nancy asked. "I could dress it real genteel, just caught up a bit in the back, so, and falling over your shoulder like this. Whyn't you let me, Miss Evalyn? I'm real good at fixing hair. Real good."

Evalyn let her try, and when, a little while later, she had been buttoned into her blue dress and had thrown her mother's Spanish shawl over her shoulders, the mirror told her she was quite presentable.

The guests had all gathered in the library when Evalyn entered. One glance around the room told her the mirror had been wrong. She looked hopelessly dowdy among the stylish women gathered there. Mrs. Covington was looking festive in a green dress of spotted silk. Young Marianne Covington was demurely lovely in a dress of pink sarcenet embroidered all over with white violets. Most breathtaking of all was Miss Trevelyan, whose elegant blond beauty was enhanced by a gown of gold-threaded gauze over mauve silk. Evalyn wanted to run away and hide, but she had learned early how to face an enemy even when hopelessly outnumbered. She put up her chin and advanced.

Lady Steele welcomed her with surprising warmth and insisted that she take a seat right in the center of the company. Accustomed to being kept on the fringes of social gatherings, Evalyn felt uncomfortable in a place of such conspicuous importance. She murmured something innocuous and sank back in her chair, hoping to divert attention from herself. But James Everard was grinning at her approvingly, and Lord Reginald bent over her and whispered, "I thay, I do like your hair that way!"

And Lord Gyllford took a glass of wine from the butler and brought it over to her himself. She accepted the wine and looked up to thank him. There was a warm glow in his eyes. Could it be a sign of approval of her appearance? Perhaps her dress wasn't so dowdy after all.

Dinner was announced, and before she rose from her chair, Evalyn's arm was claimed by the host himself. As she crossed the room in that surprising position of honor, she noticed an expression of chagrin cross the face of the lovely Miss Trevelyan. Why she, and not Miss Trevelyan, had been singled out by Lord Gyllford was extremely puzzling.

Dinner at Gyllford Manor was always relaxed and leisurely, often lasting as long as two hours. The guests did not find this wearisome, for, as Mr. Covington was fond of relating, his sister, the fashionable Lady Lofting, had often given dinners lasting five hours. Dinner turned out to be a very merry meal, for Miss Trevelyan, finding herself seated at his lordship's left hand, soon recovered her good spirits and kept

Philip's attention with a constant flow of lively conversation. Jamie deftly placed himself at the side of the pretty Marianne and, all through the meal, teased her about her new, grown-up appearance. Marianne fully enjoyed his attentions, giggling and blushing prettily and responding to his compliments with a darting glance from under trembling lashes or a whispered, "Oh, do you really think so?"

Since Philip was only occasionally permitted to turn away from Miss Trevelyan to converse with Evalyn, seated on his right, Evalyn found an opportunity to discuss with her other dinner partner, Lord Reginald, the problem of her abigail. "Forgive me for troubling you about the matter," she said to him quietly, "but Nancy and I were wondering about the arrangements for her return."

"Nancy? Nancy? I don't quite . . . ?" Reggie mumbled, perplexed.

"The innkeeper's niece. The girl you hired to be my abigail. You only engaged her for the trip, you know, and she is expecting to return to the inn tomorrow."

"Good heavens, I'd forgotten all about her!" Reggie exclaimed.

"I beg your pardon," Lord Gyllford interjected, leaning toward her, "but I couldn't help overhearing what you just said. You are speaking of your abigail, are you not? Has she given satisfactory service?"

Evalyn looked at Lord Gyllford in surprise. "Why, yes, of course. She is a delightful girl, but—"

"Then you should certainly keep her, my dear. Unless she is particularly needed at home just now. Is that the case?"

"No, I don't think she is needed at the inn . . . that is, I'm sure she could be spared . . . but it would be impossible for me to keep her with me, my lord."

Lord Gyllford smiled. "You are quite a decided young woman, Miss Pennington. Tell me, why would it be so impossible?"

"Well, I . . . you see, Lord Reginald has been pay-ing her wages, and I certainly couldn't ask him—"

"No, you certainly could not. Although I fail to understand why Lord Reginald had been required to do so."

"Not required, my lord," Reggie put in. "My privilege, I athure you! Jamie'th pocketh were a bit to let, you thee—"

"Jamie's pockets are always to let, it seems," Lord Gyllford said drily. "I thank you, Reggie, and I will deem it *my* privilege if you will permit me to take the responsibility of the abigail off your hands. With your permission, I shall add her to our household staff."

"Delighted," Reggie agreed promptly.

"But sir, I cannot permit you to go to such expense on my behalf!" Evalyn objected vehemently.

"Miss Pennington," Lord Gyllford said with mock severity, "as much as I admire decided young ladies, I cannot permit them to dictate to me the composition of my household staff. So we'll have no more discussion on this head, if you please."

"But—"

"No buts. You are not eating, Miss Pennington. You must try a little of this ragout of veal and onions. Our cook has a way with ragouts. I think you will find it quite French."

But Evalyn, although overwhelmed with gratitude at the unexpected kindness she was meeting at every turn, felt obliged to voice her objections. She could not accept such generosity. What business had a governess with an abigail? She drew a deep breath and looked up at her host, prepared to do battle. He was looking down at her, the expression on his face daring her to contradict him. She hesitated, but it was not his facial expression that deterred her. It was something far back in his eyes, an expression of such smiling warmth that her words were arrested in her throat. Never had she seen quite such a look in a man's eyes. Her own eyes wavered, and she looked down at her plate. He would have his way. There was no question about it, Lord Gyllford was quite the most disarming man ever to come her way.

The gentlemen were left lingering over their brandies, while the ladies repaired to the sitting room. Marianne restlessly wandered from the window to the fire and back again, impatient for Jamie's reappearance. Martha Covington took a seat near Evalyn, thanking her for her kindness to the twins and asking her advice on medication for an inflamed ear which was troubling one of them. Sally took the opportunity to quiz Clarissa about Miss Pennington's identity. "Who on earth is she?" Sally asked, her green eyes watching Evalyn carefully.

"A friend of Jamie's, as I've told you," Clarissa answered.

"Yes, I know. But where did he find her?"

"I believe he met her at the Carberys'."

"Come now, Clarissa, don't be secretive. Did I hear someone say that she was their governess?"

"I believe she was, yes."

"Well, then, why on earth did he bring her here?"

"Sally, don't pry. It doesn't become you. You'll know all in good time. In the meantime, it's enough for you to know that she's here on a little holiday. From what I know of Harriet Carbery, the poor girl deserves one."

"Very well, Clarissa, if that's all you'll tell me, I must be satisfied. But I must say, I don't see why you and Philip treat her as if she were a visiting duchess."

Clarissa laughed. "Dear me, you sound as if your nose is quite out of joint! But console yourself. You'd be just as put out if we were entertaining a *real* duchess. You hate playing second fiddle."

"That's right, I do. I'll say this for you, Clarissa Steele, you are frank to a fault." Sally turned away, leaned back against the sofa, and looked across the room at Miss Pennington. "My dear Miss Pennington," she purred, "do you play the piano?"

"Yes, a little. Would you like me to play?"

"Yes, I would. I imagine you are very accomplished. No, on second thought, I believe I'll do it myself. I have a lowering feeling that your playing will put us all in the shade, and, as Clarissa will tell you, I do not enjoy finding myself in anyone's shade."

Sally sauntered over to the piano, carefully draped her gauze overdress over the stool so that it fell in soft folds to the floor, threw back her head, closed her eyes, and played feelingly. The selection she chose was elegiacally moody. Clarissa watched her for an amused moment and then crossed to Miss Pennington. "Don't be discomposed by Sally's remarks, my dear," she said soothingly. "Sally likes to play the role of an *enfant terrible*. She doesn't really mean what she says."

"I quite understand, Lady Steele, and have not taken the least offense," Miss Pennington assured her. Clarissa was sure she detected a slight twinkle in Miss Pennington's eye. Evalyn leaned forward and whispered, "I think, Lady Steele, that if I put the candelabra on the piano in front of Miss Trevelyan, *no one* will be able to put her in the shade." And she rose and placed the candelabra on the piano ledge, leaving the rest of the room in shimmering shadows. Clarissa shook her head and laughed silently. Jamie and Philip certainly had the right of it: Miss Pennington was a most redoubtable girl!

When the gentlemen came in, they found the beautiful Miss Trevelyan at the piano, deep in the mood of her music and bathed in candleglow that set her hair and the golden strands of her dress in gleaming relief. They drifted to the piano, attracted like moths to the light, and applauded her performance with real enthusiasm. Sally laughed and bowed with pleasure, her petulance forgotten. Clarissa glanced at Miss Pennington. Their eyes met, and they grinned at each other. How delightful she is, Clarissa thought. I think I've found a friend.

Later, with the candles rearranged and the room restored to brightness, the guests were ready for tea and cakes. As Clarissa served and Evalyn passed around the sweets, Gervaise wandered to the window.

"Do you think the weather will hold, Philip?" he asked. "I've set my heart on some shooting tomorrow."

"I hope so, for your sake and mine," Philip answered.

"What do you mean? Are you going to join us this time instead of locking yourself away in your study?"

"No, I don't mean that at all. I mean that if you, Edward, Reg and Jamie go out, I shall have a few hours of peace in which to do some work."

"Work indeed! What on earth do you have to do that's so urgent?" Gervaise grumbled.

"Yes, Philip, do tell him," Clarissa said encouragingly. "I've long been curious about what you do when you bury yourself in your study every afternoon." She turned to Gervaise. "I suspect he only hides there to get away from us all."

"That's unfair," said Jamie loyally. "An estate of this size requires a great deal of work if it is to be managed well."

"I'm glad to hear you say so, my boy," Edward Covington said approvingly. "After all, you'll be doing it yourself one day."

But Gervaise would not be put off. "Fiddle. I handle *my* affairs too, and it doesn't take me nearly as long. He's up to something else, I'm sure."

Philip smiled. "I only disappear into my study to make it seem that my life has more purpose than that of the rest of you."

"Don't let him put you off with that bouncer," Clarissa said knowingly. "He has some secret he's afraid to reveal."

"I agree," Gervaise seconded. "I'll wager he's writing a radical tome."

Martha gasped. "That's not possible! Not Philip!"

"It's a ridiculous idea," said Sally laughing.

"But that's it, you know," Philip admitted. "How did you guess, you rascal?"

"I haven't spent hours conversing with you on Burke and Bentham and the ills of England without guessing what you're up to," Gervaise chuckled in triumph.

"A radical tome? Really?" asked Jamie in surprise.

"How exciting! About what, Philip? You must tell us," Sally urged.

"I didn't intend it to be a secret. I just don't like to prose on about my interests and make myself a dead bore."

"We won't be bored, I promise," Sally assured him.

"Indeed we won't," Clarissa agreed. "I, for one, won't rest until I know what you're up to."

"Well, briefly, I'm writing a response to a view expressed by Burke, who claimed that the British government represents, and *should* represent, the leisured classes who have education and above menial income —which means only about 400,000 of us. I contend— along with many others, like Bentham—that this is a narrow view. I'm attempting to suggest that all adults living in England make up the 'public' and should be represented."

"Good God!" exclaimed Edward. "Do you mean *everybody*?"

"Exactly so."

"I don't understand this at all," Clarissa sighed. "You mean people who receive wages? And servants and such?"

"Yes, I do."

"Well!" muttered Edward, "I've never heard such nonsense."

"Don't know but what I don't agree with you either, Philip," said Gervaise cheerfully, with keen enjoyment of an old, familiar argument. "I'm not at all opposed to the enfranchisement of tradesmen and householders who pay taxes, but—"

"But, indeed!" Edward nodded with conviction, "but the others—servants, indigents, and so on—well, I draw the line, my dear sir, I draw the line!"

Suddenly the whole room was a babble of voices,

Sally, Jamie and Clarissa supporting Lord Gyllford, and the others vociferously against. Lord Gyllford turned his amused eyes to Evalyn, who had taken a seat a little apart from the others and was calmly stirring her tea. "You have not ventured to express your view, Miss Pennington," he said.

The hubbub ceased, and everyone turned to look at Evalyn. "Since I am a member of that class against which Mr. Covington has seen fit to draw the line," she answered with a calm smile, "I had supposed that my views would be obvious. It seems to me, however, that all classes will be represented by the government before very long, whether Lord Gyllford defends them or not."

"Hear, hear!" cried Jamie and Reggie in unison, proud of their protégée.

Sally ignored them and looked at Evalyn with a sneer. "Miss Pennington puts me in mind of a job-horse who bites her master's hand because she thinks the oats he brings her are hers by right. You ought to be a little grateful, Miss Pennington, for Lord Gyllford's support for your class."

Evalyn stared at Sally in surprise and chagrin. How could her simple statement be interpreted as resentment of Lord Gyllford? "I didn't intend—" she began.

"Of course you didn't!" Clarissa defended warmly, and turned to Sally in irritation. "Sally, you are being absurd."

"It was not a fortuitous analogy, certainly," Philip said, amused. "I know you meant to defend me, Sally, but Miss Pennington has really got to the truth of it. All classes *will* be represented in time, regardless of my work."

But Evalyn lowered her eyes, struggling with her feelings of shame, frustration, and resentment. She had not intended to denigrate Lord Gyllford's writing. Yet Miss Trevelyan had deliberately tried to give that impression. What had she done to incur Miss Trevelyan's obvious antagonism? And, of more concern, was Lord

Gyllford displeased with what she had said, even though he had spoken up on her behalf? As the conversation picked up around her, she unobtrusively glanced up at Lord Gyllford's face and found, to her surprise, that he was smiling down at her with a look of fond pride. A prickle of unfamiliar excitement ran down her spine, the color rose in her cheeks, and she hastily looked down at her cup. But not before she caught a glimpse—she could not be mistaken—of a barely perceptible flicker of his lordship's right eyelid. Philip Everard, Lord Gyllford, had winked at her!

When, several hours later, the entire household had retired for the night, three people lay awake. Evalyn didn't want to fall asleep. She wanted to relive every moment since her arrival. She wanted to commit to memory Lord Gyllford's every word, every gesture, every expression that she had noted on his face. She would add these, with the other impressions of the people and events at Gyllford, to her small storehouse of happy recollections, to be pulled out and relived on some future evening when, inevitably, the loneliness and drabness of her next post threatened to depress her spirits. In the meantime, she would live each day of this unexpected holiday to the full. She snuggled contentedly into the soft luxuriousness of the bedclothes and smiled into the darkness. She didn't care if sleep never came.

Sally tossed and turned restlessly. Who was that drab little nobody, getting so much of Philip's attention? The woman was not a fool, she admitted, but she was only a governess, with no style, no taste, and no real beauty. Sally supposed that some might find the wench somewhat taking, but not in comparison with herself! What did Philip see in her? Sally could find no satisfactory answers. But she was certain of one thing: the irritating little nobody was interfering with her plans to capture Philip. Something would have to be done to get rid of her. And soon. She had not played her hand well tonight, and time was fleeting. She must think of a plan. . . .

Philip could not bring himself to lie down. He paced about his room, vaguely troubled. He knew he would not find sleep until he confronted squarely his feelings of disquiet and guilt. He paused at the window and stared out at the lawn below. The moonlight had turned the frosty grass to a silvered sea. Tomorrow would be a perfect day for Gervaise and the others to ride. Does Miss Pennington ride, he wondered? Miss Pennington. There it was. He was drawn to her as he had not been to a woman in years. Good heavens, he was jealous of his own son!

Disgusted with himself, he stalked across the room and got into bed. How amazing, he thought for the hundredth time, that twenty-two-year-old Jamie should have found in that quiet and unobtrusive girl the same gentle and clear-eyed loveliness that he had seen! But thoughts like this simply would not do. His feelings for his future daughter-in-law must be kept sternly in check and must never be permitted to exceed those of fatherly affection. He put her firmly from his mind, and, forcing himself to concentrate on his next day's writing, he at last drifted into an uneasy sleep.

CHAPTER SEVEN

The sun had not yet made an appearance when the men gathered around the breakfast board, already attired in riding clothes. Their host, Lord Gyllford, was the only one not so attired.

"Never thought to call you a spoilsport," Gervaise grumbled when Philip had repeated for the third time his intention to remain behind.

Philip laughed. "You may call me anything you please," he said to his friend, "but I have business that will not wait."

Gervaise grunted. "Your book is the business, I suppose, and if you ask me, it can wait for years."

"Thank you for the compliment," Philip said drily, "but the business has to do with the comfort of my guests."

Reggie, standing at the window, remarked amicably, "Too bad, Lord Gyllford. It lookth to be a good day for shooting."

They all turned to the window to see a faint light lining the horizon to the east. "We'd better get started, then," said Jamie, downing his last gulp of Jamaica coffee and rising from the table.

Philip walked with them to the stables to make sure they were all suitably mounted, and waved goodbye as they rode off noisily. On his return to the house, he was surprised to see young Marianne peeping into the breakfast room. Her hair was already combed and brushed into an entrancing cascade of brown ringlets, and her yellow morning dress was too becoming to have been donned for a solitary breakfast. "Good heavens, Marianne," he greeted her, "what are you doing up and about at this ungodly hour? None of the ladies will be up for hours yet."

"I was hoping to have breakfast with . . . that is, I wanted to see the gentlemen in their riding clothes," she finished lamely.

"You've just missed them, I'm afraid. Or rather, they've missed you. They would have enjoyed seeing your pretty face at breakfast. You're looking quite fetching this morning."

The shy blue eyes flickered briefly to meet his, and a small smile brightened her face. "Oh, do you really think so?" she murmured. Philip understood

that the question was purely rhetorical—merely a
group of meaningless sounds she uttered to cover
embarrassment or inadequacy with words. Some friend
of hers must have suggested it as a useful cover phrase,
to be brought out when needed. He suppressed a
smile and said politely, "Is there something I can do
for you? Can I get you something to . . . er . . . help
you pass the time?"

"Oh, no, thank you," she said, her face crestfallen.
"I suppose I'll look into your library and find a book
to read." The tone of her voice was so unmistakably
gloomy that Philip was left in no doubt as to what she
thought of that pastime. She turned, and with hanging head and slow step proceeded toward the library.
Philip watched her slow passage across the hall, wondering which of the two young men she had risen so
early to see. Reggie had shown no noticeable interest
in her the night before. Could Jamie's flirtation at the
table the night before have encouraged her interest
there? He hoped Jamie had better sense than to encourage a young and innocent female's attentions
when he was already—even if secretly—attached to
another. He sighed, and something of the gloom expressed by Marianne's retreating back entered into
him.

Evalyn opened her eyes to find Nancy pulling aside
the curtains. A cold December sun barely brightened
the room, but the look on Nancy's face seemed to
spread light into every corner. She beamed at Evalyn
with an eager smile. "Miss Evalyn, I've such news!"
she crowed.

"Good morning, Nancy," Evalyn said sleepily.
"What news?"

"You'll never credit it, I'm sure. The master sent
for me this morning. Sent for me special!"

Evalyn sat up abruptly. "Do you mean . . . Lord
Gyllford?"

"Yes'm. His lordship his very self! Hutton brought

me up—he's the butler, y'know—and his lordship, well, he smiles at me and says he'd like me in his employ, to serve as y'r personal maid, he says. To work for you *exclusive*. Then he asks me, ever so kindly, if I think I'd be happy working here. Imagine that! And I says, oh yes, sir, I'd be very happy. Then he says I'm to take me orders only from you. Then Hutton, he pokes me and whispers for me to close me mouth and make me curtsey, so I makes me prettiest one and says I'd be happy to stay as long as he'd like, and I'll try to give good service. And then Hutton takes me to the housekeeper, and she gives me this lady's maid dress and this lovely cap and says I'm to keep 'em clean and sweet-smelling at all times. See? Ain't I fine? Don't I look a proper lady's maid?"

Evalyn's head was whirling. Lord Gyllford had surprised her again. Most other men would have forgotten a promise relating to a domestic, made so casually at the dinner table. His attentions to her were as bewildering as they were pleasing. She shook her head and tried to concentrate on Nancy, gaily pirouetting before her. Smiling fondly, she watched Nancy turn, holding out the skirts of her blue bombazine dress. Nancy did indeed look every inch a lady's maid, with her starched white half-apron and the lace-trimmed mob cap which neatly covered her somewhat unruly hair. The cap looked charming with the bright blue ribbon threaded through it, and tied with a bow at the center of her forehead. "I think you look finer than I do," Evalyn laughed as she climbed out of bed, "and much too fine to be serving a mere governess like me."

"You ain't really a governess, are you? I've heard 'em whispering about you in the servants' hall like you was a fine lady—almost like you was one of the family."

"But I am a governess, truly." Nancy's face fell. Evalyn looked at her sympathetically. "Do you mind very much, Nancy?"

Nancy considered the question carefully, and her face brightened. "Well, I suppose they wouldn't think much of me in the hall if they knew, but I don't care. I suppose a real lady would scare me proper. And I ain't a real lady's maid neither, so I got nothing to complain of." She smiled her irrepressible smile. "We'll suit each other fine."

Evalyn laughed and hugged the girl warmly. "I think so too," she said.

Nancy beamed at her new mistress. Then she bustled about the room collecting various articles of clothing for Evalyn to wear. As she opened drawers and chests, the brightness again faded from her face. "I wish you had more clothes to wear," she sighed. "There ain't enough things here to keep me busy enough to earn me wages."

Evalyn shrugged into her least shabby daytime dress and let Nancy struggle with the buttons. "Then perhaps you can help me after breakfast. I mean to see what the twins are up to. If we can keep them quiet and happy, and out of the way of the other guests, we'll have deserved at least some of the unprecedented kindness we've been shown."

But Lord Gyllford had been ahead of her here too. While she and Martha stood side by side at the breakfast buffet, Evalyn asked where the children were to be found. Martha, more relaxed and at ease than she had been since her arrival, told Evalyn that Lord Gyllford had arranged for Jamie's old nurse, now living in retirement somewhere on the estate, to take charge of the children for the length of their stay.

"But that wasn't necessary," Evalyn said. "I would have been most happy to take charge of them."

"Now, my dear Miss Pennington, that would have been most unsuitable. You are a guest here, as I am. I certainly would not have permitted . . . I could not so impose on you," Martha said.

"It would have been no imposition. I most desire to make myself useful. However, I'll not trouble you further on this matter. Please remember, Mrs. Covington, that I should be glad to be of service to you and the children whenever you have need of me."

The men had left for their day of shooting early, and the house seemed quiet and somnolent. Sally had made no appearance, but Clarissa knew it was her wont to remain in bed until well into the afternoon. Noting that young Marianne was drifting about the corridors aimlessly, Clarissa suggested that the ladies take a drive. Martha and Marianne agreed eagerly, but Evalyn declined, saying that a novel she had started the night before was engrossing her. When the others had left, she found her way up to the nursery. It was not a difficult place to find—here, as in most of the great houses, the nursery was hidden away on the top floor of one of the wings. There she found the twins happily playing at spillikins on the floor before a cheerful fire. On a rocking chair nearby say a wizened old lady knitting an already overlong muffler.

"How do you do, ma'am?" Evalyn greeted her. "Are you the lady who had been governess to James Everard?"

"More of a nanny I was," the woman said, looking up with a smile. "And to his father before him." She rose from the rocker with surprising grace and agility, and came toward Evalyn with a firm, if slow, step.

"Really?" asked Evalyn in surprise. "To Lord Gyllford himself?"

"Yes, indeed. And a fair handful he was in those days. He kept me hopping, I can tell you. Mrs. Noakes, I be."

"And I'm Evalyn Pennington. I too am a governess."

Mrs. Noakes bobbed a curtsey. "And a much better than I, I have no doubt. You're a lady with learning. I could tell that the moment you opened your mouth. As for me, I could only watch over my boys and play with 'em. My boys had tutors enough to teach 'em their Latin and such."

"My charges do not learn much Latin from me either, I'm afraid. Tell me, Mrs. Noakes, do you not find it difficult to take care of two such lively boys as the twins here?"

"Not me," the old woman chortled. "It puts a spring in my step, it does, to be in the company of children again. As I told his lordship this morning, when he rode over to take me up, I'd rather be up and doing than lying about on my bed."

A voice came from the doorway. "What she said was, 'Better to wear out my shoes than my sheets!'" The ladies looked up to find Lord Gyllford smiling at them. "I see you and I have come on the same errand, Miss Pennington."

"And what errand is that, sir?" Mrs. Noakes asked.

"To see how you fare with those young jackanapes," he answered, loud enough for the boys to hear.

"We're fine, Uncle Philip," said one of the twins, not bothering to look up from the game. "We've been very good all day, haven't we, Mrs. Noakes?"

"Like two angels," she answered promptly.

"Since it still lacks an hour to midday, it won't do to praise you yet," Philip told the boys. "I'll expect a full report at your bedtime." Then, turning to Evalyn, he asked quietly, "Well, my dear, are you satisfied?"

She flushed and turned to Mrs. Noakes. "Good day to you, ma'am. I hope you'll not hesitate to call on me if you should have any need of my assistance."

She turned, and, finding Lord Gyllford holding the door for her, she left the nursery, her cheeks burning in embarrassment. Lord Gyllford walked beside her down the hall. She glanced up at him timidly. "I'm sorry, Lord Gyllford, if I seemed to be concerning myself unduly in the affairs of your household, but I had so hoped . . . to make myself useful. . . ."

"There's no need at all for you to feel embarrassment, my dear. I quite understand your feelings. However, Jamie has invited you here for a holiday, and a holiday you shall have. You may as well resign yourself to it."

"Jamie is . . . I mean, your son is very kind, but I have no wish for him to put you in a position of such . . . inconvenience in my behalf—"

Lord Gyllford stopped her with a gesture of impatience and grasped her firmly by the shoulders, turning her so that they faced each other squarely. "Try to understand, Miss Pennington, that Jamie's wishes exactly match mine in this. We—both of us, and my sister, too—have invited you to be a guest in this house. A *guest*. It is, and will continue to be, a pleasure for us to make you happy during your stay. Do you understand? Can you not accept the trifling steps we have taken to make you comfortable?"

Evalyn shook her head. "I am more grateful than I can say, but—"

"You 'but' me too many 'buts,' young lady. Just say yes."

Evalyn looked up at him. His face was close above hers, his eyes looking compellingly into her own. Again, something she saw back in his eyes made her words stick in her throat. Her heart pounded and her chest heaved with emotions completely new to her. She nodded. "Y . . . yes, sir," she managed, and dropped her eyes.

"Thank you," he said quietly, and his hands fell from her shoulders. They turned and walked down the corridor without speaking. At the top of the staircase he turned to her again. "My guests all call me Philip," he said pointedly, "and I hope you will permit me to call you by your Christian name. Evalyn is a lovely name. It suits you."

"Of course you may, my lord," she said.

"Not 'my lord,' " he corrected. "Philip."

She looked up at him, her cheeks crimson. "Oh, I don't think I . . ."

"Yes, you can. Say it. Philip."

His eyes still held that look. She took a breath, gasped, "Philip," and fled like a schoolgirl down the stairs.

Philip looked after her until she disappeared. Then he went down to his study and pulled the door shut behind him. As he crossed to his desk, he caught a glimpse of his face in the mirror over the mantlepiece. A smile—a rather foolish one, he thought—still lingered on his face. He stared at his reflection as the memory of his misgivings of the night before flooded into his mind. He had promised himself to avoid her, to keep his feelings fatherly and cool! "Oh, that was well done, Philip," he said aloud, in a tone of sardonic self-disgust, "very well done indeed!"

Evalyn forced herself to walk down the hallway toward her room slowly and with, she hoped, one last shred of dignity. She had behaved like the silliest chit of a schoolgirl, and how she was to face Lord Gyllford again she didn't in the least know. Yet something inside her was bubbling with suppressed joy, and a smile hovered at the corners of her mouth. If she were sure no one would see, she would have liked to waltz down the length of the hall. She could almost hear the music—*Philip-tah-tum, tah-tum, Philip-tah-tum*. Heavens, what was wrong with her? She'd never waltzed in her life!

But fortunately, before she made a complete fool of herself, she noticed two figures at the far end of the corridor near her room. One was Miss Trevelyan, wearing a diaphanous robe over her nightclothes, her hair still dishevelled by sleep. The other—goodness, it was Nancy! Evalyn hurried down the passageway, to be greeted by Miss Trevelyan. "Ah, there you are, Miss Pennington. You must really speak to your abigail, you know. She's kept me out here in the hallway arguing for at least five minutes. She has no idea how a maid should go on!"

"I'm sorry if she's done something out of the way. What seems to be the problem?"

Nancy sniffed in a decidedly truculent way and spoke up quickly. "She asked me to do her hair, and I won't," she said, sticking out her chin stubbornly. "His lordship said I was to work for you ex-clu-sive, didn't he?"

Evalyn suppressed a smile. "Yes, indeed he did, Nancy, and you were quite right to wait to ask my permission," she said tactfully, trying to smooth things over.

"Well, I ain't asking your permission, Miss Evalyn. She's got her own maid to do for her."

"Did you ever hear the like?" said the scandalized Miss Trevelyan. "How can you put up with such insubordination? I only asked her because my Annette is nowhere to be found. How dare this impertinent minx refuse me? If I were you, Miss Pennington, I'd pack her off this instant!"

"I think you must leave the handling of Nancy to me, Miss Trevelyan. Nancy, dear, you have been rude, and I think you must tell Miss Trevelyan how sorry you are for speaking so."

Two large tears welled up in Nancy's eyes. "I d-didn't mean to be rude, t-truly. But her m-maid, Annette, would explode l-like a firecracker at me if I was to go n-near her m-mistress's hair! And me being the n-newest on staff, it'd be for sure a slap at her pride! And the m-master did say I was to work for you ex-clu-sive, didn't he? 'Tain't right to go disobeying him on me very f-first day! So what'm I t-to do?" And she wiped her eyes with her sleeve.

"There, there, Nancy," said Evalyn soothingly, putting an arm around the girl's shoulder and putting a handkerchief into her hand. "Wipe your eyes and go down to the hall to see if you can find Miss Trevelyan's maid—what's her name? Annette? Yes, tell Annette she's wanted right away."

Nancy wiped her eyes. "Are you going to pack me off, Miss Evalyn?" she asked, her underlip quivering.

"No, of course not. Now go along."

Nancy cast her a thankful look. "Yes'm. I'll run right down and do me best to find her." And she ran off down the hall.

"It seems to me, Miss Pennington, that you have much to learn about the handling of servants," Sally Trevelyan said coldly.

A pointed retort to the effect that Miss Trevelyan herself had something to learn in that regard—seeing that her Annette was nowhere to be seen when she was needed—occurred to Evalyn, but she did not express it. It would not be pleasant for Lord Gyllford and Lady Steele if their guests were at each other's throats. So she bit back the retort and said politely, "Would you, perhaps, like *me* to do your hair?"

Sally, expecting an angry retort, was disarmed by the gentle reply. "Oh," she said in surprise, "do you think you could?"

"I could try," Evalyn answered. Sally smiled and led the way to her room. It was panelled and furnished in a manner quite similar to Evalyn's, but she noticed with some surprise that it was smaller than hers and the bed hangings not as rich. Why, she wondered, would the Everards give a governess a more elegant bedroom than they gave to Miss Trevelyan? The Everards certainly had strange ways of doing things.

Sally sat down at her dressing table and handed Evalyn her brush with a conciliatory smile. Evalyn began to brush the long, golden hair with trepidation. She knew nothing of hairstyles or the proper way of dressing a lady's hair. But before she had to admit her inexperience, a knock at the door stayed her hand.

"Yes?" called Miss Trevelyan.

"It's Clarissa, Sally. May I come in?"

There was a moment's hesitation, and Evalyn noticed an uneasy flicker in Sally's eyes. "Yes, do come in, Clarissa dear," Sally sang out in a tone of false eagerness.

Clarissa came directly to the dressing room but stopped in surprise at seeing Evalyn—and with a brush in her hand. She looked from Evalyn to Sally with a puzzled, almost troubled, expression. Then she smiled politely. "Oh, Miss Pennington, here you are! I tapped at your door not a moment ago and wondered where you'd gone. But Sally, what on earth is going on? Surely you haven't asked our Miss Pennington to do your hair?"

"Well, I didn't exactly . . . that is, I . . ." Sally began.

"Her Annette seems to have disappeared, and I volunteered," Evalyn put in quickly.

"Oh, I see," Clarissa said, but it was clear that she was not pleased. Fortunately for Evalyn's peace of mind, a breathless and contrite Annette made an appearance at that moment. Evalyn excused herself and made her escape.

"Will you wait outside a moment?" Clarissa said to Annette after Evalyn had left. Annette closed the dressing-room door behind her. Clarissa looked at Sally in the mirror of the dressing table. "I must ask you, Sally, not to play any of your . . . tricks . . . while you are here."

"Tricks?" Sally asked, all innocence.

"She may have been a governess, but all that is at an end, as you will learn in due course. While she is here and under my roof, I expect you to treat Miss Pennington like a member of the family. I trust I'll not have to speak to you on this head again." And she walked from the room, leaving Sally staring at her retreating back in both anger and embarrassment.

Annette came back into the dressing room in considerable trepidation. The petite French maid knew her mistress well, and her expression as she sat staring at the mirror boded no good. She was obviously seething with suppressed fury. "I'm so sorry to be late, Ma'm'selle, and not to have been here when you awoke, but it is so early still. I did not expect you to call until two or three. Please do not look so angry at me."

But all Annette got for her pains was a box on the ear.

Clarissa tapped again at Evalyn's door, several gowns thrown over her arm. "Come in," Evalyn called, and looked up in surprise as Clarissa entered with some hesitation.

"I . . . I'm not disturbing you, am I?" Clarissa asked a little nervously.

"Oh, no, of course not. I was just staring out the window at your lovely grounds."

"You shall see them in the spring, when all the shrubs are blooming. It's quite lovely then."

"I hope I may be invited back some day to—but what is that you carry, ma'am?"

Clarissa felt the color rise in her face. "My dear," she said haltingly, "I hope you won't take this amiss. I know you can't have much to wear, given your circumstances, and I have so many gowns that were purchased when I was much slimmer than I am now. No, please, Miss Pennington, don't refuse until you've heard me out. Believe me, my dear, when I say that I don't care what you wear. But all these lovely things are going to waste and taking up room in my chests and cupboards, and it would give me such pleasure to see you wear them. . . ."

"Oh, Lady Steele, how can I? You and Lord Gyllford have given me so much already."

"Please don't call me Lady Steele. I feel we've already become friends. And, as a friend, won't you just try one of these, to see if there is any chance that they can be altered to suit you? Please, Miss Pennington. I'd be so obliged to you."

"Well, if you agree to call me Evalyn . . ."

A delightful hour was spent among the silks and muslins and poplins. At least three gowns were found to be immediately useful, with the help of a sash here or a button there. All the rest would be suitable with only a small amount of alteration, and Clarissa assured Evalyn that she had just the woman to do it. Evalyn, standing in front of a mirror, stared with pleasure at her reflection. She was wearing a dress of lilac twilled silk, trimmed along the hem with a row of delicate white embroidery. "Oh, Clarissa," she breathed, "I don't know how to thank you. I've never worn anything so exquisite!"

Clarissa sighed with pleasure. "And I'm sure I never looked so lovely in it as you do."

Evalyn sank into a chair, quite overwhelmed. "I can't quite believe all this," she said, shaking her head as if to wake herself from a dream. "If anyone had told me, a week ago, that I would be spending a fortnight in a room like this, and wearing a dress like this, and finding friends like this . . . Oh, Clarissa, you are giving me a holiday I shall remember all my life!"

CHAPTER EIGHT

Sally curled up on the luxurious divan in her bedroom, but left her book unopened on her lap. She had more than an hour to wait before she would begin to dress for dinner. In the meantime, she had a great deal to think about. She was not doing well in her attack on the fortress of Philip's reserve. She had not been able to spend one moment alone with him since she'd arrived. It was clear that he was avoiding her, but he had always seemed to do so. She hoped that his motive was fear of her attractiveness. Many men she had known had exhibited that fear. It was as if they could sense that, if they fell under her spell, they would somehow lose control over their lives. If that was the problem with Philip, she was sure she could handle it, once she overcame this initial resistance.

But now another problem had come between her and her goal. Miss Evalyn Pennington. That Philip was attracted to her was clear. But the small and inchoate attraction did not explain Miss Pennington's position of importance in the household. That was the puzzle Sally must solve if she were to make this dreadful fortnight of rustication pay off.

The primary question to answer was why Clarissa and Philip seemed so eager to make a to-do over her. Clarissa had clearly hinted, in her scolding earlier today, that Evalyn's days as a governess were over. Why? The obvious answer was marriage. Evalyn was to be married, thus alleviating the necessity for her to earn her own living. But whom was she to marry? If she were about to marry an Everard, that would explain why Clarissa and Philip were going to such pains to make her feel at home. But which Everard? It could not be Philip, of that she was sure. Although he was obviously attracted to her, he could not be the man; he had just met her! Sally had been present at Miss Pennington's arrival and it had been obvious that they had not met before. And their conversation at the dinner table last evening indicated that no intimacy as yet existed between them.

Jamie, of course, was the logical one. Sally had the distinct impression that the governess had been invited by Jamie. They had arrived together, and had obviously met some time before. Yet he had seemed quite indifferent to her last evening and had even flirted with the Covington girl. Of course, if the announcement were to be withheld—if the engagement were to be kept secret for some reason—Jamie's behavior might have been carefully calculated to throw observers off the scent. But Sally was not the average observer. If Jamie really were attached to her, it would not escape Sally's keen eye. She would watch and see.

Of course, Reggie was a possibility. He had arrived with Jamie and Miss Pennington and had evidently been staying with Jamie at Carbery Hall. And if it were Reggie who was Miss Pennington's betrothed, there would be an obvious reason for keeping the alliance secret: Reginald Windle, Lord Farnham, would have great difficulties explaining to his family that he wanted to wed a governess. The Windles, if she knew anything of the matter, were not nearly as openminded as the Everards. On the other hand, Reggie had already succeeded to his titles and wealth, and he was in no danger of losing them no matter whom he married. No, no. She was on shaky ground with Reggie. Besides, why would Clarissa be so protective of Miss Pennington if she were *Reggie's* intended? Surely Reggie's betrothed would not have such importance in this house, would she? Well, it would be an interesting evening. If she watched closely, she might well have some answers before she went to bed that night.

The evening proved to be a complete disappointment to Sally. Not only did she fail to advance her own cause, but by the end of it she was bored, disgruntled, and as much in the dark about Miss Pennington's position as she had been earlier.

Philip took Martha on his arm when the guests went in to dinner, and Sally, though she watched her host and the governess with catlike intensity, could catch no covert glances passing between them. Philip seemed to take no special notice of Miss Pennington, even though Sally had to admit that the mousy creature looked quite lovely in a well-cut lilac gown that must have cost her a year's wages.

After dinner, Sally expected to be asked to play and sing. Instead, she was compelled to join Clarissa and Martha at the card table, and there she was trapped all evening. Gervaise joined the card players when the men rejoined the ladies, and Edward and Philip huddled over a chess board. Whenever she was able to look up from her cards, Sally studied the others, but she was unable to find any signs of a liaison between Miss Pennington and any one of the eligible men. Jamie, having exchanged the merest pleasantries with Miss Pennington, spent the evening teasing Marianne, to that young lady's obvious delight. Reggie spent most of the evening in Miss Pennington's company, but they seemed on such an easy, friendly footing with each other that Sally was convinced only a fool could read into their light badinage any signs of romance.

A light supper was served at ten-thirty, and everybody rose from their various pursuits to gather for refreshments. Now was the time Sally hoped to catch a glimpse of the truth. After supper, the goodnights would be said, and everyone would be off to bed. It was the last chance of the day for lovers to communicate with each other. Secret messages could be passed by the warmth of a glance, the twitch of a smile, the surreptitious touching of hands. Sally was determined to miss nothing. Miss Pennington was the first to say goodnight. She included the entire company in the smile she gave, and left the room without a backward glance. Reggie bore Jamie off with him, saying he wanted to show his friend the new riding coat he intended to wear on the morrow. Before he left the room, Jamie stopped at Marianne's side and whispered something to her. Sally moved a little closer.

"But you must wear something warm if we're to go driving in the curricle," he was saying. "The wind can cut right through you, riding in the open like that."

"But I hate my old pelisse," Marianne answered with a pout.

"Nonsense," Jamie said. "I'm sure it's most becoming. Anything you wear will look just the thing."

Marianne blushed with pleasure. "Oh, do you really think so?" she breathed ecstatically.

From this snatch of conversation, it was hard for Sally to believe that Jamie's heart was occupied by an entirely different young woman. Jamie's words were the words of a carefree boy. The entire matter remained very much of a puzzle.

Jamie, completely unaware of having been the object of Sally's scrutiny, entered his friend's bedroom and dropped down on the chaise, putting his feet up comfortably, folding his hands behind his head and leaning back, the very picture of a sultan surveying his *hareem*. "Well, let's see that riding coat of yours," he said to Reg cheerfully.

"Don't be tho harebrained! Do you really think I want to have your opinion of my coat? Your opinionth have no conthequenth when it cometh to matterth of thtyle."

"If that's so, why did you say you wanted to show it to me?"

"I jutht wanted a word in private with you. I haven't had an opportunity to talk to you thith evening. There'th thomething on my mind."

"Well, out with it, man. What's the matter?"

"Dash it, it ain't an eathy thing to tell one'th betht friend."

Jamie sat up abruptly. It wasn't like Reg to hold back his words, unless there were something seriously amiss. "Good God, Reg! Is there something wrong? You ain't sick or anything?"

"No, no, nothing like that. It'th only . . . well, remember the joke I made latht evening . . . about you. . . ?"

"What joke? I don't remember."

"You dropped in here before dinner and were talking about Marianne. . . ."

"Oh, yes, I remember now. You said something about me turning out to be as big a bore as Geoff."

"Yeth. Well, you are."

Jamie gave his friend a dagger look. "That's not funny, Reg."

"I'm not trying to be funny. I mean it," Reg said, looking down at his shoes in some embarrassment.

"Are you trying to tell me I'm making a cake of myself over Marianne?"

"Not exactly making a cake of yourthelf. But you may very well be turning into ath much of a bore ath Geoff if you don't watch it. You thpent the whole evening in her pocket, and you intend taking her driving tomorrow. I thought we'd be out hunting!"

"I have every intention of going hunting tomorrow," Jamie said, getting to his feet and speaking belligerently. "I only promised to take her out for a short spin in the curricle after we return."

"Well, I know how thingth can develop. You begin by taking her driving for an hour, then you take her walking for an afternoon, then you kith her in the shrubbery, and before you know it, you're an engaged man!"

"Me? Engaged? To a mere chit out of the schoolroom? You must have dipped too deep in the brandy —you're foxed."

"I'm ath thober ath you are, and I'll tell you thith, Jameth Everard—I will not remain here at Gyllford to hear you go on and on about Marianne ath Geoff did about Mith Pennington."

"Confound it! I never expected to hear such humbug from you, Reg Windle! If you think there's any similarity between me and that idiot Geoff Carbery, you're no friend of mine! Have you ever heard *me* prose on about some female? Have I ever accosted an unwilling wench on the stairs? If you don't beat all!"

Undaunted, Reggie looked at his friend calmly. "No, I ain't ever known you to behave like Geoff. But I ain't never known you to be taken with a female before, either. I've found, though, that when love attackth 'em, all men act like foolth."

Jamie glared at Reggie in irritation, until it occurred to him that he had observed the very same thing himself. His tension eased, and a laugh escaped him. "Oh, come off your high ropes, Reg! You're right about lovesick fools, of course, but I ain't one of 'em. There's a big difference between a harmless flirtation to pass the time and losing one's head over a girl, you know."

"Mmmmph," grunted Reggie, unconvinced. "I only wanted to drop a word of warning. Only a word to warn you that you're getting near deep water, that'th all."

"Don't brew up a storm about nothing. Come along with Marianne and me tomorrow, and you'll see there's no deep water."

"No, thank you. That'th not nethethary. When we get back from shooting, I intend to thpend the time with my valet. I have to dethide which waithtcoat to wear for dinner."

"If you spent any time deciding about the waistcoat you're wearing now, it was time ill-spent," Jamie said mockingly.

"What'th the matter with it?" Reggie demanded.

"Striped satin? How can you ask? It makes you look like an upholstered chair."

Reggie looked at Jamie with scorn. "Thtriped thatin ith all the rage, you ignoramuth," he said with disdain. Then he glanced down at his chest, grinned, and added, "Though I did think, mythelf, that I look a bit like a chair."

Jamie roared with laughter and fell back on the chaise. Reggie broke out in laughter, too, and it was several minutes before the two of them could catch their breaths. Finally, Jamie sobered and said, "Now, this is more like it. I was afraid for a few moments that you were going to leave."

"And I would, too, if our vithit here at Gyllford turnth out like the one at Carbery Hall."

"No chance of that, I assure you. And you will come with Marianne and me in the curricle tomorrow, won't you?"

"No, of courthe not. Whatever for?"

"For the practice. A little flirtation is good experience, so that when we meet someone who really matters, we won't make cakes of ourselves."

"Not I. I won't make a cake of mythelf. I intend to remain a bachelor all my life."

"It ain't likely. You're too good a catch. You may as well agree to come along, for I don't intend to take no for an answer."

"Very well, I'll come, but only to thee that you don't get carried away."

Unfortunately for the hunters, the morning sky showed a heavy covering of clouds. By the time the breakfasters peered out of the windows, they saw a dense fog and a cold-looking drizzle. It soon became obvious that the weather was not likely to clear in time for the day's sport. Gervaise promptly announced that he, for one, was returning to bed. Edward declared his intention of spending the morning catching up on some correspondence, and Philip headed, as usual, for his study. Jamie and Reggie looked at each other glumly. Young, energetic and eager for sport or adventure, they found the prospect of the day ahead of them filled only with boredom and gloom. With a wordless sigh, Reggie looked down into his cup and stirred his tea aimlessly. Jamie propped his elbows on the table, put his chin in his hands, and stared resignedly into space.

The brisk entrance of Miss Pennington into the breakfast room roused them both. Her expression was lively and purposeful, her morning dress of flowered muslin had an air of spring about it, and the lilt of her voice when she greeted them seemed to brighten the room. They jumped to their feet.

"Good morning, Miss Pennington. You're up and about early," Jamie remarked.

"Please sit down. Don't disturb yourself on my account," Evalyn urged. "I shall just help myself to some of this delicious-looking smoked fish and a cup of coffee and join you, if I may."

Reggie held her chair for her, and Jamie poured her coffee. She looked from one to the other in gratitude. "How pleasant to be gallanted by two gentleman at once," she said.

Reggie rather ungallantly muttered, "Well, there ain't much elthe to do." Then, recollecting himself, he quickly added, "Oh, I beg your pardon. I did not mean—"

Evalyn laughed. "I quite understand," she assured him. "The weather is so dreadful, and you've been cheated of a day of sport."

"Exactly so," Jamie sighed. "And what we're to do with ourselves all morning we just don't know."

"I should think two such intelligent and ingenious gentlemen as you are—and you certainly proved yourselves so in your handling of my problem—would have no trouble in inventing some amusements."

"I doubt that we're as intelligent and ingenious as you think," Jamie said ruefully. "We outdid ourselves with your problem."

"Quite right," Reggie agreed. "Our brainth are back to their accuthtomed lethargy."

"You'll think of something, I'm sure," Evalyn said and sipped her coffee unperturbed.

"You seem to have some purpose for the morning, don't you? What are you about, Miss Pennington?" Jamie asked.

"Nothing that would interest you, I'm afraid. I think that on a day like this, Mrs. Noakes will have her hands full amusing the twins. I intend to make myself useful to her."

Jamie's face brightened. "I say, Reggie, would you like to come up and see the nursery? I remember I had quite a good collection of toy soldiers in all kinds of battle regalia, from the Normans to Marlborough."

Reggie made a face. "How exhilaráting," he said drily.

"I know it doesn't sound very appealing to you, Lord Reginald, but only think how exciting it would be for the twins!" Evalyn suggested with a gleam in her eyes. "It would be the very thing for a rainy morning like this. Would you mind very much coming along with me? The boys would so enjoy seeing Mr. Everard's soldiers—they are the very things boys like."

Reggie let himself be persuaded, and the trio made their way upstairs to the nursery. As they approached, they heard the sounds of a commotion and came to the door to find the twins on the floor, pommelling each other, with poor Mrs. Noakes standing over them wringing her hands and squeaking remonstrances in a quite ineffectual manner. Reg and Jamie rushed to the rescue, Reg lifting one of them and holding him in firm restraint while Jamie lifted the other and stood him on his feet.

"All right, young man," Jamie said to the boy who, by the tears running down his face, made clear that he had been getting the worst of it, "what's amiss here?" And he wiped away the tears as unobtrusively as possible.

"Freddie kicked me," the boy answered truculently.

"I did not!" shouted the other, twisting powerlessly in Reggie's grip.

"So your brother's name is Freddie," Jamie said to his charge. "What's yours?"

"T-Ted—Theodore."

"Oh, I thay!" Reggie said, exchanging amused looks with Jamie. "Freddie and Teddie!"

"That was Mamma's idea, not ours!" said Freddie, still struggling to free himself of Reggie's grip.

"Be quiet!" Reggie said sternly. "A boy who kickth hith brother ith not worthy of lithening to."

The boy twisted around and looked at Reggie with interest. "You said that wrong," he accused. "You talk peculiar."

Reggie nodded matter-of-factly. "It'th a lithp."

The boy giggled. "What's a lithp?"

Jamie frowned at him. "A lisp. That means he doesn't pronounce the letter 's.' But bigger men than you have learned not to make sport of this gentleman's way with words. There's nothing wrong with the way he uses his fists, you see."

The boy's eyes grew round. "Oh, are you a boxer, sir?" he asked Reg with dawning respect.

Reggie grinned. "I've thtepped into the ring a few timeth," he said.

"He has a punishing right, that I can tell you," Jamie added, rubbing his jaw for emphasis.

"Can you show us how to box?" the twin called Teddy asked eagerly.

Evalyn, who had been standing with Mrs. Noakes and watching the proceedings with amused interest, felt it was time to step forward. "Not here, I'm afraid. But these two gentlemen have come upstairs purposely to show you some wonderful toy soldiers, and to tell you about the battles their uniforms represent. Isn't that kind of them?"

"Tell them *what*?" Reggie asked with an air of a man who had been unwittingly trapped. He met Jamie's pleading look with a grimace, and then shrugged. "Oh, very well. Go ahead and find the thilly thingth. We haven't anything better to do."

Lord Gyllford, when he chanced to look into the nursery an hour later, was startled to find a number of his guests gathered there. A table had been set up in the middle of the room, and lined up upon it were several dozen little painted toy soldiers. On the far side of the table, Reggie and Jamie were acting out the Battle of Crécy. On the near side sat Evalyn, Clarissa, Martha and Marianne, and the twins, watching the display in rapt fascination. And in her rocker, contentedly knitting, sat Mrs. Noakes. He listened for a moment, smiling over the liberties his son and Reggie were taking with history, then tiptoed stealthily away.

By the time the Battle of Blenheim had been won, the clouds had lifted and the day had brightened considerably. After a late luncheon, Jamie reminded Reg of his promise to ride out in the curricle. Reggie demurred. "Three will be a crush," he said.

"Rubbish. Marianne will take only a small space. I won't have you backing out now."

Marianne, positively glowing at the thought of two escorts, was quite ready. Her pelisse was serviceable rather than becoming, but her bonnet, with its high poke and bright red bow captivatingly tied under her left ear, more than made up for it. Jamie helped her up and tucked a blanket around her legs, the two friends climbed up and took their places on either side of her, and they set off. Their destination was the nearby town of Ashwater, about ten miles to the northwest. Jamie chatted happily about the points of interest along the way—the neat cottage belonging to the bailiff of the Gyllford estates, the home woods where, in season, the quail and pheasant were plentiful, and the notorious "hanging tree" where once, before Jamie was born, a highwayman had met his end—to which Marianne responded with her eager "Really?" Reggie was silent except for a few negative comments on Jamie's way with the horses. "Took that turn a bit too fatht, didn't you?" or "Watch out for that rut! You'll dump uth in the ditch!" Jamie blithely ignored the warnings until a wheel chanced to catch in a deep rut just as he was rounding a turn at a good clip. There was the sound of a crack, the curricle lurched wildly to the right and came to a sudden stop, the horses plunging and rearing frighteningly. One of the horses broke from the reins and galloped off into the underbrush and out of sight. Jamie jumped out of the carriage with a shout and ran to calm the remaining animal. Reggie glanced worriedly at Marianne, who sat stunned. "You're not hurt, are you?" he asked.

She shook her head.

"It ain't anything but a broken wheel, I expect. Don't worry." He patted her hand awkwardly and climbed down gingerly from the lopsided vehicle. Hurrying to Jamie's side, he helped his friend get the horse under control. Jamie looked at Reg shamefacedly.

"It was the damned road. I hope you're not thinking that I let the horses get away from me, are you?" he asked belligerently.

"Of courthe not. Don't be a gudgeon."

They walked to the side of the curricle and surveyed the damage. The wheel had broken from the axle and lay useless and crushed under the weight of the carriage. "Well, what now?" asked Reg.

"There's only one thing for it. I must get to the village and rent us another conveyance. This wheel will not be repaired in a day."

"I'll go, Jamie. I can ride the horthe. You remain here with Marianne."

"No, that won't work. The road has so many turnings and forks, you'd never find the way."

Reggie stared at him in horror. "You're not thuggeththing that I remain here with her!"

"Come now, Reg, don't be a saphead. It will only be for an hour or two."

"An hour or two! It may ath well be a month! No, no, I couldn't."

"But Reggie, you must!"

"No, wait," Reggie said, thinking desperately for a way out. "Why don't you take her up on the horthe with you, and I'll walk alongthide?"

"That would slow me up too much. Besides, I'll have enough trouble riding without a saddle to worry about having anyone else up with me."

But Reg was adamant. "Thorry, old man, but you'll have to think of thomething elthe. I told you that girlth, particularly young oneth, are not in my line. I wouldn't know what to thay to her for two minuteth, let alone two hourth."

"Be reasonable, man! I must be the one to go, for I know the way and I am known at the stable in the village, so I won't have any trouble procuring a conveyance. Someone must stay here with Marianne. We cannot leave her alone, can we? Even *you* must see that!"

Though he cast about urgently in his mind for another solution to the problem, poor Reggie could find none. He glumly shrugged his acquiescence. Jamie grinned, clapped him on the shoulder, and hurried to face the shivering, frightened Marianne. With Reggie's help, they lifted her down from the tilted curricle and set her on the ground. Jamie expressed his regrets for the accident in the briefest terms possible. Then he unfastened the reins from the horse, jumped on its back, and galloped off down the road.

Reggie looked down at his charge with trepidation. "You are shivering, Mith Covington," he said with concern. "Pleathe let me give you my coat."

Marianne looked up at him gratefully, but shook her head. "Oh, no, Lord Farnham. I'm not c-cold. Only f-frightened."

"No need to be frightened. No real harm done," Reggie assured her. "Jamie will be back before you know it with a hired hack."

There. That was the extent of his conversation. What else was he to say to her? He took a quick glance at her face. She was peeping at him from under the brim of her ridiculously grown-up bonnet with an air of expectation. Heaven help him, how was he to fill the two hours looming up formidably before him?

CHAPTER NINE

Philip looked up from his desk at the sound of a knock at his study door. "Come in," he called.

Clarissa peeped in hesitantly. "May I come in?" she asked. "I don't want to disturb you."

"What is this unwonted timidity?" Philip asked, cocking an amused eyebrow at her. "You've always come in without the slightest qualm."

"That was before I realized what important work you do here, my dear. I'm much more respectful now that I realize you're an author."

"And very proper, too. But now that you've demonstrated this admirable humility, you may stop being a peagoose and come in."

Clarissa laughed and entered, closing the door carefully behind her. When she saw his desk, covered with closely written pages, her expression changed. "Oh, dear," she said regretfully, "I *am* disturbing you. Perhaps I should wait until later to talk to you."

"Nonsense. I am not writing another New Testament. The world can wait indefinitely for these words of mine. Come now, sit down and tell me what's on your mind."

"Are you sure you don't mind?"

"Quite sure. I was about to clear my desk and join our guests anyway."

"Oh, I'm so glad of that. That's what I've come to ask you to do. I find myself in a bit of an embarrassment. . . ."

"Embarrassment?"

"Yes, and it's your son's fault."

"Jamie? What's he done?"

"He's gone off in the curricle with Marianne and Reggie and left poor Evalyn here to her own devices. Not that she's shown the least sign of being upset, but still—"

"Do you mean to say he's gone off without even asking her to join the party? Surely he couldn't have done that! He *must* have asked her. Perhaps she didn't want to go and told him she preferred to remain at home."

"No, Philip, he didn't even ask her. She knew nothing about the expedition until Martha mentioned to me, in Evalyn's presence, that Marianne and Jamie had gone off together. Martha had a decided matchmaker's gleam in her eye. I think she's beginning to believe that Jamie and her Marianne may make a match of it."

"Oh, my Lord!" Philip exclaimed in disgust.

"Just so," his sister sighed. "Knowing that Evalyn had overheard all this had me ready to sink!"

"I could wring Jamie's neck."

"So could I. Except, of course, that Evalyn was not in the least discomposed. She's been helping me weave the Christmas wreaths, and there she sat working as calmly as you please, as if it were the most natural thing in the world for one's fiancé to go off with another girl."

Philip got up and paced about, musing. "I've noticed this strange behavior myself. Jamie neglects Miss Pennington shamefully. But I've never seen her look in the least constrained. Do you think it's something they've decided between them?"

"I don't know what you mean," Clarissa said, puzzled.

"Well, we told them that we'd make no announcement until after the new year. Perhaps they've decided that we wanted them to keep their feelings secret from our guests, and so they pretend not to notice each other."

"But how foolish! I never intended for them to dissemble in that way. In fact, it is quite the worst way to prepare society for the news of their engagement."

"Now I don't know what *you* mean," Philip said.

"It will be a shock enough when society learns that James Everard is betrothed to some girl unknown to the polite world. If they have been seen together—seen to be taken with each other—there will have been at least some . . . oh, what shall I call it? . . . preparatory gossip."

Philip made an impatient gesture. "I don't care a fig for the gossip of what you call the polite world. It's Miss Pennington I care about." He suddenly stood stock-still, realizing he had said more than he'd meant to. "Miss Pennington's feelings, I mean," he added lamely.

"If what you surmise is true—that they are behaving this way to keep their relationship secret—we need not worry about her feelings," Clarissa said sensibly. "However, I do not credit it. It's too foolish a plan."

"Then how do you account for Jamie's behavior?"

"I don't know. I only know that I cannot like having poor Evalyn so neglected."

"Neither can I. You may be sure I shall speak to Jamie at the first opportunity. Meanwhile, one would think that Sally could keep her company."

"Sally is a—! Never mind. I don't want to tell you what I think of Sally. You will only think me small-minded, and remind me that you told me not to invite her. It's enough to say that I don't think she and Evalyn have quite taken to each other. Besides, she's gone riding with Edward and Gervaise, and I don't expect to see them again until almost tea time."

"I see. Well, what can we do?"

"I was hoping that you could squire Evalyn about a bit. It would please her, I know, to have Jamie's father's attention and approval."

Philip was silent. Clarissa looked at him curiously. He was staring out into the middle distance, as if his mind were on something else. "Philip?" she asked, "is there something wrong? It cannot be that—? Don't tell me that you don't *like* Evalyn."

Philip stared at his sister. "Of course I like her," he said, "but I . . . I am rather busy, you know, with our guests and the book, and I've been thinking that I ought to start planning for Boxing Day and the rest. . . ."

"If I didn't know you better," said the puzzled Clarissa, "I would take you for the worst of curmudgeons. This rationalization is not at all the sort of thing you have ever before indulged in. What's come over you?"

Philip sighed. "You're right. I *am* behaving like a curmudgeon. Come, let's go into the sitting room. I shall be delighted to rescue Miss Pennington from the boredom and neglect she is no doubt suffering in your company."

Miss Pennington did not look in the least as if she needed rescuing. She and Martha were seated at a large table which was completely covered with greens and ribbons. There were evergreen branches, shoots of holly boasting bright clumps of red berries, strands of ivy, sprigs of mistletoe, and a profusion of ribbons and candles. The ladies were happily fashioning a number of "kissing boughs." These were gaily-decorated baskets made by shaping evergreen boughs and tying them in place with ribbons. Within the baskets would be placed a few apples and candles, and each would be hung from a doorway, with the lively, white-berried mistletoe hanging like a tassel underneath. While they worked, Martha and Evalyn were pursuing a lively discussion about the possible dangers to the morals of a young lady like Marianne of reading novels like Miss Burney's *Evalina*. Philip and Clarissa entered the room in time to hear Martha stating earnestly, "I am convinced that such reading weakens a young lady's moral fiber."

Philip nodded to the ladies and sat down at the table, looking at Evalyn with interest to hear what her response to this would be.

"I don't think so, Martha," she said in her straight-forward, unaffected way. "A young girl has so much to learn about life. The reading of novels provides her with experiences without the necessity of living through these experiences in actuality. Thus she may be spared the dangers and pain of real experiences, while gaining wisdom from the vicarious ones."

"Is that how *you* became so wise, Miss Pennington?" Philip couldn't resist asking. "Have all your experiences been from books?"

Evalyn blushed and answered laughingly, "What other experiences should a lady in my circumstances have had, sir?"

"That's tipping me a leveler for my impertinence!" Philip acknowledged with a grin. "I humbly apologize, Miss Pennington. But if a mere man may give his views on novel reading—"

"By all means, Philip," Martha urged. "I should love to hear them."

"You may not, when you learn that I won't give you much support. I don't see any danger to a young woman's morals in such reading. However, I do see a danger in Miss Pennington's view. It would be too bad, Miss Pennington, if a young woman used novels to substitute for life's experiences. Vicarious living is not a proper substitute for reality. Joys can never be as fulfilling in books as they are in life, and even dangers and pains are more meaningful when they are real."

"I have to agree with you about the joys," Evalyn admitted, "but I think that life brings enough dangers and pains without our seeking them. Just reading about them would be enough for me."

Philip's grin widened. "What? *Cowardly*, Miss Pennington?"

"Merely cautious," she returned promptly.

Clarissa was pleased to see how well they got on. Whatever maggot had got into his head earlier seemed to have disappeared. "Evalyn was asking earlier about the portraits in the gallery, Philip," she said. "You must take her through one day and tell her about the rogues in our family's past."

"I'd be delighted," Philip agreed cheerfully. Turning to Miss Pennington he suggested, "Would you like to go now?"

"If you have the time," Evalyn said, "and Clarissa can spare me . . ."

"Of course," Clarissa agreed. "Go along, both of you."

Philip rose. "How about joining us, Martha? Or have you already made the acquaintance of our illustrious ancestors?"

"More than I want to, thank you. Clarissa and I will be quite content to stay here and have a good gossip while we finish these wreaths."

The gallery, which was really a long corridor connecting two wings of the manor house, was designed cleverly. The wall which faced west was lined with windows, thus letting in the very last of the setting sun. The east wall was unbroken by any windows or doorways, and was completely lined with portraits. They were of a wide assortment of sizes and styles, from tiny, gay miniatures to enormous canvasses of gloomy pomposity. Philip pointed out an impressive, though distant, relation who had sailed with Drake; a sweet-faced, grossly overweight matron surrounded by seven children who was his great-grandmother; a slim, dark-eyed beauty who was his great-aunt and who, he said, had openly claimed to have been a mistress of George the Second; and his grandfather, the second Earl of Gyllford, whose grizzled hair and humorous eyes seemed to Evalyn to be very like the man who now stood beside her. "He's quite the handsomest man in the collection," Evalyn said impulsively.

"Do you think so?" Philip asked. "I'm not surprised, of course. They say that Jamie is very like him."

"Jamie? Oh, I thought rather that . . ." She stopped in confusion. "That is . . . I mean . . . I hadn't noticed that."

Philip looked at her curiously. If she and Jamie had agreed to keep their alliance hidden, they surely needn't play the game with *him*! Was she embarrassed to acknowledge to Jamie's own father that she thought Jamie handsome? Blast the pair of them, he thought. They were certainly puzzling.

Evalyn moved quickly to another portrait. "I've been wondering about this gentleman," she said, pointing to a painting of a thin, sharp-nosed old man with a completely unsuitable, heavily powdered, many-curled wig, and a great number of rings on his fingers.

"Why did you single out Uncle Joshua? You are looking at the late and unlamented Joshua Alexander Sebastian Selkirk Gyllford, known far and wide for taking more than six hours to dress for dinner. Sir Joshua reputedly spent twelve of the sixteen hours of his waking day in his dressing room. I have it on excellent authority that he employed three valets at once, since no one valet could stand the strain."

Evalyn laughed. "I singled him out because I have the perfect mate for him. She hangs in my bedroom. She has a nose every bit as . . . er . . . important as his, a wig as high as an urn and hung with all sorts of pins and jewels and fripperies, and wears at least three rings on each finger."

"They sound a good match, though I can't say I recall the painting. I wonder if it could be his wife, Aunt Caroline."

"Would you like to come and see her?" Evalyn asked.

"Yes, indeed. It would be a great joke for the family to know that Uncle Joshua had been so suitably matched. If it is indeed Aunt Caroline, I may hang them side by side."

"But how will you know? Will you recognize her?"

"I met her only once or twice, when she was quite old, but it is possible that I may recognize her."

They started back through the gallery. Suddenly Evalyn stopped. "Oh!" she said softly.

"What is it?" Philip asked in concern.

"Something silly. I . . . I'm afraid you will think me miss-ish. . . ."

"I already think you miss-ish," Philip teased, "so don't hold back on that score."

She laughed. "I'm afraid I am. You see, I'm not always certain about just what is proper in your circles. Is it . . . perhaps . . . not the thing for me to take you to my . . . ?"

"Your bedroom?" Philip gave a snort of laughter. "Haven't your novels taught you that? It will be quite proper, my dear, I promise you. We need only leave the door ajar, and you will not be compromised." And he tucked her arm under his and proceeded down the corridor.

The lady in question hung on the wall opposite Evalyn's bed. Philip needed only a moment to recognize her. "It is Aunt Caroline to the life! I don't remember seeing this painting before, but if I had, I would never have consigned it to hang in a guest room. What a dreadful sight she is, to be sure. When I think of all the guests who have slept in this room, and who must have suffered untold nightmares from the sight of her, I'm quite contrite. I shall have her removed instant—"

At that moment, his lordship was interrupted by the precipitate entrance of a dishevelled, wild-looking Nancy, Evalyn's unconventional abigail, plainly agitated in the extreme. She rushed across the room to the window, the words spilling out of her as she ran. "Oh, thank the good Lord you're here, Miss Evalyn. Only take a look out the window. It's Joseph, the under-footman, got hisself stuck on the ledge out-side, and so terrified that he'll not move a hair to get hisself off!"

"Nancy, I don't understand a word of what you're saying. Are you telling me there's a *man* out there on the ledge?" Evalyn asked.

"Yes'm," cried Nancy, almost jumping out of her skin in impatience. "Come, look for yer—" Turning as she spoke, she caught her first glimpse of Lord Gyllford. Her mouth dropped open and she gasped in horror. "Oh, no!" she groaned.

"Please don't trouble yourself about my presence, girl," Lord Gyllford assured her, "but I'm sure you must be mistaken. There couldn't be a man out there —we're three stories above ground!"

"B-b-begging your pardon, me lord, but there *is*. It's Joseph, y'see. Standing right out there too scared to move."

"Then stand aside, please, and let me see to him," said Philip firmly.

"Oh, no, me lord, not you!" Nancy almost shrieked, and, like the intrepid girl she was, she stretched out her arms across the window to bar the way.

"But, Nancy," Evalyn said reasonably, "surely his lordship is the only one of us strong enough to handle a fully grown man. Step aside, as he's asked you, and let us have the man in before he falls."

Nancy, though shaking and tearful, refused to budge. "You don't understand. He can't move because he's so scared. If he sees his lordship, that'll send him over the edge for sure!"

"The girl may be right," Evalyn said to Philip. She turned to the window without another word, opened the casement and peered out. When she turned back, her face was pale and her mouth tense. "He's out there, all right," she told Philip tensely, "frozen to the spot and trembling in every limb."

"How far from the window?" Philip asked.

"About ten feet, I'd say."

"Too far to reach. I'd better get some men organized down below, and he can jump into a blanket," Philip said and started for the door.

"Oh, no, please!" Nancy begged. She ran to Philip, dropped down on her knees in front of him and grasped his hand. "Annette asked me *particular* not to say anything to anyone but Miss Evalyn. It'd be the end of her if anyone else learns of this! Oh, please sir! Once you go out o' this room, there won't be no way to keep it quiet."

"Don't be a fool, girl," Philip said, his voice gently at variance with his words as he lifted her to her feet. "You don't want the man to die, do you?"

"There may be another way," Evalyn ventured.

"I knew you would think o' something," Nancy said, looking at Evalyn with adoration and relief.

"What do you suggest?" Philip asked.

"Let me try to coax him to move. He'll have no reason to be frightened of me. And if you stand behind the casement, right alongside me, you can be ready to grasp him as soon as he gets close enough."

Philip nodded his agreement and came across the room in three strides. Evalyn opened the casement and looked out again. A stone ledge ran the length of the outside wall, extending from the wall about a foot, except under the windows where the ledge curved outward to form small, circular balconies. The balconies were edged with low, wrought-iron grilles which permitted the inhabitants of the rooms, should they desire to do so, to step outside in safety. The footman, however, stood on the narrow part of the ledge, halfway between Evalyn's balcony and the one belonging to Sally's room. He stood immobile, his back against the wall, his shirtsleeves flapping in the wind, his hands clutching the coat of his livery, pressing it in a crushed bundle against his chest. His eyes, wide with terror, were fixed on the ground three stories below.

Philip put his hands on Evalyn's waist and lifted

her over the sill, and she stepped out on the tiny balcony. Philip climbed up after her, but remained hidden by the casement.

"Good afternoon," Evalyn said to the footman in so calm and ordinary a voice that Philip stared at her in amazement. "You are Joseph, are you not?"

Joseph's head remained fixed, but the pupils of his terrified eyes slid to the corners in his attempt to see who was speaking to him.

"You needn't turn to look at me," Evalyn continued in her calm way. "I'm only Miss Pennington. You've gotten yourself into a fix, haven't you? Well, don't be concerned—we shall soon get you out of it." Without a pause, she continued to speak in her everyday, softly modulated voice. "I think—don't you?—that it would be best not to turn your head or look around, but perhaps you had best not look at the ground either. Looking straight ahead should serve us best, I think. Yes, just like that. Very good. Now, then, it seems to me that all you need do is slide your right foot toward the right a very little way. There's no danger, you know; the ledge is very firm. I'm standing on it myself. Just a little way to the right. Yes, just so. Good. Now you need only to slide your left leg to meet it. There! Very good indeed. All we need are a few more movements just like that, and we shall have you safe. A bit to the right again. Good. Now the left . . ."

Thus, bit by bit, Evalyn coaxed him closer to the balcony. The moment he was close to the railing, Philip caught him under the arms and pulled him over the grille onto the balcony. Evalyn caught the footman's coat as it dropped from his hands, and she and Philip gently helped the shaking man over the sill and into the bedroom.

Nancy embraced Joseph in her enthusiastic relief. "Oh, thank goodness," she exclaimed ecstatically. "Thank goodness!"

Joseph, beginning to get his color back, turned to

thank his benefactress, and for the first time saw Philip. His face turned ashen, and he fell to the ground in a dead faint.

"Confound it!" Philip muttered in disgust. "My presence seems to do nothing but add complications."

Evalyn's lips twitched. "Not at all, my lord. You were indispensible. How could we have hauled him over the railing of the balcony without you?"

Philip frowned at her. "Throw me no sops, my girl. I have the most lowering feeling that, had I not been here, you and your intrepid abigail would have managed very well, and I'd never have heard a word of this entire affair. But never mind that now. What shall we do to bring the fellow round?"

"Nancy, go to Annette and see if she can give you a bottle of vinaigrette."

Nancy returned shortly, but it was Annette herself who carried the restorative. She bobbed a quick curtsey to Philip and Evalyn, and promptly knelt at Joseph's side, holding the vinaigrette under his nose, and murmuring endearments in her native tongue. Joseph shivered, groaned, and opened his eyes. He looked at Philip, winced, and struggled to get to his feet. But Annette held him back. "No, no, *mon cher*, you are not to get up yet," she said tenderly.

Joseph pushed her arm aside and got to his feet awkwardly. "M-m-my lord," he stammered.

Annette jumped up and took a heroic stance in front of him. "You'll not scold my Joseph, milord," she said bravely. "It is all my fault. To me must come all the blame."

"Annette, be still," Joseph whispered fiercely. "His lordship's business is wi' me, not you! Be off to your lady, do y'hear me?"

"I'm glad to see you've got your courage back," Philip remarked drily. "For a while I was very much afraid I had a jellyfish in my employ."

"It was only the height, my lord," Joseph said earnestly. "Ever since I been a tot I been terrified o' heights. Even if my mum stood me on a table I'd yell like a screech owl."

"If you're so afraid of heights, how is it we found you outside a third-story window?"

Joseph stiffened. "Can't tell you that, my lord."

"I can tell him! Me, Annette! I have to be ashamed of nothing, *moi!*"

"Be quiet, girl," Joseph hissed at her. "Do y'want to get us both sacked? Get back to y'r lady before she misses you."

"If you don't mind, Joseph," Philip said with some asperity, "I'll decide who goes or stays. Now, I don't care to pry into your private doings, but I can't allow my guests to be troubled with incidents like this. Unless I learn, and quickly, why you were outside Miss Pennington's window, I'll sack the lot of you."

"No, no m'sieur! I deserve it only! You are a good, kind man—so everyone says downstairs. I will explain it to you. . . ."

Joseph began to interrupt. Philip stayed him with a glare. Annette said to Joseph softly, "Do not be angry with me, *mon cher*. Someone must explain. It is *amour*, milord. Joseph and I . . . we are for many months . . . how you say? . . . betrothed. But we cannot marry. Joseph supports his *maman* and has not yet enough savings for me to leave the employ of Miss Trevelyan. And Miss Trevelyan does not like for her dresser to be married. So we must wait, and wait . . . *comprenez?*"

Philip said impatiently, "Yes, of course, but what has this to do with being outside the window?"

Annette hung her head. "The rest, it is more . . . *difficile* . . . difficult to say. . . ."

Joseph stepped forward. "I'll tell him. Y'see, sir, gossip spreads real quick in the servants' hall, and if Miss Trevelyan ever should get word that Annette and me is planning to be wed, well, you can be sure that'd be the end of Annette's position. So we ain't ever told nobody about it. Well, you can see that it would gall a man . . . never being able to walk out with his girl or nothing . . . so, when Annette tells me that Miss Trevelyan is out riding for the afternoon—and I not needed this afternoon neither—well, then, I fair jumped at the chance to see Annette alone. I slipped up to Miss Trevelyan's room and Annette let me in—"

"Yes, yes, enough!" Philip cut in, with an embarrassed glance at Evalyn. "There's no need to explain further. I take it that Miss Trevelyan returned from her outing a bit earlier than expected, is that it?"

"Yes, sir, that she did. And there was no place for me to go but out the window. I knew I'd never make it to the next room, but there was just nowheres else to go!"

"But there's something I don't understand," Evalyn said. "What had my Nancy to do with all this?"

"I was passing by, on me way to check your clothes for this evening," Nancy said, "when Annette comes out o' Miss Trevelyan's room looking so white and desp'rate-like, it fair pulled me heart out o' me. She was half crazy with fright. She told me what had happened, so I ran to find you."

"I see. But Nancy, I thought you and Annette were at swords' points."

Nancy shrugged. "That's true enough. But if she was that desp'rate, I had to help her, didn't I?"

"Yes, of course. You did the right thing," Evalyn assured her.

Annette embraced Nancy warmly. "And I never forget, Nancy. Annette never forgets a kindness. For you, and you, Miss Evalyn, I will prove someday my gratitude," she said with feeling.

All eyes turned to Philip, who was staring at them nonplussed. "I suppose you're all hoping that I will excuse you and forget the whole sorry incident," he said glowering at them. "Very well, I will." He turned to the footman and thrust his coat into his arms. "Here, go along. But see that there are no more clandestine meetings, and that you never again go climbing walls."

A chorus of thank-yous greeted this announcement, but Philip only glared. Nancy and Annette curtseyed hurriedly and ran out. But Joseph would not be put off. "I don't know how to thank you proper, my lord," he said with real gratitude.

"Joseph," said Philip softly, "I will speak to Hutton about raising your wages." Joseph stared at Philip openmouthed. "Well, we must see what we can do to get you married without too much delay," he added gruffly. "Now, go along, man, go along." Joseph made an attempt at a bow and almost ran to the door, shrugging himself into his coat at the same time. "And walk with some dignity," Philip said in disgust, "some dignity, if you please. We don't want to set the whole house talking!"

At the door, Joseph made another attempt to express his thanks, but Philip waved him out. When he had left, Evalyn smiled at Philip warmly. "That was very kind in you, my lord," she said.

"My lord again? I thought we had agreed on Philip. May I say, *Miss Pennington*, that Jamie was right when he said that you were a most redoubtable girl?"

"Did he say that of me? I must thank him, if it is indeed a compliment."

"Can it be otherwise? Of course it is a compliment. Your calm and composure out there on the balcony were quite remarkable in a woman. Most ladies would have fainted or had hysterics."

"You're not being very kind to my sex. As for me, I couldn't have behaved otherwise. My father was a soldier and would not have permitted fainting or hysterics in anyone living in his house."

Philip, standing close to her, lifted her chin and looked down at her with sympathy. "Poor Evalyn," he said softly, "were you not permitted even tears?"

"Oh, no! Tears would have been considered the worst weakness."

"It must have been a difficult childhood. I most sincerely feel for you."

A twinkle appeared in Evalyn's eyes. "Don't feel regret for my *childhood*, my lord," she said, "but rather feel it for me *now*."

"Now?" Philip asked.

"Yes. You see, I am being compromised."

Philip recognized the twinkle. "Compromised, my girl? By me?"

"Yes, I'm afraid so," she said in her almost perfectly serious way. He dropped his hand from her chin.

"And how am I compromising you?" he asked in a tone of almost perfect severity.

"You see, I am alone with you in my bedroom."

"Yes, but I explained earlier how that fact need not be compromising."

"Yes, I remember," Evalyn assured him, "but I'm afraid your Joseph has closed the door."

Philip gave a shout of laughter. "Vixen!" he said. "You have garrotted me again! Very well, Miss, I'll go. And I shall take Aunt Caroline with me." He lifted the portrait from the wall and strode to the door. There he paused and looked back at her. "But I shall retaliate, never fear. I shall replace this portrait with the one of my great-aunt Lucy Gyllford Axminster. She is the lady who murdered her husband in cold blood, convinced the magistrates that the deed was done by a highwayman, and attended the funeral as calmly as you please, without troubling herself to shed a single tear. I think you and she should deal extremely well together!"

CHAPTER TEN

Reggie's nose was red and his fingers frozen. The sun had already sunk below the horizon and would very soon take with it the last of the light. To make matters worse, a sharp wind was whipping up. No matter how often he looked down the lane he could see no sign of Jamie or the carriage he was supposed to hire. He glanced at Marianne trudging along doggedly beside him as they tried to keep warm by pacing back and forth along the road. She appeared to be extremely cold and uncomfortable, but he had to admit that the girl had made no complaint in the almost two hours since Jamie had left them. It had been a dreadful time. Reggie had wracked his brain for topics to discuss so that the time would pass comfortably. He had tried to discuss horses, but Marianne admitted to being afraid of them. He had brought up the subject of travel, but Marianne had never been anywhere. He broached the subject of the London season, but Marianne was not yet out and had no knowledge of it. Her monosyllabic answers to his questions were dampening in the extreme, and his head ached from casting about for a subject on which he could draw her out. For a while, he was quite ready to strangle her with the ribbons of her ridiculous bonnet. But now, looking down at her rosy-tipped nose and blue-tinged lips, he found himself touched with sympathy for her plight which, he belatedly realized, might be even worse than his own.

"Pleathe let me give you my coat," he pleaded for the twentieth time. "You mutht be freezing."

"No, I assure you," she said with a pathetic little smile. "I'm doing quite well, really. It's only—"

"Only what?" asked Reggie in consternation.

"My fingers. They're stinging me so. If only I had thought to bring my muff. It's lined with fur and would have been such a comfort."

"I have an idea," ventured Reggie bravely, feeling suddenly imbued with a sense of gallantry toward the poor creature. "Why don't we thit down on that tree thtump, and I'll rub your handth. That'll warm them up a bit."

"T-thank you," she said in a quavery voice, and sat down on the stump. Reggie sat down beside her, took her hands, and rubbed them vigorously. When he looked up to see if she were feeling any better, he found that she had turned her face away from him, and that her shoulders were heaving gently.

"My word!" he exclaimed in real agony. "Mith Covington, you're not crying, are you?"

She nodded, and a sob escaped her. Reggie felt sick. He was absolutely incapable of dealing with a sobbing female. He glanced quickly down the road in a desperate hope that he might see a sign of Jamie, but there was none. He felt an overpowering urge to run down the road as fast as his legs could carry him, but he resisted—he was born and bred a gentleman, after all. With real courage he turned to her again and asked, "What ith it? Your fingerth? Did I hurt you? Pleathe, you muthtn't cry!"

The shoulders heaved more violently, and the sobs became louder as Marianne shook her head. "N-no, of c-course n-not!" she managed. "It's n-nothing *you've* done. It's m-me!"

"I don't understand," Reggie groaned in mounting desperation. "Ith there anything I can do? Here, take my coat."

"Don't your d-dare take your coat off!" Marianne cried, hastily turning to him. "I w-won't have you c-contracting an inflammation of the l-lungs because of m-me!" And her tears resumed.

"Ith *that* what'th worrying you?" Reggie asked amazed. "What a goothe you are! I am wearing a coat and a waithtcoat under thith greatcoat. I'll be fine." He stripped off his greatcoat and put it around her shoulders.

"I know I'm a goose," she sniffed. "You've been so p-patient with me, and s-so g-good and k-kind, and I've been such a b-bore!"

"A bore! How can you think thuch a thing! I've never heard thuch thtuff and nonthenthe," Reggie exclaimed with perfect sincerity. "It'th all my fault. I never know what to thay to young ladieth."

"It's you who are talking stuff and nonsense now," Marianne sniffed. "You've been a perfect gentleman, and you t-tried so hard to c-converse with me. But I can n-never think of things to say. And I so wanted to be interesting!" And with a fresh flood of tears, she dropped her head on Reggie's shoulder.

It seemed only natural for Reggie to support her by slipping his arm about her waist, and patting her back sympathetically with his free hand. If Marianne were not wearing that terrible bonnet, he would have put his cheek against her soft brown ringlets. An unfamiliar feeling of warmth and strength flowed through him, and he found himself hoping that Jamie would not turn up just yet. "There, there, Marianne, don't cry," he heard himself murmuring over and over. Without quite realizing what he was doing, he lifted her chin and, with the exquisite, lace-edged handkerchief he pulled from his pocket, he tenderly wiped her cheeks.

"I'm s-sorry to b-be acting like s-such a b-baby," Marianne said, her voice still quivering with tears, her wet lashes fluttering enticingly over melting blue eyes. Entranced, Reggie bent closer. She lifted her face to his and, to his utter surprise, their lips met. For a few seconds, neither of them moved. Reggie felt dizzy, as if his head were flying off into the air. Then he realized what he was doing. He was kissing a girl! *Jamie's* girl.

"Oh, Lord!" he groaned and jumped to his feet. Marianne stared up at him in trusting and innocent surprise. "Marianne!" he said in a choked voice, "I mean, Mith Covington . . . I'm very thorry. I don't know what to . . . I don't know what came over me! It wath unforgivable, I know, but I give you my word it will not happen again."

"Oh," Marianne said in a tiny voice, and a tear started down her cheek again.

"Good God, you're not going to cry again!" said Reggie in despair. "I know what I've done can be very upthetting to a young girl, but it wath not tho very bad, really. Pleathe, Marianne," he begged, sitting down beside her and grasping her hands. "Truly, you can trutht me. I've given you my word. I won't break it."

"I don't w-want your w-word!" she said between sobs.

"Marianne! What can you mean? You cannot *want* me to kith you!"

"Why not?" she asked, sniffing into his handkerchief.

"Becauthe . . . becauthe . . . well, for one thing, everyone knowth I've no way with the ladieth. I'm much too fat, and I lithp—"

Marianne's usually limpid eyes flashed. "You have a way with *me*! And you are *not* fat! Everybody says you always look in the height of fashion. Jamie says you're top-of-the-trees! I heard him! And as for your lisp, well—"

"Well—?"

"I think it's . . . lovable!"

Reggie gaped at her in astonishment. "Lovable? I don't with to be rude, Marianne, but are you thure you're not touched in your upper workth?"

Marianne was forced to giggle. "Oh, Reggie, you're so droll!"

A distant sound of horses' hooves brought a sense of urgency to Reggie's next words. "That'th all very well, Marianne, but you mutht promithe me to forget what . . . what'th happened here today."

"But why?"

"I haven't time to explain. Jamie'th coming. You do like Jamie, don't you?"

"Oh, yes, but—"

"And he liketh you. Therefore, you mutht promithe me—"

Marianne looked dangerously close to tears again. "I don't understand. Don't *you* like me?"

Reggie looked toward the approaching vehicle in desperation. Jamie was practically upon them. "It don't matter whether I like you or not," he explained hastily. "He liked you firtht, you thee?" A rather shabby phaeton was drawing up in front of them. Reggie pulled Marianne to her feet. "You do underthtand, don't you? And you won't cry, will you? That'th a good girl!"

Jamie, cheerful and self-satisfied at having rescued his party from a nasty fix, was full of the adventures he'd encountered. He'd found, on his arrival at Ashwater, that the livery stable where he was known had no one in attendance, and that he had not a penny in his pockets. His account of his attempts to establish credit made for a lengthy and humorous monologue, which occupied him through the entire trip home. If his passengers were somewhat preoccupied and unusually quiet, Jamie seemed to take no notice at all.

Clarissa knew that the evening would not go well. All the signs of trouble were apparent even before nightfall. First, one of the horses that Jamie had taken appeared at the stable wild-eyed and riderless. When she had finally found Philip, who had unaccountably disappeared for over an hour, he calmly told her not to worry, that Jamie was quite capable of handling any emergency on the road. His reassurances fell on deaf ears, for she knew that Martha would fall into hysterics if she got wind of the news that something had happened to the curricle in which her daughter was riding. By the time Jamie and his party finally appeared, looking cold and exhausted, it lacked only half an hour to dinner time. The rest of the household had already gathered in the drawing room, and the necessity of keeping them amused for an additional half-hour while Jamie, Reggie, and Marianne dressed, severely taxed her nerves.

The second trouble sign was the news that Martha imparted to her. Freddie, one of the twins, was complaining of an earache. Clarissa tried to make light of it to Martha, assuring and reassuring her that children often have complaints in the evening which disappear magically in the morning. But earaches were often symptoms of severe infection, as Clarissa well knew, and the fear of a serious illness invading her household hung over her like a cloud.

But the trouble that most depressed her spirits was her relationship with Gervaise which, he had made clear this afternoon, was approaching some sort of climax. He wanted her to marry him. He had always, as long as she could remember, wanted her to marry him. He had been an admirer in her youth, and she knew that he had never married because of a strong sense of loyalty to her, although she found it hard to believe—his protestations to the contrary—that his love for her could persist into middle age. She believed that it was simply a habit with him to think of himself in love with her. Nevertheless, his unwavering devotion had been a source of comfort to her through many years. He had been a trusted adviser, an escort, a gentle and cheerful friend. She counted on his support, enjoyed his company, and found his comfortable companionship one of the necessities of her life.

But now he was threatening to withdraw these from her. He had made it clear that he wanted a wife, not a friend. He had told her quite firmly this afternoon that he wanted some time alone with her as soon as she could arrange it. She knew what he would say. And she knew what her answer had to be. She had other obligations. She could not marry. But she did not want to lose his friendship. Why, oh why, had he chosen this time to force this dilemma upon her?

He ought to have realized that the Christmas season was the worst time of year for additional pressures. She had so much to see to and to organize. Christmas eve was only two days off. There were the Christmas baskets still to get ready for distribution among the tenants, the Yule log ceremony, and the transportation to midnight mass to arrange, to say nothing of the late supper they would have afterwards. Then the enormous Christmas dinner for the next day had to be planned—a particular problem since she never knew how many neighbors would be dropping in. Then there was Boxing Day following, when it would be their turn to prepare the feast and entertainment for the servants' special day, and give them their Christmas boxes. Trust Gervaise to muddle her at such a time!

Sitting at the foot of the dining table, Clarissa surveyed her guests carefully. The snatches of conversation she heard sounded cheerful, the food was delectable and abundant, the candlelight gave the faces a warm, lively glow. But Martha looked strained and seemed to have her mind elsewhere. Sally, flirting with Philip outrageously, nevertheless seemed to be watching everyone with those cat's eyes of hers, as if she were a French spy trying to ferret out some dreadful secret. And Reggie was a little silent tonight—not like himself at all. Jamie, however, was persisting in his attentions to little Marianne, who was in high color tonight and looking very lovely. Evidently Philip had had no chance to speak to his son and was endeavoring to make up for it by keeping up a lively conversation with Evalyn. Well, things could be worse, she thought. We might brush through this evening after all. She stole a glance at Gervaise, seated at her right. He was regarding her with his apple-cheeked smile. "So," he said teasingly, "now that you've checked all your other guests, you finally give me a glance."

"Oh, pooh," she laughed and patted his arm affectionately. "I don't trouble about you. You're quite one of the family."

His smile faded. "I suppose I have been so," he said, looking down into his plate, "but you must take no one for granted."

Hutton, the butler, came up behind her at that moment and leaned over her, asking for instructions on serving the second course, so Clarissa didn't have to give Gervaise an answer.

While waiting for the men to finish their port, the ladies sat in the drawing room somewhat dispiritedly, Sally playing the piano without her usual enthusiasm, Marianne pacing about the room in obvious boredom, and Clarissa staring at the fire abstractedly. Evalyn, noticing the worried frown on Martha's brow, approached her and said, "You seem to be a little troubled this evening, Mrs. Covington. I hope there's nothing wrong with the twins."

Martha looked up eagerly and made room for Evalyn on the settee. "I *am* a bit troubled," she admitted. "Freddie's complained of an earache. Clarissa thinks it will go away by morning, and of course she's probably right. But it's my nature to fear the worst. If it should turn out to be an infection, I'm sure I shall suffer a *collapse*, for I don't know what I can do for him. Our doctor at home is quite capable and knows the twins so well, but he is too far away to be brought here, and I have no confidence at all in strange doctors."

"I'm sure that, if a doctor were needed, Clarissa will know of a capable one," Evalyn said comfortingly.

"Yes, but strangers are strangers, no matter how well recommended they may be. And a strange doctor would not know Freddie as he should."

"But he need not be familiar with his patient if you or Mr. Covington can give him an accurate history of Freddie's past illnesses."

"Oh, Mr. Covington is no help at all in these matters. He always says that I make fuss enough for two and retires to his study. Tell me, Evalyn, do you think I should give the boy some medication? I've brought some James's Powders with me, and some mint water, too. And I've heard that putting a roasted onion in the ear can be quite beneficial."

Evalyn looked dubious. "Why don't we go upstairs and see if he is sleeping comfortably? Perhaps he has already gotten over his pain, and your mind would be at ease."

"Oh, *would* you go with me? I know I shan't relax until I am convinced that the dear child is not suffering."

The two women left the drawing room and did not return for over an hour. When they came back, they found that Philip, Gervaise, Edward, and Jamie were enjoying a lively game of silver-loo. Sally was still at the piano, Reggie turning the pages for her, and Clarissa listening to the music with all the attention she could muster. And Marianne was gazing moodily out of the window at the moon. Martha took a seat beside Clarissa, who leaned over and whispered, "How is Freddie? Is he sleeping comfortably?"

"He is now," sighed Martha with relief. "Your Evalyn is a gem, truly she is. We found Freddie cross and uncomfortable, and quite unable to sleep. But Evalyn soothed him, and had her Nancy make him some herb tea and heat up some oil which she dropped in his ear. And before I knew it, he had dropped off to sleep. We stayed and watched over him for quite a while, but he seems to be sleeping so contentedly that we came away."

"Oh, I'm so glad," Clarissa said, relieved.

"Yes. You can imagine how grateful I am. Do you think, Clarissa, that Evalyn would consider taking a position as governess with us? I know she is a guest here, and I wouldn't dream of asking her without your permission, but do you know anything of her plans for after the holidays? Does she return to the Carberys, or has she another post?"

Clarissa smiled enigmatically. "I'm delighted that you found her so helpful. She is truly a remarkable young woman. But I'm quite sure that after the holidays, she will be . . . er . . . otherwise engaged."

Evalyn, meanwhile, had joined Marianne at the window. "What a lovely moon," she remarked.

Marianne looked downcast, and sighed feelingly. "Yes, very lovely," she said.

"I suppose you are thinking that it is a night on which to be gazing at the moon with an interesting young man, rather than to be making polite conversation with a prosy, chattering female," Evalyn said with an understanding smile.

Marianne looked stricken. "Oh, no, Miss Pennington, not at all! I hope I didn't . . . that is, I never intended . . . I mean, I didn't mean to offend—"

"Of course you didn't. You haven't given me any reason to be offended. It's only that I know I would have felt, when I was your age, that a night like this is wasted if it isn't shared with a young man."

"I don't feel that way. I find young men quite confusing and difficult, and I wouldn't care in the least if I never spoke to any of them again."

"Oh, how cruel! There is at least one gentleman in this very room who would be very sorry to hear you say so."

"No, there isn't. If you mean Jamie, you can see that he sits across the room laughing over his silly card game and has not exchanged a word with me all evening. And as for Reginald Windle, he has been languishing over Miss Trevelyan in the most odiously deferential way, just as if nothing whatever had happened between—" And here she stopped and blushed in embarrassment.

"I don't wish to pry, of course," Evalyn assured the girl gently, "but Lord Reginald is a particular friend of mine, and I'm sure he would never have offended you knowingly."

"Oh, he didn't offend me, exactly," Marianne hastened to reassure Evalyn, and before she was aware, she had confided to Evalyn the whole story of her adventures of the afternoon. "So you see, Miss Pennington," she concluded, "that is why I am so confused. How can a gentleman kiss a girl one minute and ignore her the next?"

"It certainly is a puzzle," Evalyn agreed, "but it seems clear that Lord Reginald feels honor-bound to leave the field to Jamie."

"Do you really think so?" Marianne asked hopefully. "You do not think he has forgotten me already?"

"I don't believe he could have done so. But honor is important to gentlemen, you know. More important than love, I think. So you must not blame him too much for putting his honor before his heart."

"Oh, Miss Pennington, you make him sound quite romantic! Do you think I should put him out of my heart, too?"

"I'm sure I don't know. Are you certain that he's really there? I was under the impression that Jamie is the one who attracts you."

Marianne sighed again. "Oh, dear, I wish you hadn't said that. I don't know which of them I prefer. Do you think that means I'm . . . flighty?"

Evalyn bit back a smile. "No, of course not. I think it means that you are not acquainted with them for a long enough time. In due course, your instincts will tell you which one you love."

"Are you sure, Miss Pennington? Do you think I will ever be certain?"

"Oh, yes. When you are truly in love, your instincts

will point him out to you, just as the needle of a compass points north."

Marianne gazed at her with something like adoration. But even as she spoke, Evalyn was uncomfortably aware that, instinctively, her own eyes were about to turn toward the gaming table. It was only by a physical effort—not unlike the effort of keeping the needle of a compass from pointing north—that she was able to restrain herself from turning to look at Philip's face.

CHAPTER ELEVEN

Sally bid everyone goodnight with her brightest smile, floated off gracefully to her room like a blond goddess on a cloud of mauve silk, closed the door gently behind her, and kicked over the nearest chair with a vicious swing of her foot. "What an idiot I am!" she said aloud. She paced the room, her hips swaying angrily. What was she doing in this rustic backwater? She belonged in London, in a whirl of balls and soirées, gambling games and masquerades, intrigues and flirtations, and the thousand other diversions with which she was accustomed to give excitement to her daily existence. She was so bored here she wanted to scream! She had known, in maneuvering her invitation, that she was condemning herself to a fortnight of quiet evenings and lazy days, but she had not expected to be humiliated, to be forced to take a back seat to a nobody of a governess. Why, even that seventeen-year-old chit, Marianne, was arousing more interest among the men than she! What was the matter with these men? Were they blind?

She picked up a taper with shaking fingers and lit all the candles of a large candelabra. She carried it to her dressing room and set it on the dressing table in front of the mirror. In the strong reflected light, she studied her face with intense concern. Her green eyes glinted back at her as brightly as ever, subtly accented by the blacking with which she darkened her lashes. Her skin was smooth and unmarked by a wrinkle, freckle, or blemish, and the soft pink color of her cheekbones was due as much to nature as to art. The long, tear-drop diamond earrings made glittering highlights on her cheeks, and emphasized their smoothness. Her neck was long and graceful, her shoulders smooth as ivory. The only fault she could find with the picture in the mirror was in the arrangement of her hair. She had felt, earlier this evening, that Annette's suggestion for her coiffure was very becoming, with its part down the center and a cascade of tight curls falling over her ears. But now, in contrast to the insufferable Miss Pennington's simple style, it looked ornate and artificial.

There was a light scratching at the door, and Annette entered diffidently. "You have come up to bed early, Ma'm'selle," she ventured.

"You are late!" Sally countered angrily. "I expect you to be here waiting for me when I come up to bed!"

"But, Ma'm'selle, how am I to know—?"

"I'll brook no arguments, girl!" Sally cut in. "Stop jabbering and take down my hair. And by the way, don't fix it in this style again. It's dreadful."

"*Zut!* Did you not say to me earlier that—?"

Sally narrowed her eyes threateningly. "Are you going to talk back to me about everything? Watch your step, Annette. You can be replaced quite easily, you know. I don't know why I've put up with you this long."

Annette had heard these threats many times before and was unmoved. "You did not have much amusement

downstairs tonight, eh?" she asked impertinently, pulling the pins from her mistress's hair.

"Amusement! It was the greatest bore I've ever been
forced to endure. I don't think I can stand much
more. I'm tempted to pack up this very night. I'd
get to London if I had to travel on the public stage!"

Annette drew in her breath and opened her mouth
to object. The possibility of being forced to leave Joseph so soon came as a shock. Although Lord Gyllford
had been true to his word and had arranged for a pro-
motion for Joseph, the pair had not yet had time to
benefit from the new arrangement. It would be terrible
to be forced to leave him now, when she had been expecting to spend another ten days in his company.
But she knew that she could not hope to sway her
mistress by argument. Perhaps she could soothe her
out of the sullens. A better mood might make the idea
of rushing back to London less appealing. "Perhaps
Ma'm'selle is only a little tired," she suggested amicably.

"Ma'm'selle is not in the least tired. How can I be
tired? I haven't been dancing, have I? I haven't done
anything that would tire a dowager in her eighties!"

Annette, having taken down Ma'm'selle's hair, now
undertook to unhook her gown. She remained silent,
trying desperately to think of some way to make the
stay at Gyllford appear more attractive to her willful
employer, but nothing occurred to her. She helped her
Ma'm'selle into her filmy nightdress, a costly trifle
made of layers of gauze, each layer a different shade
of blue, and picked up the garments Miss Trevelyan
had discarded. Ordinarily, she would have departed
with them, but tonight she lingered in the dressing
room, pretending to be busy putting things in order,
hoping that she would learn more of Miss Trevelyan's
plans.

Sally, not in the least sleepy, stretched herself lux-
uriously on the chaise and mulled things over. Philip
had been unapproachable ever since her arrival, but

she had seen nothing to make her think that he had designs in other quarters. While Miss Pennington's position in the household still remained a mystery, she was almost convinced that Philip was not involved in it. There was no reason to feel that her campaign was lost. She might win him still, if she could get near to him. She would have to make him more approachable. She would have to waylay him in his study, or surprise him by appearing early at breakfast. . . . She was clever—she would find ways. As for Miss Pennington, if her presence should become a threat to her plans, Sally would find a way to discredit her.

Annette made a noise in the dressing room. "Are you still here?" Sally asked. "I don't want you any more tonight. Go to bed."

"I only wish to put away your things. Look, you have left your diamond earrings lying here. Do you not want to lock them away in your jewel box?"

"Oh, bother. Just leave them there and go away."

"But how foolish, Ma'm'selle! It is not at all proper to leave such things lying about for anyone to pick up."

"There's no one here who would—" Sally stopped and rose slowly from the chaise. She walked to the door of the dressing room and leaned against the frame. "Perhaps you're right," she said to Annette, a strange smile turning up the corners of her mouth, her eyes showing a calculating gleam. "One should never be too careless with valuables, no matter where one is, don't you agree? You are very right to caution me. Here, I'll put them in the box, Annette, and you must make sure I lock it carefully. You must be sure we do this every night, all the time we stay here. Will you remember to remind me, *chère* Annette?"

Annette ogled her mistress in suspicion. What was the meaning of this sudden emphasis on the safety of her jewels? And the sudden affection with which she was speaking? Annette didn't like the glitter of those green eyes. Ma'm'selle was planning some devilment, of that Annette was sure. "As you say, Ma'm'selle," she said carefully.

"Every night, for as long as we stay here, we must remember to do this, *n'est-ce pas?* It is your own suggestion, after all."

"But, yes. It is of all things the most sensible," Annette said, watching her mistress carefully. "Does this mean we are to remain here?"

Ma'm'selle Trevelyan smiled enigmatically, locked the jewel case, and tucked the key under a powder puff in a glass dish on the dressing table. "Yes," she said thoughtfully, "I think we'll remain for a little while. This rustication may prove to be somewhat enjoyable after all."

Reggie woke early the next morning and drew aside the window curtains to find the ground covered with a light sprinkling of snow, and the sky heavy with the threat of further precipitation. Blast! he thought, another day of enforced inactivity. Another day in which he would be obliged to linger about the house, making polite conversation, and playing silly card games. And worst of all, he would have to see Marianne and pretend to indifference and distance, while all the while he would remember their warmth and intimacy. He climbed back into bed and tried to go back to sleep. There was no point in dressing now. No one would be down to breakfast before ten on a day like this. He closed his eyes and tried to will sleep to return to him again, but he felt obstinately wide awake. His mind returned, as it had done repeatedly the night before, to the little patch of woods where he had spent the previous afternoon. He could see the tree stump, the fading sunlight lighting the bare treetops, the wet lashes of Marianne's eyes flickering tremulously against her cheeks. He could see her lift her eyes, and then her face, close to his. And he could feel again the surprising warmth and softness of her lips against his own.

He sat up, leaned back against the pillow, his eyes wide open. Of all the men in his wide circle, he was the last expected to lose his head over a girl. Reggie was the one to whom the others came with their problems in matters of the heart. Old Reg would be sure to take it all as a great joke and a bore, and tease them out of the doldrums. Anyone could have predicted what Reggie's future would be: a rich and fat old bachelor, riding to the hounds, organizing shooting parties and elaborate and well-attended dinners. Not that he was at all averse to keeping a ladybird or two for amusement. But ladies of the muslin company did not count in this regard. They never affected one's emotions. One did not become involved with them in any serious way.

But a naive, innocent girl like Marianne—one whose birth and station in life were similar to his own— well, that was quite a different case. One kiss and he could have been a doomed man. Fortunately, Jamie had staked the first claim. Reggie had no intention of altering his plans for the future for any girl, and certainly not for a chit just out of the schoolroom, not yet "out," with no *savoire-faire* or address. She could barely make civilized conversation!

He sighed. All that was far from the truth, and he knew it. Why, when they had sat together on the tree stump, her conversation had been utterly charming. Where, oh, where could he ever again find a girl who would describe his lisp as "lovable"?

But he mustn't dwell on it. He must discipline himself to put her out of his thoughts. He must find some other way to occupy his mind. He cast his eyes around the room. There on the mantle was the very thing. He hadn't spent any of his time in such pursuits since his days at Cambridge, and even then he had avoided it as much as possible. But there was nothing else he could think of. Yes, there was nothing for it but to get out of bed, get that book from the mantlepiece and spend the morning reading. He sighed. Love can get a man into preposterous situations. He crossed the room barefooted and lifted the book from the shelf. It was somewhat yellowed and covered with dust. He blew it clean and looked at the title—*The Life of Mr. Jonathan Wild the Great*. Well, it sounded as good as any. Reggie pattered back to bed and propped himself up among the pillows. To what ignominy had he fallen! As he turned stoically to the first page, he hoped fervently that word of this activity would not leak out to his friends. He would never be able to live it down!

Evalyn was also spending the morning in a novel way. She had been trying to find a solution to a problem that had been disturbing her since her arrival at Gyllford; she wanted to express her thanks to her hostess in some sort of tangible way, but she had nothing in her portmanteau that would make a suitable gift. Her Spanish shawl was the only one of her personal effects which might answer, but Clarissa had in her possession several shawls much more beautiful. Yesterday, however, in a chance conversation with Joseph, she had come upon a solution. She had met the footman in the hallway and had entered into polite conversation with him. During this, she learned that he had once been employed in Birmingham in a factory owned by a Mr. Henry Clay, who had patented a process for making *papier-mâché*. This material had become very popular throughout England, and was used for things as diverse as buttons, paper cases, tea trays, and coach panels.

The material was very easy to make at home, Joseph said in response to her questions, needing only strips of paper soaked in glue or size. The wet paper could then be shaped on a mold or any solid surface. When dry, it had the consistency of thin wood and could be varnished, lacquered, painted, or decorated in any number of ways. Evalyn, who had seen many objects made from this material, immediately decided that she would try to make a button box for Clarissa out of this ingenious material.

This morning she, Nancy, and Joseph had paid a visit to the kitchens, where she had procured some flour, a large bowl of water, and some heavy paper. This they took to Evalyn's room where, under Joseph's supervision, they tore the paper into strips, soaked it in the ready-made glue, and shaped the strips around a porcelain box which Evalyn had found on her dressing table. Joseph assured her that when the paper had dried it could easily be lifted off the porcelain, which could then be returned to its original condition simply by washing it.

When the makeshift mold had been covered, Joseph returned to his duties, and Nancy and Evalyn washed up. Evalyn looked at the morning's work with a pleased smile. The box and the lid had been neatly set to dry on a table before the window. Tomorrow, she would remove the mold and begin the process of varnishing and decorating. It would not be a valuable gift, but it would be delicate and colorful, and she was sure Clarissa would be pleased with something made with such loving care.

This morning was an important one for Gervaise, too. Rather carefully attired in a rose-colored coat with slightly rolled lapels, and a pair of blue pantaloons fitting tightly from waist to ankle in the new Parisian style and trimmed with a row of buttons down the outside of each leg, he entered the library nervously. He looked around with a sigh of relief to see that the large room was unoccupied. He had insisted on a meeting with Clarissa and now was beset with doubts and misgivings. It was not at all his style to force her hand, although he had long felt that his dog-like devotion to her all these years was somewhat demeaning to his sense of his own manhood. Middle-aged and corpulent as he undoubtedly was, he was still a man of some stature and dignity, and to be forever dangling after a woman who could not make up her mind did not seem to him to be appropriate behavior. The time had come to call a halt.

He was sure that his instincts in this matter were sound and rational, yet misgivings crowded in on him. After today's interview with Clarissa, his life would not be the same. If she agreed to marry him, he would, of course, be obliged to give up some of the comforts of a bachelor's existence—the freedom to come and go as he pleased, to run his house to suit himself, to plan his amusements, his meals, and his wardrobe without interference. This he was more than willing to do, to dispel the gloom with which his frequently recurring periods of loneliness enveloped him. If, on the other hand, she refused him, he would be cut off from his hitherto easy access to the one place where he felt at home and happy, Gyllford Manor, and from the sense of exhilaration and contentment which her companionship had provided all these years.

The high, starched points of his shirt collar cut into his full cheeks uncomfortably, and his coat felt annoyingly tight over his abdomen as he walked stiffly to and fro across the Oriental rug covering part of the library floor. Why had he let his man trick him out in so formal a style? His pantaloons, which earlier today had seemed to him the height of fashionable elegance, now seemed singularly inappropriate for country wear. His coat, which Weston had cut himself, and which had fit him quite admirably when he had first tried it on, now seemed positively ill-fitting. And finally, to his chagrin, he discovered that he'd been nervously twisting a waistcoat button and it had come off in his hand.

Staring down at the irritating button, he came to a decision. He would immediately return to his room and send his man to Clarissa, informing her he was not feeling up to snuff this morning. He started for the door and, true to his luck, came face-to-face with her. "Of course, you would arrive at this moment!" he muttered.

"Oh, dear," said Clarissa, confused, "have I misunderstood the time?"

"Not at all," Gervaise answered. "You are as precise and punctual as a tax collector."

"What a charming simile," she murmured drily.

"No offense meant, dear lady, I assure you. It's only that I am not quite dressed this morning, it seems." And he held out the button sheepishly for her inspection. "I was about to leave for repairs."

Clarissa laughed. "No need to run away," she assured him. "Often and often I've seen you with a button missing. I'm not at all put off by it."

Seating herself on a sofa before the fire, she patted the place next to her and urged him to sit down. He shook his head. "I'm afraid to chance it. If I sit, I fear that more of these blasted buttons may come loose."

"Poor Gervaise. Then why do you choose clothing with such an inordinate number of buttons? Look at those pantaloons! There must be at least sixty buttons on them!"

He looked down at the pantaloons awkwardly, his cheeks reddening in embarrassment. "I thought these pantaloons would make me look quite up to snuff—the complete man of fashion," he said, crestfallen.

"And so they do. Truly. Even without the button, you look complete to a shade," she assured him, regretting her hasty criticism.

He cocked a knowing eye at her. "No need to flummer me, my girl. But perhaps this is a good moment to point out that when we are married, you may, if you please, take complete charge of my wardrobe."

"And thus we come to the point," she said with a sigh.

"Yes, we do. Clarissa, I can no longer be put off. I cannot stomach this life any longer. I have a big empty house which depresses my spirit every time I set foot in it, because you are not there to greet me. I have a steady stream of invitations which I refuse, because I do not like to go alone. I have a French cook who overfeeds me, because I have no one to supervise and curtail his excesses. I have an overweening valet who dresses me like a counter-coxcomb, because I have no wife to select my wardrobe. I have—"

"Enough, enough!" Clarissa cut in with a voice tinged half with amusement and half with annoyance. "I shall provide you with a housekeeper of taste and character who will be happy to handle most of your problems in return for an extortionate wage, which I know you can well afford, and which shall be much less costly than providing yourself with a wife."

"That is unworthy of you, Clarissa. I don't think our problem can be solved with levity."

"Yes, you're right," she said, chastised. "I'm sorry, my dear."

"Well, then, what have you to say to me?"

"What can I say, Gervaise? I value your friendship more than I can say."

"Friendship, *faugh!*"

"Don't sneer at it so unkindly. I will admit to you that your friendship has sustained me through many years that might otherwise have been unbearably lonely."

"Do you admit that? Then you must know that I feel it, too." Heedless of his buttons, he sat down beside her and grasped her hands. "But Clarissa, my dear, I've not made a secret of the fact that your friendship has never been enough for me. When you were married to Steele, I had no choice but to keep you my friend. But it was always your love I wanted. After his death, I hoped . . . But you know all this. Why should you keep me waiting now? We have not so many years ahead—"

She waved him to silence and turned her head away. "Please, no more. I shall weep and disgrace myself. We mustn't talk like this. You know my situation. I cannot marry and ignore my obligations."

Gervaise sighed and rose awkwardly from his seat. "I can no longer accept that excuse," he said, leaning against the mantlepiece and staring down into the fire. "It had some validity when Jamie was a child. A woman was badly needed here then, and you were the only one who could fill the void. I understood and accepted it. But Jamie is twenty-two! He'll be married himself before long. There's no reason any longer for you to postpone your own life—your own happiness. Unless—"

"Unless?"

He turned to face her. "Unless you don't believe that marriage to me will make you happy," he said, looking at her levelly.

She dropped her eyes. "I think . . . I *do* believe that I would be happy with you, Gervaise. . . ."

He was beside her in an instant, kissing her hand tenderly. "Oh, my dear!" he said, moved.

"But, dearest, I cannot marry you. Not because of Jamie, but Philip. He is accustomed to my presence. He has never coped with the running of a household, as you have. He would be in a terrible muddle. I could not desert him, I could not!"

Gervaise raised his head, and eyed her with anger. "Nonsense! You don't do the man justice. He is quite capable of looking after himself. He would be the first to tell you not to make such a sacrifice of yourself."

"Yes, so we must never tell him. Never. I insist upon that, Gervaise."

He stood up and drew himself up to his full height. "There is no need to tell me that, Clarissa. You know better than to think I would run to him for aid behind your back!"

"I know. I'm sorry to have offended you, my dear."

"Offended me! What a peagoose you are. You have severed our relationship without a qualm, and you worry about trifles."

"I have many a qualm, I assure you. Must our relationship be severed?"

"Yes, I've determined on it," he said stubbornly.

"But why, my dear? Why can't we go on as before?"

"No, I can no longer abide it. I must have a wife. I'm too dashed lonely without one. If it can't be you, then I must cast about for someone else." He gave her a quick, shrewd look from the corners of his eyes. "I may be a fat old clown, but I'm still able to attract a few good-natured females. One of them will agree to share my life and wealth."

Clarissa snorted. "Don't be so damned humble with *me*, sir. I'm well aware of the lures that Gussie Monks has been casting in your direction these ten years, and she with a fortune that quite dwarfs yours. She's good-natured enough for anyone, if one doesn't mind the addled brain that goes with it. And you needn't think," she added, getting up and walking quickly to the door, "that you can weaken my resistance by making me jealous, because it won't wash!" And she slammed the door behind her.

"Is that so?" he shouted at the closed door. "Well, we'll see how you feel when you're a guest at my wedding!"

The door opened, and Clarissa stood on the threshold, looking contrite. "Did you say something?" she asked innocently. She stepped inside and carefully closed the door behind her.

"Never mind. What did you come back for?"

"To ask if you intend to remain or to leave in a huff."

"Under the circumstances, I certainly can't remain, can I?"

"You certainly can and you certainly should. I'm counting on your support through the Christmas festivities, Boxing Day and the rest. You would be a malignant churl if you deserted me now."

"A malignant churl?" he repeated, a smile forcing its way to the corners of his mouth. "I scarcely find that an accurate or fair description of my character."

Clarissa's mouth also showed signs of a smile. "I suppose not. But if you agree to remain, I promise to give some more thought to our . . . difficulty."

"More thought? I was under the impression that you'd been doing that these past ten years!"

"So I have," she answered pertly. "I'm a very slow thinker."

"Oh, go along, you nodcock, and leave me to my misery."

"But you will remain, won't you?"

"Yes, fool that I am. That gives you ten days to think. Ten days. Not a moment longer."

"Good," she said. She blew him a kiss and left the room. He looked after her with an expression of amusement mixed with disgust. She had deftly managed to keep him dangling by offering him just enough encouragement to keep his hopes alive. Well, he thought as he left the room, she did say she loved me, didn't she? If memory served, she had *almost* said it. Absorbed in interpreting her remembered words, he didn't notice Reggie coming down the hall until they almost collided.

"Sorry," said Gervaise. "Wasn't looking where I was going."

"No harm done," Reggie assured him. "If you're on your way to breakfatht, I'll join you. There wath no one in the breakfatht room a moment ago, and I hate to eat alone."

"Don't blame you a bit, my boy," said Gervaise feelingly. "Don't blame you a bit. I hate to eat alone myself. I was going to change my clothes, but I'll keep you company at breakfast first."

"Much obliged," Reggie said. "But I would change after breakfatht, if I wath you. Thothe pantaloonth are not at all the thing. However did you perthuade yourthelf to wear them?"

CHAPTER TWELVE

The snow started again before noon and fell heavily and steadily for the next three hours, covering the landscape with a thick blanket of fluffy whiteness. The sight pleased everyone, with the possible exception of the twins, who were unconditionally refused permission to go out and play in the drifts. Freddie, whose earache had disappeared, leaving him with only a mild case of the sniffles, was still considered "under the weather" and had to stay indoors. Teddy, though exhibiting no signs of sickness, was similarly imprisoned until, his mother said, she could be sure that he had not caught the illness from his brother.

But Clarissa could not help noting that the rest of the household was surprisingly and delightfully cheerful. Even Sally, who yesterday had shown unmistakable signs of boredom, was vivacious and utterly charming. She had broken in on Philip in his study and had managed to coax him out to join the party for luncheon. It had been a very merry meal, with Jamie making jokes, Marianne in such good spirits as to actually have uttered several full sentences to the group at large, and Sally teasing and flirting shamelessly.

Even the house had an air of cheerfulness. Holly wreaths had already been placed on all the mantlepieces, and delicious smells were emanating from the nether regions, where all sorts of delicacies were being prepared for a splendid Christmas dinner. Clarissa herself felt more cheerful, now that she and Gervaise had had it out. Nothing was solved, and the problem still loomed before her, but she had managed him so far and, with a little luck, she felt confident she could do so again.

After luncheon, Philip and Edward had ridden out on horseback through the snow to find a tree from which they would cut a huge Yule log for this year's festivities. They would choose a tree of appropriate height and width, cut it down, trim it, tie a rope around it, and bring it back to the house by dragging it along the ground between them. It would be kindled on Christmas Eve by first lighting a piece of last year's log, which had been saved for this purpose. It was a ritual the whole family enjoyed. Clarissa was afraid that Jamie had felt a bit of resentment when he was asked to surrender to Edward his place in the search for the tree. But Jamie didn't seem to mind. Instead, he had offered to teach Marianne how to play billiards, and that pastime seemed now to be occupying them quite happily. Clarissa was therefore free to spend the afternoon in making plans with the housekeeper and cook. Her guests were doing very well without her.

Clarissa was unaware that one guest at least was less than happy. Reggie had put a good face on it, but things were going hard with him. After luncheon Jamie had asked him to help teach Marianne to play billiards. Reggie refused. Jamie couldn't understand it. "Why not?" he demanded. "What else do you have to do?"

"I . . . er . . . have thomething to do in my room," Reggie told him, and turned to go.

But Jamie restrained him. "What on earth have you to do there?" he asked. "It's too early to pick out your waistcoat for dinner."

"I have other wayth to thpend my time," Reggie declared proudly. "I don't need to uthe all my time to confer with my valet."

Jamie eyed him suspiciously. "Well, then, what will you do?"

"Private buthineth."

"Private business? Do you take me for a flat? What private business?"

"If I tell you, it will not be private."

"Since when do you have private business you can't tell me about? You're doing it much too brown, Reggie. Something's amiss, and I'm going to get to the bottom of it."

Reggie capitulated. Jamie was his best friend, after all. "I doubt you'll believe me, but I'm going to my room to read."

Jamie gaped. "To what?"

"You heard me. To read."

"To read? A book?"

Reggie glared at him. "What elthe would I read? A receipt for mushroom and kidney pie?"

"Cut line, Reggie! Do you expect me to swallow a whisker like that? I've never seen you read a book in all my life!"

"I'm reading one now."

"Then tell me the name of it!" Jamie challenged.

"*The Life of Jonathan Wild* or thome thuch title. Very interethting, really. About a magithtrate who ith thteeped in corruption. . . ."

"Spare me, please. I've heard enough for one day. Reading a book!" Jamie shook his head, unbelieving. "You must be *sick!*"

"Take a damper, Jamie," Reggie said threateningly. "Remember that I can flatten you when I've a mind to. And you are not to tell anybody about thith. If you breathe a word, you'll have to anthwer to me, even if you *are* my betht friend."

"Do you think I have windmills in my head? No one would believe me anyway."

"Good. Then we have nothing to worry about." And he turned and walked off down the hall.

Jamie went to the billiard room much shaken. That Reggie should have turned bookish was an occurrence a man could not take lightly. He would have to look into this problem, and soon.

Evalyn had spent the early part of the afternoon telling the twins a story while spooning hot soup down Freddie's throat. Now, with everybody in the household busy at various amusements and occupations, she found a few hours before her to spend as she wished. She put a last coat of lacquer on her *papier-mâché* box, and as she looked up from that completed task, the sight of the fresh snow on the gardens below made her yearn for the outdoors. She donned her thickest boots and her one sturdy cloak, and made for the front door. As she crossed the wide front hallway, Philip and Edward clumped in, laughing and shaking the snow from their boots and hats.

"Good afternoon, Miss Pennington," Edward greeted her. "Come out and see the enormous log we've prepared for the Christmas fire."

Before Evalyn could reply, the library doors opened and Gervaise emerged, yawning. Philip pointed to him and laughed. "Look at what you've done, Edward. For shame! Your crowing has awakened our lazy friend from his afternoon nap."

"Not at all," Gervaise declared, unperturbed. "I had already awakened when you two burst in the door."

"A likely tale. Many's the afternoon I've had to rouse you and send you on your way with barely enough time to dress for dinner," Philip teased.

"Balderdash. Don't listen to him, Miss Pennington. He has a hidden, nasty streak, which makes him enjoy cutting up the reputations of even his oldest and dearest friends."

Evalyn laughed, but couldn't resist coming to Philip's defense. "It must be a well-hidden streak," she said, "for I've never seen the least sign of it."

"Oh, well said," purred a female voice behind her,

and all eyes turned to find Sally poised gracefully on the stairway, a vision in wine-colored kerseymere. Clarissa stood just behind her, smiling benignly at everyone.

"Ah, there you are, Edward," Clarissa said. "I hoped you had returned. Your wife has been asking for you. She has developed a crick in the back of her neck and claims that only you know the trick of setting it right."

Edward sighed a patient, long-suffering sigh. "Yes, I do. After all these years of matrimony, there's scarcely a problem which I've not developed the trick of solving." He handed his coat to a waiting footman and, making a little bow, hurried off up the stairs.

"Philip, my dear," Sally said invitingly, "I've come for *you*. We are organizing a game of billiards, and I need a partner."

"Thank you, but I should not be an asset to you. It's been years since I handled a billiard cue."

"Never mind that. I am expert enough for both of us," she countered smoothly.

"You must excuse me, I'm afraid," Philip said, unbudgeable. "I have some rather pressing matters which need attending to."

The color rose in Sally's cheeks and her eyes glinted; nevertheless, she managed to smile. "Very well, then, I'll have to persuade Gervaise . . ."

"A much better choice than Philip, if I do say so myself," Gervaise said with aplomb. "I'm a far better billiard player than anyone you're likely to find within a hundred miles."

"Spoken with truth and appropriate modesty," Philip said smiling.

Gervaise climbed the stairs, took Sally's arm, and tucked it under his own. "Come, my dear, let's go and defeat the enemy." And he led her up the stairs, giving Clarissa a saucy glance as he passed her by. Clarissa favored Philip and Evalyn with an amused shrug, then followed the billiard players up the stairs.

Evalyn tied the strings of her cloak, lifted her hood,

and started toward the door. Philip, shrugging out of his coat, looked at her in surprise. "Do you mean to go out, Miss Pennington?"

"Why, yes."

"But not alone, surely?"

Evalyn smiled. "I'm not a schoolroom miss, Lord Gyllford. Surely I'm old enough to take a little walk unattended."

"I see you have relapsed into formality and are calling me Lord Gyllford again."

"But did you not, a moment ago, call me Miss Pennington?"

"Did I? I apologize, but I will not be put from the point. Why is Jamie not keeping you company?"

"Jamie?" she asked in surprise. "Why on earth should he?"

"Surely he cannot like to see you spending so much time alone. If you will postpone your walk for a minute or two, I'll find him. I'm sure he'll be delighted to keep you company on your outing."

"I won't hear of such a thing," Evalyn said, shocked. "Disturb Jamie merely to accompany me on a little walk? I'll not go at all, if you think my walking alone is improper, but I wouldn't for the world have Jamie's billiard game disturbed."

"You young people are indeed a puzzle to me," Philip said, shaking his head in perplexity. "But of course, there is nothing improper in your taking a little walk by yourself, if you're sure you want to."

"Yes, I do. I love fresh-fallen snow. I've been wanting to get out in it all afternoon."

"Then of course I won't prevent you," Philip said. Evalyn made a quick curtsey and turned to the door. "Wait, Miss Pennington," he called after her. "I wonder . . . would you object to *my* company?"

"Of course I wouldn't, if I had not just heard you say that you have pressing business to attend to."

Philip grinned guiltily. "You listen to me too carefully, my dear. I admit to you, on the expectation that you'll not give me away, that I have pressing business only when asked to play billiards."

Evalyn smiled, but shook her head. "You are being kind, I think. I cannot feel easy thinking that my silly walk is taking you away from more urgent matters. Please, sir, if my walking out alone troubles you, I shall gladly stay indoors and think no more about it. I'd be very grateful if you can do the same." And she quickly untied the ribbons of her cloak.

Philip went to her, took her hands from her cloak, and tied its ribbons again. "We are both being over-zealous and foolish, I think. You shall certainly have your walk, and alone if you wish it so. I only ask you to believe that I would truly enjoy joining you, if you will have me. You're not the only lover of new-fallen snow, you know."

He was looking down at her earnestly, with the glow of warmth in the back of his eyes that had, at least twice before, caused her heart to lurch and her spine to turn to jelly. She said nothing, her throat suddenly too constricted to permit her to speak. "Well, Evalyn," he asked with his endearing grin, "may I come?"

She nodded shyly, and he turned and signalled to the footman who had retired discreetly to the stairway while they spoke. Before she'd caught her breath, he had put on his many-caped greatcoat and, leaving it unbuttoned, with his muffler hanging untied from under its collar, he had taken her hand and led her out the door. The air was crisp and a light wind blew the powdery snow into their faces. They came down the steps and walked along the curved avenue. Philip glanced down at her. "Are you sure that light cloak is enough?" he asked.

Evalyn cocked her head and looked at him askance. "I begin to think, Lord Gyllford, that you would make a better governess than I. Your overwhelming solicitude quite befits the profession."

Philip threw back his head with a shout of laughter.

"I do sound like a clucking old hen, don't I? Very well, Miss Acid-Tongue, not another solicitous word will you hear from me."

"Good, my lord. It will be an immeasurable aid to our future conversation."

"There it is—'my lord' again. Why do you suppose, Miss Penn—Evalyn, that we find it so difficult to call each other by our Christian names?"

"I'm not sure," Evalyn answered slowly, giving the question more serious attention than Philip had intended, "but I think it may be that our inequality of rank makes it difficult for us to be comfortable together as friends."

His smile faded, and he turned to her almost angrily. "What nonsense! Do you think I see a *governess* before me every time I look at you? What a pompous fool you must think me!"

"Not at all," Evalyn answered in the calm, reasonable voice he so much admired. "But you can scarcely expect us to forget completely the very great gulf that our so-different stations in life have built between us."

"I would forget your so-called 'station' completely, if you didn't keep reminding me," he stated flatly. "You must try to be a little less belligerently *poor*, my girl, and try to accept the truth of what you really are."

"What am I but a governess, and an unemployed one at that?"

He grasped her by the shoulders angrily. "I could shake you! Can you truly believe that the word 'governess' has anything to do with the you that I—that anybody with eyes—must see when we look at you?"

Evalyn stared up at him. "I have no idea wh-what you see when you look at me," she said breathlessly.

His anger was instantly dissipated by the ingenuous look in her eyes. "A lovely girl," he said quietly, "a warm, witty, serene, kind, lovely girl. Will you remember that?"

She nodded wordlessly, and he dropped his hands

from her shoulders. They walked on through the deep-ening shadows. "I suppose it is too much to hope that you can see anything but 'his lordship' when you look at me," he remarked somewhat ruefully.

"You must know," she answered in her forthrightly way, "that I see a great deal more than that."

He grinned down at her. "I see a great deal more than that, *Philip*."

She smiled back. "I see a great deal more than that, Philip," she repeated obediently.

"Where did you get this overly strong sense of class differences, I wonder? Was it your family?"

She told him, hesitantly at first, but more comfort-ably after a while, about her father and their life to-gether. "It was not he who ingrained my sense of my 'place' into me," she said at last. "It was, I suppose, a result of holding the post of governess in three rather noble households."

Philip frowned. "Treated you shabbily, did they? I could wring their necks."

"Not at all. They were very kind, really. It's just . . . how can I explain? You like to deny its existence, but there is an invisible sort of barrier set up between the classes. When one inadvertently moves to pass through it, the disapproval is unmistakable. One learns to recognize the lines of demarcation rather quickly."

"Well, my dear, you shall never feel that disap-proval again," he said fervently, "and that I promise you."

"In your own home, perhaps," she corrected gently.

"Anywhere! Ev—" he began, but a gust of wind shook the trees above them, and a small avalanche of snow fell on top of them. Philip's tall hat was knocked to the ground. Laughing, he shook the snow out of his hair and brushed it from his shoulders. Then he turned to Evalyn and brushed it from her hood and cape. "There, that's better. Are you all right?"

"Yes, of course."

"I know I promised not to be old-henish, but I can't

help noticing how very thin your cloak is. You must be frozen." He pulled the muffler from his neck and wound it twice around her throat. The daylight was fading rapidly, but in the dim glow he could see her face quite clearly. His hands, still holding the ends of the muffler, were stayed, his breath arrested. Her eyes were smiling up at him gratefully. A few snowflakes, which had clung to her cheeks and caught in her lashes, gave her face an enticing sparkle. For a moment neither of them moved. Then, as if impelled by some irresistible instinct long dormant in him, he pulled her to him. She lay against him unmoving, her face tilted up. His heart was pounding so loudly that he knew she must hear.

Evalyn heard. She couldn't think—she couldn't analyze the meaning of any of this. He was holding her in his arms, his heart pounding against her. That was enough for her now. She would think later. Now she could only feel an enveloping sense of joy unfolding like a flower inside her. She recognized on his face, so close above her own, the look she had seen before, lurking deep behind his eyes. Now it seemed to be shining from his whole being. She waited, breathless, for the kiss she knew was coming. But suddenly, shockingly, before her startled gaze, the warmth in his face faded, instantaneously replaced by an expression she could only describe as horror. His body stiffened, and he abruptly thrust her from him. "Oh, my God!" he groaned. "What am I doing?"

She did not ask for an explanation—she couldn't have uttered a word. And he gave none. Instead, he dropped his eyes from her face and said in a constricted voice, "It grows dark. We'd better go back."

Evalyn bent down and picked up his hat. She held it out to him, her eyes searching his face. He looked at her briefly, a look of chagrin and shame, took the hat from her and turned away. They walked back to the house in silence.

A waiting footman sprang to attention when they

entered the dimly lit hallway. Philip waved him away and turned to Evalyn. "I must apologize for my unaccountable behavior," he said in a distant voice. "I've never before heard of a case of midsummer madness striking anyone in the dead of winter, but it is the only explanation I can offer—"

"Please, Philip, don't joke. I don't underst—" Evalyn began.

He went on as if she hadn't spoken. "I can only thank you for permitting me to accompany you," he said, "and to assure you, Miss Pennington, that I shall not so offend you again."

She gasped. "*Miss Penning—?*"

But he had turned away and was striding across the hallway. He took the stairs two at a time and was gone, leaving Evalyn staring after him, the snowflakes melting on her cloak and dripping down to form little puddles on the floor around her.

CHAPTER THIRTEEN

Wellstock said later to his cronies below stairs that he'd been sure that his master had been digging deep in the bottle when he looked into the bedroom that evening. There Lord Gyllford sat, one boot on, the other in his hand, staring ahead of him at nothing. Wellstock had stood in the doorway for at least five minutes, waiting to be recognized, and his lordship did not move the whole time. Finally, Wellstock had coughed discreetly, walked in, and pulled off the other boot. Still his lordship did not seem to notice him at all!

"Are you all right, sir?" Wellstock had asked in deep concern. He had never known his master to make indentures. Not at all a drinking man. Lord Gyllford had slowly focused his eyes on Wellstock's face. "Oh, it's you, Wellstock," he'd said in a dead—but not a drunken—voice. "Go away, man. I'll not be needing you."

"But you're not dressed, my lord, and dinner is scarcely a half-hour off," Wellstock had remonstrated.

"Look in on Jamie, will you? I can dress myself tonight," Lord Gyllford had said shortly.

Wellstock had taken himself off, but he'd looked back before he left, and there was his lordship in his stockinged feet, sitting exactly as he had been when the valet arrived.

Philip knew very well that he had to dress for dinner. He just couldn't seem to rouse himself. A deep depression had taken hold of him and seemed to weigh him down like lead. The prospect of facing everyone at dinner time and making cheerful conversation only added to his misery. He felt an urge to hide away somewhere, in a corner of the cellar or the attic, as he had done when he was a little boy and had been severely reprimanded by his usually adoring and adored mother. What humiliating feelings these were for a man with a son of his own, a son whom—heaven help him!—he'd been on the verge of betraying. How could he so have forgotten himself?

His only excuse—though he knew his behavior had been inexcusable—was a strong sense (a feeling he'd not before put into words) that Jamie and Evalyn did not suit. She seemed older than Jamie, more mature, more—how could he describe it?—more at peace with herself. Jamie seemed still to be a boy, still playing games with life and flirting with adulthood. But Philip realized that he might well be rationalizing. His analysis of the situation could no longer be trusted. His objectivity had been hopelessly impaired ever since he'd laid eyes on the girl his son had chosen to marry. There was only one realization he could accept as truth: that he loved her. He could no longer fool himself about that. For almost twenty years he'd guarded himself against this emotion, only to tumble into it with the one person he should most have avoided. What evil fate had decreed that his son should attach himself to the one girl whose nature, face, and voice seemed especially designed to penetrate the strong defenses behind which he had walled himself for so long?

But was he mistaken about Evalyn's nature? This question was more painful to face than the awareness of his own weakness had been. Her true character could be other than what it appeared. He accepted fully the entire blame for what had happened this afternoon in the snow, but Evalyn's behavior, too, had not been above reproach. He had lived too many years and was too experienced to have misinterpreted what he'd read in her face as he held her in his arms. She had accepted his embrace with eagerness, even joy. Could she have forgotten Jamie as completely as he had? Yet he alone had shown signs of guilt. And afterwards, how could she have stared at him with those eyes so full of painful and complete innocence?

If he didn't know Evalyn—if this had happened to a pair of strangers and the story had come to him—he would have been able to explain the situation well enough. He would have said the girl was an adventuress, trying to see if she could permanently attach the richer father before letting go of the bird-in-hand son. But he couldn't, knowing Evalyn, believe it of her for a moment. Perhaps he was completely besotted, but he would swear that there was not a trace of deceit or avarice in her.

Yet he could think of no other explanation for her behavior. The expression in her eyes when she looked at him had been no more daughterly than his had been fatherly. Could she be an adventuress, making a game of him and Jamie both? An adventuress could be successful only if she didn't behave or look like

one. Was her straightforward manner, her completely
convincing air of innocence, the polished performance
of an artful dissembler? The mere suspicion made him
feel sick. He could not—would not—believe it of her.

These nagging questions could not now be answered. But his overriding sense of guilt could be
dealt with. He could not again allow himself to be
alone in her company, not until she had married Jamie
and he had learned to contain his feelings for her
within strict bounds. In time he would rebuild the
protective walls behind which he had successfully barricaded himself in the past. In the meantime, he must
find some outward means by which to separate himself from her. Sally! How fortunate that she was present for the holidays. Sally had made it quite clear
that she would enjoy his attentions. Well, she would
have them. He knew it ill became him to use her in
this way, but he trusted himself to keep his attentions
well within the bounds of gay companionship. Sally
was quite up to the mark and would recognize easily
the difference between a sincere courtship and a harmless flirtation.

Philip hurried down and entered the drawing room,
meeting Clarissa's frown with an apologetic smile for
his extraordinary lateness. He scanned the room quickly, helpless to keep himself from searching out Evalyn's face among the others looking up at him. He
did not immediately see her, and he wondered if she
had been too upset by his behavior to make an appearance this evening. But she was there, sitting a
little apart from the others, and looking pale and
strained. He ached to go and comfort her, but he
forced himself to look away. It was Jamie's place—
not his—to soothe the worried lines from her forehead,
to coax the color back into her cheeks. Philip could
only hope fervently that Jamie was aware of what his
duty was.

He turned and greeted his guests, apologizing pro-
fusely for keeping them waiting. The butler, who had

had to tell the cook twice to return the succulent chops to the fire, anounced dinner in a tone of voice which scarcely revealed his relief. Philip went directly to Sally and bowed. "You are a vision tonight, my dear," he said, "all draped in velvet. What do you call that splendid color you're wearing?"

Sally looked up at him with a cautious glint. "I believe my *modiste* calls it Venetian red."

"Yes, it does put one in mind of an Italian painting. But perhaps you should have waited until tomorrow evening to wear it. What a perfect color for Christmas eve."

"If it pleases you, your lordship," Sally said with coy smoothness, "it is appropriate at any time."

"It does indeed please me. So much so that I have an unquenchable desire to escort such Venetian loveliness in to dinner. May I have your arm?"

The cautious look was still in her eye as she glanced up at him, but he favored her with the most disarming smile he could muster. "Thank you, my lord," she said, pleased with herself, and gave him her arm. As she swept past Evalyn, she did not neglect to cast the governess a look of triumph.

Sally had had a busy afternoon. From the window of the billiard room, she had seen Philip and Evalyn walk down the avenue together. Even from that distance, Sally could discern their complete absorption in one another. She saw Philip stop and turn to Evalyn, speaking to her with an intensity that Sally could almost feel. She had to recognize at last that the attraction between Philip and the governess, however inexplicable, was quite real. The time had come for her to put her plan into action.

As soon as she could, she had escaped from the billiard room and hurried to her bedroom. She closed the door behind her and locked it against any chance intruder. A commotion behind her, coming from her dressing room, made her jump. "Who's there?" she called sharply.

"Only me, Ma'm'selle," came Annette's voice, and the maid came hurriedly from the dressing room, smoothing back her hair and adjusting her cap with nervous fingers. It occurred to Sally that Annette had been up to some mischief.

"What are you doing here?" Sally demanded.

"I make ready the things for you to wear tonight," Annette said with a shrug. "Are you not early, Ma'm-'selle?"

"I'm a bit tired. You may go for an hour or so, Annette. I want to rest."

Annette cast a hurried glance over her shoulder into the dressing room. "But, Ma'm'selle," she objected, "I must brush the velvet most careful, to make the nap to shine. I will close the door to the dressing room. Annette will be quiet like a mouse. You will not be disturb', I promise."

Sally clenched her teeth. "Must you argue about everything I say to you? I want to be alone. Get out. I don't want to see your face for an hour."

Annette bit her lip, bobbed a quick curtsey and went to the door. She cast another glance back at the dressing room, unlocked the door and went out. Sally locked it again and went to the dressing room. She took her jewel-case key from beneath the powder puff, unlocked the case and removed her diamond drop earrings. With a satisfied smile, she held them up so that the light from the window shone through them. They were large, many-faceted stones shaped like tear drops, and were the most expensive of all the valuables in her possession. She dropped the jewel-case key on the dressing table and crossed to the dressing room door. There she paused. It wouldn't do, she decided, to leave the key lying on the dressing table. Annette would notice the theft too soon. She went back, locked the case and replaced the key in its hiding place. Then she went swiftly from the dressing room.

She dropped the gems into the bosom of her dress, unlocked the door and looked out into the hallway. It was empty. She closed her door quietly behind her and walked silently down the hall to Evalyn's room. She scratched at the door. There was no answer. Stealthily she turned the knob. The door was open. She entered, closed the door behind her, and looked about her in surprise. The room was unmistakably larger than hers! The governess had been given a grander room than her own! Her green eyes flashed angrily. To think that she had been made to take second place to a mouse of a female without station, breeding, or beauty! But Evalyn's favored position in this house would be short-lived. Sally's lips curled as she reached into her gown and took out the diamonds.

Her eyes roamed the room for a suitable place to hide them. The hiding place must be carefully chosen. Evalyn must not discover the jewels. They must be discovered—and only after careful search—by a magistrate or by Philip himself. Hiding them among Evalyn's articles of clothing would not serve—Evalyn or her obnoxious little abigail would be sure to come upon them. Under the mattress was too obvious and unimaginative. Dropping them into a jar of face powder or a pot of rouge might do, but Evalyn's dressing table held no such objects.

Sally's eye fell on Evalyn's work table near the window. On it sat a little *papier-mâché* box which Evalyn had obviously just made. It had been charmingly lacquered and set out to dry. Sally touched it gingerly. Fortunately, it had dried completely. She opened the lid. A satin lining, stuffed with cotton wadding, had been glued inside. Sally smiled. She had found the place. She pulled a corner of the lining loose and slipped the diamonds in behind the padding. Then, confident that it would come loose again at the slightest touch, she pressed the corner back into place. She was satisfied that a careful searcher would feel the sharp outlines of the diamonds through the padding. She replaced the lid, and swiftly left the room.

Now, sitting at the dining table, basking in the glow

of Philip's rather marked attentions, she wondered if perhaps she'd been hasty. Perhaps the whole thing had not been necessary—perhaps she _had_ overestimated the extent of Philip's interest in the governess. Her green eyes flicked to Evalyn's face. The girl was pale and looked to be under a strain. Philip, too, had a look of strain, and she noticed that he rubbed the bridge of his nose from time to time, as if he had a headache. Something had passed between them, Sally was certain of that. No, she had not made a mistake; she would let the diamonds play their part.

For Evalyn, the dinner was a continuation of the nightmare that had begun when Philip left her, cold and trembling, in the empty hallway. She had gone to her room and knelt before the fire where Nancy had found her—she didn't know how much later—still wearing her wet cloak. Nancy had immediately embarked on a tirade of scolding until she glimpsed Evalyn's face.

"Miss Evalyn," she gasped, "what's happened to you?"

Evalyn looked at the girl's honest face, and its expression of warm and sincere concern was too much for her to bear. Unaccustomed tears began to roll down her cheeks. Nancy was aghast. "Oh, my lady," she whispered, awed, "who's hurt you? I ain't never seen you cry!" The girl lifted Evalyn to her feet and led her to the bed. Evalyn put her face into the pillow and sobbed until her body felt wracked and empty. It was as if all the tears she hadn't shed since her childhood had been stored up inside her and had finally broken loose. When the flood subsided, and she looked up, she found Nancy still regarding her, wringing her hands in helpless and agonized concern. Evalyn tried to smile and reassure the girl. "I don't know what's come over me," she said in a tremulous, unrecognizable voice. "It's really nothing, Nancy. I'm just a bit blue-devilled, that's all."

Nancy didn't believe a word of it. "Blue-devilled!" she exclaimed. "Do you take me for a clodpole? It's plain as pikestaff someone's hurt you bad. It ain't me place to know your business, Miss Evalyn, and it's just as well you don't tell me, because if I was to learn who upset you like this, I'd wring her neck for sure!"

Evalyn gave a hiccup of a laugh and tried to pull herself together. "I must make myself presentable and go down to dinner," she said helplessly. Nancy rose to the task, bathing her swollen eyes and reddened nose until she looked more like herself, and helping her into her clothes, as if Evalyn were a baby. All the while, Nancy kept up a stream of talk about nothing at all, hoping to divert Evalyn from brooding about whatever had so disturbed her. But Evalyn could not be diverted. Philip's face, with its shocking expression of horror and self-disgust, could not be blotted from her mind.

Evalyn had no one to blame but herself. She had been enjoying her few days of luxury and attention and had not wanted to think about the consequences or the future. She had responded with instinctive naturalness to the warmth in Philip's eyes and to the obvious pleasure he had found in her company. She'd been aware that she was drawn to him as she had never been to a man before, but she had not let herself analyze or identify her feelings. Then he'd taken her in his arms, and the truth became blindingly clear. She had fallen heedlessly and headlong in love with a man who was completely beyond her sphere.

She was not a fool. She knew that he had been attracted to her almost as strongly as she to him. Perhaps he had drifted into it as thoughtlessly as she had done, only to realize suddenly that the attraction led to a dead end. "What am I doing?" he'd said in that horrified voice. There, on the verge of kissing her, he had realized how impossible a situation he was in. For all his kindness to her, for all his courageous words about his disregard for her "station" in life, a man in his position could not marry an impoverished governess with no family. He must have realized, too, from what she'd told him about her upbringing, that she was too properly reared to accept a *carte blanche*. He'd awakened himself with that dreadful look of horror and had uttered, "What am I doing?" in the nick of time. She wasn't angry. She shouldn't even feel hurt. She understood perfectly. All she had to do now was to pick up the pieces of her heart and paste herself back together again. All it took was a little courage and the ability to withstand some pain. She was her father's daughter; those were the things she had learned early.

But here at dinner she began to realize how difficult the job of putting herself together would be. Every time Philip laughed into Sally's face, which he was doing with repulsive frequency, she felt he was dealing her a dagger blow. Every time he turned his eyes away from her, a pain cut through her chest. Every time she had to smile and make rational remarks to one or another of the people around her, it required an effort of will she was not sure she was strong enough to make. She could only hope that her courage would hold until enough time had passed to allow her to say her goodnights and make her escape.

After dinner, Sally was asked to entertain, and she played and sang with great enthusiasm for almost an hour. "We must have some carols tomorrow evening," Clarissa requested when Sally at last rose from the pianoforte. "Carols are what I most enjoy about the Christmas festivities."

"Really?" Jamie asked in surprise. "I could name a dozen things I enjoy as much, or more."

"Pooh," challenged his loving aunt, "name one thing that captures the spirit of Christmas festivities half as well."

"You are altering the point, aunt. You were speaking at first of enjoyment. If it is *spirit* we are speaking of, then the answer must be the Christmas Mass. But if it is the festivities we are discussing, then my enjoyment lies in many other things besides the singing of carols."

"Well, what then?" his aunt persisted. Everyone looked at Jamie with amused interest.

"Do you want the shocking truth?" he asked his aunt with a twinkle.

"The truth, of course."

"Then I would choose, without hesitation, the Christmas mistletoe!" His answer was greeted with a loud laugh, and he glanced at Marianne and winked broadly at her. "All the ladies be warned," he said. "I shall be lurking behind every doorway as soon as my aunt has hung the kissing boughs."

"A good choice," chortled Gervaise, "but, as much as I enjoy kissing the ladies, there is something I would choose even ahead of mistletoe."

"It's not hard to guess what that is," Clarissa teased. "The Christmas goose!"

"I was going to say plum pudding, but in truth it is hard to choose between them," Gervaise said laughing.

"What?" asked Martha. "And you call yourself English? How can you have overlooked our good roast beef?"

"Shall we combine all of them and agree that it's the entire Christmas dinner that is the crowning glory of the festivities?" suggested Edward, ever the compromiser.

"I'll agree to that," Gervaise said.

"You look dissatisfied, Reggie," Clarissa said. "I hope that you will support me in my feeling that there are things more important than food and kissing."

Reggie roused himself from the gloom in which Jamie's wink at Marianne had sunk him, and he smiled politely at his hostess. "I don't know if you will think thith ith thupport, but nobody hath mentioned what I find to be motht enjoyable: the wathail bowl."

"Hear, hear!" Edward cheered. "The wassail bowl by all means! What would Christmas be without it?"

Sally leaned forward. "Let's not forget the dancing. When all the neighbors gather and the musicians break into a lively tune, I do love to dance with a handsome partner. Don't you agree, Philip?"

"I would not forego any of it," Philip answered, "the mince pie and the plum pudding, the turkey and the goose, the wassail and the home-brew, the songs and the dancing, they all have my support. But if I had to choose only one thing—the one indispensable festivity of the day—I think I would choose the Yule log. I love to see the great blazing fire. Have you noticed how everybody is, sooner or later, attracted to it? It becomes the heart, the visible center of the room, and all the faces gathered in a semicircle around it seem to shine in the dancing glow of the flames."

"Oh, Philip, how right you are!" sighed Martha, much moved.

"Yes, I'll have to agree," Gervaise said reflectively. "How perfect it is on Christmas Day to sit round the fire, listening to the hiss of the roasting pears, smelling the chestnuts, while the wind howls away outside the windows. What are those lines of Milton—something about a storm outside—?"

"I know the ones you mean," said Philip. "'And out of doors, a something storm o'erwhelms . . .' No, I'm afraid I've forgotten them."

Evalyn's voice came softly from somewhere behind him. "'And out of doors, a washing storm o'erwhelms/ Nature pitch-dark, and rides the thundering elms.'"

Philip turned to look at her, unable to keep from his eyes the look of appreciative pleasure she'd roused in him. Their eyes met and held, and it was several seconds before either of them could look away.

CHAPTER FOURTEEN

Snow fell again during the night, and the dawn of the
day before Christmas was barely perceptible behind
the heavy clouds which gave a sullen look to the sky.
A gusty wind had blown up, rattling the windows and
blowing the snow into drifts. Clarissa forced herself
out of bed before her abigail appeared to waken her.
She pattered across the icy floor quickly, knowing that
the day held too few hours for the completion of all
the tasks she had left herself to do. She had to see to
the hanging of the rest of the Christmas greens—the
holly wreaths and the kissing boughs which she, Martha, and Evalyn had wrought so painstakingly throughout the week. She had to speak to Hutton about pre-
paring the things needed for the Christmas eve games,
like Jamie's favorite, snapdragon. And, most difficult
and time-consuming, she had to arrange for the baskets
(after she filled them with sugar cakes, pails of her
special Christmas punch, plump Christmas birds, and
trinkets for the children) to be labelled, each with a
personal note, and loaded into a carriage so that Philip
could deliver them that afternoon.

She dressed quickly and left her bedroom, closing
the door quietly so as not to disturb the sleeping
household. To her surprise, she found that Evalyn,
fully dressed, was emerging from her room.

"Evalyn, my dear," she whispered, "why have you
risen so early? I doubt that even the servants are up
and about."

"I knew this would be a very busy day for you, and I hoped you would permit me to help."

"Of course, my dear. But this is supposed to be a holiday for you. I don't wish you to give up your rest on any account, even mine."

"I am not accustomed to sleeping late," Evalyn assured her. "It was no sacrifice to get up early."

"Then I thank you most sincerely. I'll enjoy both your assistance and your company. But, Evalyn, you do look a little fagged. There are shadows beneath your eyes. You must promise me that you'll lie down for a rest later today."

A few minutes later, wrapped in huge white aprons, they stood ladling the punch into pails, and carefully wrapping the sugar cakes to keep them from crumbling in the baskets. Neither one took notice of the fact that they were strangely silent until they both sighed at once. Clarissa looked up in surprise, caught Evalyn's eye, and laughed. "Dear me," she said, "we neither of us seem to have captured the holiday spirit. Such heartfelt sighs! How do you account for our mutual depression?"

"I certainly can't account for mine," Evalyn said with what she hoped was a reassuring smile. "I'm having the most wonderful holiday of my life. It must be the weather that has lowered my spirits."

"I can't blame the weather for mine," Clarissa admitted. "I rather like the snow at Christmas time."

"Then it must be something more serious that is troubling you," Evalyn suggested, not wanting to pry but offering a sympathetic ear.

"Yes, I find it serious, although you may think it foolish in a woman of my years to be troubled by such a thing."

"I'm sure I couldn't think lightly of anything that troubles you," Evalyn said earnestly.

"But you will think me foolish when you learn that I'm fretting over a proposal of marriage. Imagine! At my age, to carry on in my head like the veriest school-girl!"

"A marriage proposal! But Clarissa, how wonderful! Is it . . . I hope you'll not think me forward to ask . . . is it Gervaise?"

Clarissa looked at her in surprise. "However did you guess, Evalyn?"

Evalyn smiled. "It was not at all hard to guess. I've noticed many times that often, even when he is speaking to someone else, his eyes seek you out."

Clarissa blushed with pleasure. "Do they? I was not aware . . ."

"Oh, yes. And when you're not in the room, he seems to be watching for you to come in the door."

"Oh, dear. That *is* touching, when you think how many years we— Evalyn, I almost wish you hadn't told me. How can I face him and tell him I cannot accept him when you have painted this tenderhearted picture of him?"

"But why must you refuse him? It cannot be that you don't care for him."

Clarissa cocked her head and looked at Evalyn with a twinkle. "Why do you say that with such assurance? Have you caught *my* eyes searching *his* out?"

Evalyn laughed. "Perhaps not. But you tease him so affectionately, and . . . I don't know. I felt sure—"

Clarissa sighed. "I don't deny you're right. But I cannot marry him. And I cannot bear to tell him so."

Evalyn's smile faded. "I'm so sorry, Clarissa," she said softly. "It is dreadful when 'impediments' prevent 'the marriage of true minds.' "

Clarissa's eyes misted over and, to her embarrassment, two tears rolled down her cheeks. She quickly brushed them aside with the back of her hand and laughed tremulously. "Isn't it amazing how Mr. Shakespeare has something appropriate to say for every occasion?"

"Yes, but even his words don't really help," Evalyn

said regretfully. "I wish *someone* could help you, Clarissa."

"Someone could, if only he realized . . ." Clarissa began. "But no. I am not being fair. I cannot expect Philip to marry just to please me."

Evalyn caught her breath. "Philip . . . ? Marry?" she asked.

"Well, yes. You see, he's the impediment, the poor dear. I cannot leave him alone in this great house, especially now with Jamie about to set up his own establishment." And she gave Evalyn an arch smile. "To leave him at this time would be unthinkable," she went on. "Philip would be in a complete domestic muddle within a month if he were left to manage by himself."

"Perhaps you underestimate him," Evalyn ventured.

Clarissa regarded her with some surprise. "That's what Gervaise says, too. But I don't agree. You see, Gervaise has managed his household beautifully all these years and thinks it quite easy. But Philip is the sort of man who is always preoccupied with serious concerns. He wouldn't pay attention to the thousands of domestic details that must be attended to. That's why I cannot marry Gervaise. He doesn't need me as much as Philip does."

"I see. That's why you hope Philip will marry . . ."

"Yes. I've been pushing him to do it for years and years! Not only for myself and Gervaise, of course—I'm not as selfish as that—but for Philip's own happiness. The lengths I've gone to to put eligible females in his way! The ruses and excuses I've devised to lure him to social events! I've been positively shameless, but to no avail. The man is quite immune."

Evalyn, her eyes fastened on the package she was wrapping, said hesitantly, "Perhaps he will surprise you one day . . . soon . . ."

Clarissa shook her head. "You are thinking of Sally, are you not? No, there's not a chance of that. Philip dislikes her, I think, even though his attitude did seem to be softening last evening. But I myself don't wish them to make a match of it. I don't like her above half. Evalyn, I'm at my wits' end! He'll soon be too old to attract a proper female—"

"Old?" Evalyn said in genuine surprise. "How can you say so?"

Clarissa smiled at her fondly. "There are not many girls your age who would *not* say so, my dear. Forty-four is a far cry from youth."

"Forty-four is a perfect—! I mean, a very good age for a husband," Evalyn said, her eyes lowered and her cheeks revealing a flush. "There must be hundreds of girls even younger than I am who would think themselves lucky to . . . to marry a man like Lord Gyllford."

"You are a darling," Clarissa said warmly, and patted her hand with affection. "Just talking to you has lifted my spirits immeasurably. You can have no idea how happy I am that Jamie has brought you to us!"

Later that morning, Jamie peered into the breakfast room to find only Marianne present. She looked charming in a morning dress with ruffles of lace at the neck. But she sat stirring her tea in a decidedly listless manner. "Good morning," Jamie greeted her cheerfully. "Am I the last to come down?"

"No, not quite," Marianne said in a small voice. "Everyone's been here but . . . your friend."

"Reggie? Is he still abed? That's not like him."

"He has not seemed . . . that is, does it seem to you that he . . . ?"

"That he what, Marianne?"

"That he has been . . . avoiding companionship these last few days?"

"Now you mention it, yes, I have," Jamie answered, his brow wrinkling. "He's been acting dashed queer, as if he's in some sort of hank. Been meaning to look into it. If you'll excuse me, Marianne, I'll do so right now."

Determined to get to the bottom of the mystery of Reggie's strange behavior, Jamie marched firmly up the stairs and into Reggie's bedroom without so much as a knock on the door. Reggie was sitting up among the pillows, his nose deep in a book he'd evidently more than half finished.

"Good God!" Jamie exclaimed. "Not reading again!"

Reggie started. "Well! of all . . . ! What'th the idea of thneaking up on me like thith? You didn't even knock!"

"You can get down off your high ropes, Reggie Windle, and don't try to tip me a rise. I came in without knocking to catch you unaware. Something has pitched you into a bumble bath, and I mean to find out what it is."

"Nothing to find out," Reggie said flatly, sticking his nose back in the book.

"You'll tell me," Jamie threatened, "or you'll feel my fists. Spending your time reading! Why, it ain't even *healthy*! And you've been avoiding me . . . don't deny it. Even Marianne noticed it."

"Oh, she did, did she?" asked the voice behind the book. "Well, it ain't any of her conthern."

"Stop hiding your face behind that book and look at me," Jamie demanded. "Something has put you out of frame, and I want to know what it is." His voice lowered, and he asked in a troubled voice, "Have I said or done anything to offend you, Reg? You know I'd rather cut my tongue out than hurt your feelings."

"Don't be a beetle-headed flat," Reggie said, laying the book aside and looking up at Jamie with a troubled frown. "Maybe I'm homethick. I've been thinking that I might go home to Farnham tomorrow . . ."

"Farnham?" Jamie exclaimed impatiently. "Whatever for? There's no one there except the servants!"

"To my thithter, then. She athked me to come for the holidayth."

"Yes, I remember. And you said you'd rather spend a month in prison than a week with your sister. Damn it, man, I'm your best friend! Can't you tell me?"

Reggie twisted the edges of his comforter with nervous fingers. "Hard to talk about it," he said slowly. "Dathed embarrathing."

Jamie perched at the foot of the bed. "Embarrassing or not, you'd better get to it, because I'm not moving until you do."

"Damned babblemonger," Reggie muttered. Then, after a pause, he sighed and plunged in. "It ain't anything you've done. It'th me! I've gone and done the motht addlepated thing. I've been an even greater lobcock than Geoff Carbery."

"Geoff Carbery?" Jamie asked in complete bewilderment. "Whatever can you . . . ? You don't mean you've done something stupid in the petticoat line?"

Reggie nodded glumly.

"I don't believe it! You?" A thought struck him like a lightning bolt. "You don't mean that *you've* accosted Miss Pennington!"

"No, of courthe not!" said Reggie, outraged.

"Well then, who?"

Reggie glanced at his friend with an expression ridden with guilt. "Marianne," he said tragically.

Jamie blinked. "Marianne? That child? You couldn't have behaved improperly to such an innocent! I'll not believe it of you."

"Well, it wouldn't have happened at all, if you hadn't made me remain with her on the road the other day. I mean, what would you have done if she'd been crying, and she looked up at you with thothe big eyeth of herth, and thaid that *you* were handthome and kind and . . ."

Jamie, beginning to understand, felt an irresistible urge to laugh. Struggling to keep his expression serious, he asked, "Said you were handsome and kind, did she?"

"Yeth, and . . . and . . . that my lithp was lovable . . ."

"L-lovable? She said your lisp was love—*lovable* . . . ?"

"Yeth, she did! I mean, *any* man would have kithed her . . . !"

It was too much for Jamie. He put his head back and roared with laughter. The more he thought of Reggie's lovable lisp, the more he laughed. Reggie stared at him in mounting vexation. "I don't thee what there ith to laugh about," he said coldly. "She ith *your* young lady, after all."

"Y-you're doing it much t-too brown, Reg," Jamie gasped, wiping his streaming eyes with his sleeve. "I'll believe the h-handsome and k-kind part, but a l-lovable lisp—!" But Reggie's words reached him at last, and his laughter faded away. "W-what did you say?" he asked.

"I thaid there ith nothing to laugh about," Reggie repeated rigidly.

"No, no, the other part. About Marianne being my young lady."

"Well, what about it?"

Jamie stared at Reggie in sudden understanding. "Is that it? Have you been hiding away behind a book because you thought that Marianne and I—?"

Reggie glared at him angrily. "You're not going to pretend that you're not attracted to her, are you? You told me you were, the very firtht night we arrived!"

"Reggie, you gudgeon! You cannot have thought I was serious! I like her, of course, but nothing beyond the ordinary. There aren't any other females here to flirt with, and I wanted to pass the time . . ."

"Do you mean it, Jamie?" Reggie asked urgently. "You really don't care for her?"

"Of course I mean it. How many times do I have to tell you I ain't in the petticoat line? Besides, now that I think about it, it seems plain that she's liked you better from the first. If you ask me, she's been looking blue-devilled ever since you began avoiding us."

A gleam of hope lit Reggie's face. "Do you really think tho?" he asked.

Jamie had to laugh again.

"Now what'th tho funny?" Reggie demanded.

"You," Jamie said between gasps. "The way you said, 'Do you really think so?'—well, you sounded just like Marianne!" And Jamie roared again. Reggie blinked, tried to look severe, and then slowly collapsed into helpless laughter.

"Of course," Jamie added, when he could manage to speak, "she doesn't have your l-lovable lisp!"

Reggie's response was a well-aimed barrage of pillows flung at Jamie's head.

The snow had stopped falling and the sky had lightened by the afternoon, and over luncheon several eager voices joined to beg Philip to permit them to accompany him on his rounds of the tenants. Sally, whose vivacious quality was blooming under the warmth of Philip's attention, spoke feelingly of the pleasure of riding through the snow. Reggie, happily restored to the society of his friend and Marianne (the story of *Jonathan Wild* forgotten), seconded Sally's views and immediately claimed two seats in the carriage— one for him and one for Marianne. Jamie promptly demanded a seat next to them.

"Mutht you came along?" Reg had asked, *sotto voce*.

"Yes, I must," Jamie had answered decidedly. "Just because you've won the fair lady, don't think you'll get *me* to retire with a book!"

The group gathering in the front hallway that afternoon made a gay assemblage. There was much laughter, the clump of heavy boots, the commotion of several footmen helping the men into their greatcoats. Mufflers were wound around throats, muffs and mittens found for eager hands. In the midst of the turmoil, Philip noticed Evalyn walking quietly up the stairs. At Clarissa's insistence, she was going to her room for a rest. Philip nudged his son. "I think you should ask Miss Pennington to join us, Jamie. It seems to me that you've become neglectful of including her in your activities."

"Oh?" Jamie asked, puzzled. "I didn't realize that I was expected to—of course, I'll ask her." He ran up a few steps and caught her arm. "Miss Pennington," he said, "we're all about to go riding in the snow. Why don't you join us?"

"Do come!" called Sally from below. Her watchful eye had missed nothing of this byplay. "It promises to be a most amusing outing." She took Philip's arm possessively and laughed up at him.

"Thank you," Evalyn said, "but I prefer the warmth of the indoors."

"Come now, Miss Pennington," Philip said in his most avuncular manner, "I heard you say not long ago that you loved new-fallen snow."

Evalyn lifted her chin and regarded him with her disconcertingly direct stare. "You must have mistaken me, my lord," she said. "The sight of it brings back associations that are not at all pleasant to me. I'm afraid I'm not in the least tempted." With a little curtsey, she turned and walked purposefully up the stairs and out of sight.

Jamie looked at his father curiously. "If I didn't know better, sir, I would think you'd been given a very decided set-down."

"It certainly seems so," Philip said gruffly, his ears a little red.

"The girl acts more like a duchess than a governess," Sally murmured, half to herself, with reluctant admiration.

"I told you," Jamie said, "that she's a very—"

"Yes, we know," Philip cut him off drily. "A very redoubtable girl."

Evalyn closed the door of her room behind her and leaned against it, trembling. She considered throwing herself on the bed and sobbing her heart out, but without Nancy's restraining presence, she might not be able to stop. Sobbing, as she had discovered yesterday, did very little good. It was a momentary relief at best, and it reddened the eyes, caused the lips to swell, and left one utterly drained and numb. No, she had better keep her wits about her and decide what to do. She could not continue in this fashion, that was clear. She could not pull herself out of this dejection if she were obliged to see Philip every day, to watch him dance attendance on Sally, to hear his voice, to see his face in the firelight, to catch the glances he threw at her occasionally, and store them up to feed on later, like a starving bird in the snow. The look he had given her last night, when she had recited those lines of Milton's, had sustained her all night long. No, she must go away. It would be foolish to subject herself to more of this feeling of hopelessness and pain.

She still had the money in her reticule which she had saved from her wages. With careful management, it would see her to London. And she still had the address of the unknown cousin who might provide her with a place to stay until she could find work. Quickly, before she allowed the warmth and luxury of the room and the kindness of the people in this house to change her mind, she pulled the battered portmanteau from under the bed and began to pack.

When Nancy found her, she was almost finished. The girl gaped at her openmouthed. "Miss Evalyn! What're you doing?" she squeaked. "You're not leaving?"

"Hush, Nancy. I want no one to know about this. Quickly, now, I shall need your help."

"Well, you ain't going to get it! You was supposed to stay here 'til the new year. Where're you going? And why?"

"Don't ask any questions, Nancy. I must go today. You know that I would not be doing this if it weren't necessary. Don't make this harder for me than it is already."

"Oh, Miss! You're breaking me heart, for sure. It has something to do with yesterday, don't it?"

Evalyn merely nodded.

"I knew it. You ain't been the same since. It was something bad, I know. Miss Evalyn, I ain't asking you to tell me what it was, but if you could see your way clear to telling his lordship . . ."

"His lordship?"

"Yes, Miss Evalyn. He has a good head and a kind heart. Everyone says so. And he likes you, I could tell that when you was both helping to get Joseph out of trouble. He would help you, I know he would."

"He couldn't help me, Nancy."

"Are you sure? Positive sure?"

"Yes, dear, I'm positively sure," Evalyn said with a small smile.

Nancy's lip quivered. "Miss Clarissa then. She might be able to . . ."

"Nancy, don't. There's no one to help. Please don't look at me so, or I shall start to sob again." But it was Nancy who sobbed. Evalyn put her arms about the girl's shoulders and tried to soothe her, but Nancy was inconsolable.

"N-nobody was ever s-so g-good to m-me b-before," she cried. "It ain't r-right for someone l-like you to have to g-go away. And on C-Christmas eve, too. It ain't right."

When Nancy's tears had ceased, Evalyn rose and said in a firm, steady voice, "You must help me now, Nancy. Do you think you can?"

Nancy sniffed and nodded.

"Good. Now, listen. You must find Joseph for me and ask him if he can take the curricle without anyone knowing and drive me into Ashwater. Tell him we can do it when everyone is dressing for dinner—in about half an hour. Then, Nancy, you must stay in here for the night. If anyone knocks and asks why I haven't come down to dinner, tell them I'm not feeling well and have gone to bed."

"B-but they'll be bound to find out sooner or later," Nancy said.

"Yes. Tomorrow you're to find Miss Clarissa and give her this letter. I also want you to give her this box I've made for her. If you can find some silver paper, we can wrap it up before Joseph comes for me. And give her these gloves that I've knitted for the twins. Tell them they're from Father Christmas."

"Oh, Miss Evalyn . . ." Nancy whimpered.

"And Nancy, this is for you. It's my Spanish shawl. It was my mother's. It would make me so happy to know you have it."

"Oh, no, Miss Evalyn, I couldn't. It's too pretty for me. . . ."

But Evalyn put it around her shoulders. Nancy burst into fresh tears, and the two embraced. "Oh, Miss Evalyn, what's to become of me without you?"

"I've written about you in my note. I'm sure Miss Clarissa can find a place for you, if you want it. Now, go along, Nancy dear, and get Joseph for me."

Half an hour later, Evalyn put on her cloak, picked up her portmanteau, and looked around the room. The portrait of Philip's aunt gazed at her coldly. She could hear Philip's voice. . . . "You and she should deal extremely well together." The walls glowed dimly in the late afternoon light as they had done on the day she arrived. She could see through the window the outlines of the balcony railing over which she and Philip had pulled Joseph to safety. She looked at the dressing table where she had left the few packages which were all she had to express her thanks. And thanks she owed in full measure to all the people in this house. Despite the pain she carried with her, a pain for which no one was to blame but herself, she realized that she had experienced more of the emotions of living, had felt more of the pleasures, the joys, the excitements and—yes—the sufferings than in all of her days before. Yet, as she crept stealthily down the back stairs to where Joseph sat waiting in the cur-

ricle, she realized with a shock that since the day
she had left the house of Lady Carbery less than one
week had elapsed.

CHAPTER FIFTEEN

Sally looked with pleasure at the dress laid out for
her on the bed. She had chosen it especially to wear
tonight—Christmas eve. It was of the loveliest Flor-
entine silk in a green that exactly matched her eyes
and was cunningly designed to drape across the bosom
in the most flattering way. The tiny puffed sleeves
could be pulled back off the shoulders, and the high
waist admirably suited her figure. It was a deceptively
simple creation, the only trimmings to be found in a
wide band across the bottom, where a classic design
had been intricately woven into the material and
edged with seed pearls.

Annette had already dressed her hair. It was
brushed back into a knot at the back of her head, with
only a small part of the front escaping into little curls
that surrounded her face. A jewelled band circled her
head, and later she would thrust a tall ostrich plume
into the center of it.

A gasp from Annette in the dressing room widened
her smile. "Ma'm'selle! Come quick!" the girl cried.

"What is it, Annette?" Sally asked in a voice that
was calculatedly casual.

"Your diamond earrings, Ma'm'selle! I cannot find
them!"

"I don't want to wear the diamonds tonight, I told
you. I want the pearl drops."

Annette appeared in the dressing room doorway, looking distraught. *"Mais, non! Vous ne comprenez pas!* They are gone!"

"What do you mean, gone?"

"I mean gone! Disappeared! *Perdu!*"

Sally strode quickly to the dressing room and surveyed the open jewel box. "Are you sure?" she asked, looking through the contents hurriedly.

"But of course I am sure. Did you not put them here yourself, in this very compartment?"

Sally carefully emptied every compartment and every tiny drawer, while Annette watched nervously at her elbow. "How strange. . . ." mused Sally. "Only you and I know where I keep the key. . . ."

Annette straightened up and spoke haughtily. "You are not suggesting, Ma'm'selle, that I am responsible for such a thing! You cannot believe that I—! I am no thief, *moi!*"

"Oh, be still, Annette! I'm not accusing you. It would be stupid for you to have done so, and you are not stupid. Irritating and disrespectful, yes, but not stupid."

"For that, I suppose, I should make thanks. But why do you think it would be stupid of me to have done it?"

"You would be the first one suspected, as you well know. No, you are not the culprit. I think you had better go and bring Lady Steele to me. She must be informed at once."

A moment later Clarissa, wearing a loose wrapper, her hair only half dressed, hurried into the room. "What is it, Sally? Annette says you've something to tell me. Of the greatest moment, to use her words."

"Well, it is of some moment, I'm afraid. I hate to trouble you with this matter, my dear, but I don't see what else there is to do. My diamond drops have disappeared."

"Diamonds drops? You mean those magnificent diamond earrings?" Clarissa gasped. "Are you sure?"

"Oh, but yes, *Madame*. We have looked most carefully," Annette said earnestly. "They have assuredly disappeared."

"You see," Sally explained, "Annette has instructions that she's to stand by me and make sure I lock them away in my jewel box after every time I wear them. I'm inclined to be somewhat careless, so we devised this system between us, didn't we, Annette?"

Annette eyed her employer curiously. Something in Ma'm'selle's voice put Annette on the alert. She knew her Ma'm'selle very well. The "system" was devised only two nights ago, and at the time, Annette had not been comfortable about the manner of its devising. She had felt then that Miss Trevelyan was up to some trick. Now she was sure of it, but what it could be she did not know. There was nothing she could do but answer the question. "Yes, we did," she said reluctantly. She would have liked to add "two nights ago," but decided to hold her tongue.

"I see," said Clarissa, who looked quite pale, her brow furrowed in worried lines. "You think that someone in this house may have stolen them?"

"I don't see what else I can think," Sally said.

"There are other possibilities. When was the last time you saw them?"

"The night I wore the mauve silk, isn't that so, Annette?"

"Yes, Ma'm'selle. Two nights ago. Then we put the earrings away here in the box."

"Are you sure you haven't worn them since?" Clarissa persisted.

"Quite sure. Last night I wore the Venetian velvet and decided not to wear any jewels with it. We did not even open the box."

"Oh, dear. I don't know what to say. A thing like this has never happened before. Sally, do you think we might wait a day or two before we do anything about this? It is so awkward, especially on Christmas eve, to start questioning servants and so on. . . . Perhaps if we wait, the earrings will turn up."

"I don't see how they possibly can," Sally said, masking her impatience for her plan to unfold, "but I wouldn't dream of upsetting your holiday festivities. I'm sure I can rely on you to handle the matter tactfully. Do just as you think you should, Clarissa. I leave it entirely in your hands."

"Thank you, my dear," Clarissa said. "I regret that such an occurrence should have taken place in my home, but I'm sure the earrings will be restored to you before long." But her worried frown did not disappear as she retreated, much disturbed, to her own bedroom.

The kissing boughs had been hung over the doorways of several of the downstairs rooms, and Jamie and Reggie, coming down to dinner early, had placed themselves on either side of the drawing room doorway. As each lady made her entrance, the two young men bent and kissed her cheeks simultaneously. First, Martha arrived, bearing a twin by each hand. The boys, dressed in long trousers, white shirts with turned-down collars trimmed with lace, and blue coats exactly like their father's, had been permitted to join the adults for dinner for this occasion. When they saw their mother caught under the mistletoe by two gentlemen at once, they went off in a fit of giggles. Their sister followed. Marianne, her brown ringlets shining from an hour of energetic brushing, looked—to one man at least—the very essence of feminine loveliness in her demure evening gown of ruby-colored lustring. When she was kissed, her brothers giggled again, louder and longer. It became infectious, setting off the entire room when Clarissa entered, and climaxing in a paroxysm of merriment when Sally at last came in.

Almost an hour later, the guests had still not left the drawing room to go in to dine. Hutton had twice put in his head to see if he could enter and announce dinner and had twice withdrawn, because one of the company had not yet put in an appearance. Finally, Clarissa beckoned to him and whispered instructions to dispatch a footman to see what had detained Miss Pennington. Philip watched the interchange and quietly and unobtrusively left the drawing room. The returning footman found his lordship pacing the hall. "Well, where is Miss Pennington?" he demanded abruptly.

"She begs to be excused, my lord. She is not feeling well."

"Did she say what was wrong?" his lordship asked in concern.

"No, my lord. I did not speak to the young lady. Her abigail informed me she had retired."

"I see. Very well, you may tell Hutton to announce dinner. I'll inform Lady Steele."

He returned to the drawing room and told the assemblage that Evalyn had retired early. He informed Clarissa in a low voice that Evalyn was not feeling well. Clarissa shook her head. "I told the girl she was looking fagged. I'm glad she decided to go to bed, though I'm sorry she will miss the Christmas eve celebrations. Don't look so worried, Philip. I'm sure she'll be right as rain after a good night's sleep."

After an excellent dinner, the guests gathered in the drawing room for an evening of Christmas games. First they played hunt-the-slipper, as a favor to the twins. Then forfeits, by popular demand, with Marianne unanimously chosen as the crier of the forfeits. She surprised the entire group by devising forfeits of great ingenuity, and announcing them in a voice that could be heard at least by those who were close by or listening with attention. And, at last, Jamie's favorite, snapdragon, was announced.

Hutton entered with great ceremony, bearing a broad, shallow bowl filled with brandy. He was followed by two footmen, one carrying a tray of raisins and the other a table, which was placed in the middle of the room. The bowl was set on the table, the raisins dropped into the brandy, and then Jamie lit a long stick and ignited the brandy, to a chorus of oohs and aahs. The blue flame jumped merrily. The guests were requested to pull the flaming raisins from the bowl and pop them into their mouths. This was to be done to the accompaniment of the snapdragon song and, if the experience of the past gave any clue, much clapping of hands and derisive laughter.

> "Here he comes with flaming bowl,
> Don't he mean to take his toll,
> Snip! Snap! Dragon!"

they sang as Edward gingerly put his fingers into the flame and hastily withdrew them, empty.

"No, no," Jamie cautioned him. "You must be very quick about it, like this." And he thrust his hand into the brandy with a darting motion and had popped three flaming raisins in his mouth in the wink of an eye.

"Doesn't it hurt?" asked Teddy, awed.

"Not a bit, if you're quick. Here, you try." And he lifted the bow over the bowl.

> "With his blue and lapping tongue
> Many of you will be stung,
> Snip! Snap! Dragon!"

The boys were quick learners and popped the raisins in their mouths with amusing bravado. Sally, graceful and quick, took her turn to prolonged applause. Marianne was too timid to try, so Reggie fed her with the raisins he'd procured. Everyone managed to take a turn before the flame died out, and, to the twins' disappointment, the game ended as they all sang the final stanza:

"Don't 'ee fear him, but be bold,
Out he goes, his flames are cold,
Snip! Snap! Dragon!"

The game was such a success that nobody, not even Sally, noticed that Philip had quietly slipped out of the room. He ran up the stairs and knocked softly at Evalyn's door. A wary, frightened Nancy opened it a crack and peeped out. "Good evening, your lordship," she said in a quivering voice.

"Good evening, Nancy. I've come to see your mistress. May I come in?"

"Oh, no, sir," she exclaimed. "She's fast asleep!"

"I see. Is she very ill? What did she say was troubling her?"

"Only a headache, sir. Nothing to worry over."

"But perhaps I should send Clarissa up—just to see if she's feverish. . . ?"

"Oh, she ain't feverish, sir, I promise you that. There ain't no use disturbing her now."

Philip scanned the girl's face closely. "Very well. But you will stay with her all night, won't you? And be sure to send for me if she should wake and need anything, will you do that?"

"Oh, most certainly, sir. I won't leave this room all night. You have me word on it."

"Yes. Well, goodnight then," he said, and reluctantly turned away.

Philip found the rest of the evening very nearly unendurable, but he played the part of host so well that nobody suspected it. One thing beyond his control was the weather which, it was soon discovered, had become so bad that the plans for the evening were adversely affected. The snow fell so heavily that attendance at the midnight service would not be possible. Instead, Edward was asked to conduct a brief family service, carols were sung with gusto, and the little group gathered for the late supper in a happy Christmas spirit. Philip, however, could not help giving a sigh of relief when the company finally disbanded and headed for their beds.

Edward Covington had had a memorable evening. Not only was he proud of being asked to conduct the service, but he had had a talk with Reggie that had induced in him a most unaccustomed, fatherly glow. A brief talk with Marianne, just before she retired, had increased his sense of exhilaration, and it was with a pleased, self-satisfied smile that he readied himself for bed. His man dismissed, he put on his frogged dressing gown and tapped at the door which connected his bedroom with his wife's.

"Come in," Martha called. As he entered, Martha's abigail, who had been administering nosedrops to her mistress, glanced at Edward's dressing gown, replaced the bottle of medication, and hastily withdrew.

"What is it, my dear?" asked Edward with a suppressed sigh. "Another cold?"

"Oh, no," his spouse reassured him, sitting up among the pillows and patting the space beside her invitingly, "it's only a preventive measure. You know how I am in such weather."

Edward sat down on the bed and took her hand. "Yes, my dear, I know how you are. But I don't know if it's altogether wise to take medication before it is needed."

"Why would it be unwise?" she asked him reasonably. "If the medicine is beneficial when one is sick, why should it be harmful when one is well?"

Edward opened his mouth to respond, found himself nonplussed, and shut it again. He shrugged. "Never mind that now. I have some news that will surprise you, I think."

"News? You surprise me already. What news can you possibly have? We left each other scarcely an hour ago."

"Did you notice tonight that, during the games, Reg-

gie took me aside? He asked me to step into the library
to have a word with him."

"No, I can't say I noticed. What on earth did he
want with you?"

"Prepare yourself for a shock, my dear. He asked my
permission to pay his addresses to Marianne!"

Martha's mouth dropped open, and she stared at
her husband, speechless. She felt for a moment as if
she were in a dream. She could not have heard him
properly.

"Did you say Marianne? He wants to court *our*
Marianne?"

"So it would seem."

"You cannot have understood him! You've made a
mistake. Marianne is only a child! She'll not have her
come-out until next year!"

"So I told him," said her laconic husband with irritating calm.

Martha caught her breath and clutched at his arm.
"What did you tell him? Edward!" she almost
screamed. "You didn't *refuse* him!"

"Hush, my dear, don't get so excited. One minute
you say she's too young, and the next you say you
don't want me to refuse him. You must try to be calm
and compose your mind."

"Compose my mind! How can I compose my mind
when you tell me you whistled the Farnham fortune
down the wind!"

"I didn't do any such thing. Do you take me for a
fool?"

"Well, then, what *did* you do? Will you stop talking
and tell me what you said?"

"I can scarcely stop talking and tell you anything,"
Edward responded with asperity.

"What?" asked Martha. "Sometimes, Edward, I find
it extremely difficult to follow you."

Edward sighed. "Very well, my dear, suppose we
start all over again from the beginning."

"Yes," agreed his wife, leaning back against the pillows, pressing her hands against her breasts and taking deep breaths to calm herself, "that"—she breathed—"would be a very good"—she breathed again—"idea."

"Well then, I repeat. I accompanied Reggie to the library where he told me, in an excellent, succinct style, that he had grown attached to our daughter—"

"How remarkable," exclaimed his wife in gratification. "In less than a week! I must say I would not have believed she had it in her."

"You are not to interrupt with irrelevancies, ma'am. As I was saying, Reggie said he had grown attached to our daughter and would like my permission to pay his addresses to her."

"Yes, yes. Well?"

"Whereupon, after I had gotten over my surprise, I pointed out to him that she was only seventeen and had not yet been presented—"

"Very true. Just what you ought to have said."

"Thank you. Then Reggie said he was aware of that, and that he was willing to give her a chance to have her come-out and see a little more of the world before extracting a firm commitment from her."

Martha clapped her hands together gleefully. "Did he say that? How considerate of him! I must say, I'm thoroughly delighted with the boy. I think that should serve very well, don't you? It will give me plenty of time to persuade Marianne that putting up with a little lisp is nothing but a trifle when compared with the Farnham fortune and the right to be called a viscountess."

"I don't think you'll need that time. When I told Marianne what had transpired—"

"You told her?"

"Yes, of course. I stopped in at her bedroom before coming here. She threw her arms about my neck and said she was the happiest girl in the world!"

"Oh, Edward, I can scarcely believe it! Our daughter . . . to be a viscountess, the lady of a great house in the country, a London residence, all the horses and carriages she could want, the servants, the gowns, the pin-money . . . Edward, I think I'm going to faint . . . !"

Edward stood up abruptly and frowned down at her. "If you do," he said severely, "I'll march out of here and leave you where you fall. It's bad enough to have you fainting when trouble occurs, but if you begin to do it when *good* things happen, you'll get no help from me!"

Philip lay in his bed that night, staring up at the shadows cast on the ceiling by the flickering firelight. For the fourth night in succession, it was Evalyn who had caused his insomnia. Tonight it was an uneasy feeling of guilt that was keeping him awake. He feared that she had taken to her bed because of the treatment she had received at his hands. And at Jamie's hands, too. His irritation at his irresponsible son was chaffing him severely. What sort of man had his son become? The beetlehead had not shown a moment's concern over Evalyn's absence this evening. He had enjoyed his Christmas eve completely and had indulged in his silly games with the light-hearted enthusiasm of a child without a care in the world.

Two days ago, Philip had promised Clarissa to take Jamie to task, but he'd not yet been able to bring himself to deliver that much-needed lecture on the duties of a prospective bridegroom to his bride. Obviously, he could put it off no longer. Tomorrow he would have it out with Jamie. He went over in his mind the various instances of neglect of which Jamie had been guilty. Yet it would not be advisable to throw a recital of Jamie's thoughtless acts at his head. Perhaps it would be better to encourage Jamie to announce his engagement immediately, so that he and Evalyn could feel free to exhibit publicly their attachment to each other. But Philip would not neglect to point out to his rackety son the necessity of giving his bride his undivided affection and attention. Philip rehearsed several speeches in his mind and imagined the scene with Jamie in several diffrent ways. Somehow, though, no matter how calmly and reasonably each scene started, Philip found himself concluding each imaginary encounter by firmly wringing his blasted son's neck.

CHAPTER SIXTEEN

The ten-mile drive to Ashwater took more than two hours, for although the curricle was light, the passage through the snow was difficult. The open carriage did not afford much protection from the elements, and Evalyn and Joseph were chilled to the bone by the time they drove into the inn yard. Joseph shook his head worriedly as he helped Evalyn down from the carriage. "I hope you know what you're about," he said, voicing his disapproval for the fourth time that hour. "You'll never get a hack on a night like this, and even if you do, you'll not make it to Launceston. And if you do get to Launceston, you'll not see the Exeter stage 'til this snow clears."

Evalyn looked at the snow swirling about the inn yard. It seemed to be coming down more heavily than before, and the wind was growing stronger. Drifts were beginning to form around the gateposts and along the walls of the inn. "Perhaps you're right, Joseph," she said, a worried frown creasing her forehead, "but I shall contrive somehow. Meanwhile, come in and get warm before you set off for home."

The Bull at Ashwater was a small, cheerful inn, with a taproom that was usually filled with lively activity at this time of evening. On this night, however, a solitary drinker sat in one corner, and Mrs. Fern, the landlord's wife, knelt before the fireplace adding wood to an already lively blaze. Otherwise, the place was deserted. Hearing footsteps, Mrs. Fern looked up to see Evalyn and Joseph standing in the doorway. "Bless me," she exclaimed, "where'd you come from? I ain't heard no carriage."

She bustled over to Evalyn and took her cloak. "Here now, Missy, sit you down near the fire. You're shivering something fierce."

"Get the lady something hot to drink," Joseph said, putting down the portmanteau. "She's chilled to the bone."

"And you, too, by the look of you." She hurried off muttering to herself on the peculiarities of folk who would venture out on a night like this, and Christmas eve, too. She returned in a moment with a pot of hot tea and two steaming mugs of mulled wine. Joseph took the wine and drank as quickly as he could swallow the hot brew. "I'd best be getting back, Miss Evalyn, before the drifts get too deep," he said.

"Yes, I'm worried about that, Joseph. What will happen if you get stuck in a drift?"

"I'll dig myself out, don't you worry none about me. It's you what's got me concerned."

"You're so kind to worry about me when I may have gotten you in a devil of a hobble."

"Not me," he assured her with a grin. "If I been missed, I'll tell 'em that I took the curricle to see my sick mum in Bridestowe. I ain't never seen you tonight, Miss Evalyn, and that's a fact." He winked at her broadly and wrapped his muffler tightly around his neck. "Well, I best be off. You take good care o' yourself. Good luck to you, ma'am. I hope you get some good o' this night's work."

Evalyn watched through the taproom window as Joseph drove off in the snow. Then she returned to the fire, sat down and sipped her tea slowly. The enormity of her predicament slowly overwhelmed her. Perhaps she had been foolish and hasty. The trip to London would be long and costly, even in the best weather. She had to get to Launceston to pick up the stage to Exeter, the last stop of the London-Exeter stage. Each change would require additional funds for tipping the ostlers who handled her luggage, for accommodations if a long wait was required between connections, and for goodness knew what other exigencies which might arise. She had no idea of the cost of a hack to Launceston, but her meagre funds would certainly not provide for more than one or two nights' lodging while waiting out the storm.

There was one consolation. The snow would surely prevent anyone at Gyllford from coming after her, if they were inclined to do so. Not that she expected anyone to follow her. She was a stranger to them, after all. Kind as they had been to her, they had known her for only a week and had no obligation to be concerned for her welfare, especially after they learned that she had chosen to run away from them. She sighed. Would Philip miss her? she wondered. What would he think of her foolish disappearance? She remembered the warm gleam in his eyes, his slight, teasing smile when he had taken the portrait from her bedroom wall. How amazingly close they had been at that moment, as if each one could read the other's thoughts. It was too painful now to think about. What would there be in his revealing blue eyes when he learned that she had gone? Would they be scornful of her foolishness? Angry at her thoughtlessness? Or would they be completely indifferent? Would he dismiss the news with a shrug and turn his eyes to the beautiful Miss Trevelyan?

She was shaken from these ruminations by a cough at her elbow. Mrs. Fern stood looking down at her. "Has your man gone?" the puzzled woman asked. "You ain't meaning to stay here tonight, are you?"

"I'm not sure. Is there a hack and a driver I could hire to take me to Launceston?"

"Tonight?" Mrs. Fern asked wide-eyed. "You couldn't expect man or beast to be abroad on a night like this! Besides, it's Christmas eve!"

"Oh, dear. I had hoped—"

"Let me call Mr. Fern, dearie. He knows more about hiring out hacks than what I do. He's out in the kitchen, eating a piece of tomorrow's ham."

The innkeeper, Mr. Fern, a burly man with a bald head and a great walrus moustache, came from the kitchen, a look of curiosity clearly discernible in his face. "I wouldn't ask a driver to take you out tonight," he told her firmly. "Wouldn't be safe, ma'am."

"Do you think you can get someone for me tomorrow?" Evalyn asked.

Mr. Fern turned to the solitary man in the corner. "Sam'l?" he asked, "would you be able to drive a hack to Launceston in the morning?"

The man looked up from his tankard and shook his head. "Doubt it," he said shortly. "The snow ain't goin' to stop so soon. Not this'n."

The landlord shrugged. "If old Sam'l thinks not, you can lay odds you won't get out o' here tomorrow morning neither."

"Old Sam'l knows the weather, he does," Mrs. Fern agreed.

Evalyn shook her head, crestfallen. "I hope he may be wrong, this time," she said worriedly. "But in the meantime, do you have a room for me?"

"That we have, ma'am, with the house so empty. Don't you fret. We'll have you snug in no time," Mr. Fern said kindly.

"That we will," agreed his spouse. "The best bedroom for you tonight. Mr. Fern will bring you a bit of ham and some greens, while I go up and start a nice fire and warm your sheets. Some food and a warm bed'll get you out of the dismals, you'll see."

Evalyn smiled weakly and resumed her seat. Mr.

Fern filled a tankard, wordlessly placed it before old Sam'l, and went out to the kitchen. He returned a moment later with a platter heaped with several slices of ham, potatoes, and turnip greens, which he placed on a nearby table with a flourish. He held the chair for her, and Evalyn sat down gratefully. "It smells delicious," she said. "I suddenly feel quite hungry."

"We thought you might be, Mrs. Fern and me. Nothing like a hot meal to get rid of the dumps."

The innkeeper went off to the kitchen, and Evalyn began to eat. The ham was surprisingly well prepared. She had just begun her third slice when there came a sound of a carriage in the yard. An angry voice shouted, "Ostler! Ostler! Where the deuce is everybody?"

Mr. Fern hurried from the kitchen and out the door. "Everyone's gone home," she heard him explain. "It is Christmas eve, you know."

A confusion of footsteps and noise in the entryway made Evalyn aware that a number of people had arrived. There were several children's voices and the sound of a baby crying. "Merciful heavens! Ye'll not bring us in there!" said a woman's voice, distinctive for its Irish brogue. "I won't have my wee ones in a taproom. A private parlor, if ye please."

"The parlor's closed, ma'am. I ain't got no fire going in there tonight."

"Well, then, don't stand there gawkin'! Start one! And when ye've done that, bring some more candles. Dark as a tomb in there, it is. And, Charlie boy, stop that! Take Mary into the parlor and sit her down. You, Sean, stop kicking the wall—the snow'll melt off y'r boots soon enough. Meggie, let Cathy help ye off with y'r cloak. Well, come along, then. The sooner we finish, the sooner we'll be home." The slam of a door stilled any further sounds.

Evalyn watched in amusement as the innkeeper hurried back and forth from the kitchen to the parlor bearing trays of loaded dishes. Mrs. Fern, returning from upstairs, was quickly impressed to assist. The two of them were too busy to do more than throw Evalyn a harried glance as they ran by. "Don't know what such a fam'ly's doing out on Christmas eve," Mrs. Fern whispered to Evalyn as she returned from her third trip to the parlor. "Those children should be home waiting for Father Christmas." And she ran off to the kitchen.

"Eating our whole Christmas dinner, too," grumbled her husband as he followed hastily behind her.

Evalyn, patiently waiting to be shown up to her bedroom, was surprised by the sound of sniffling coming from the doorway to the taproom. She looked around to see a little girl peeping in at her from the passageway. The child couldn't have been more than three or four years old, for she was still in short petticoats. Her red, curly hair was dishevelled, and her eyes and nose were running. A white tucker had been tied around her neck, and she wore only one shoe. Evalyn smiled at her. "Good evening," she said. The child sniffed forlornly but didn't move. "If you come here," Evalyn said invitingly, "I'll give you a bit of my biscuit. Would you like that?"

The child advanced toward her cautiously, her hands hidden behind her back. A few feet away, she stopped and eyed Evalyn with suspicion. Evalyn got up from her chair and held out her hand. The child backed away. Evalyn pulled out a handkerchief, knelt down and beckoned. The little girl advanced shyly. "There, now," Evalyn said soothingly, "no need to be afraid of me, you know. May I wipe your face with my nice handkerchief?"

The child nodded and toddled across the few feet still separating them. Evalyn wiped her eyes and nose. "You've been crying, haven't you?" Evalyn asked sympathetically. "Is it because you're hungry?"

The child shook her head. "No, ma'am," she said timidly, and brought her hands from behind her back. In one was a grimy doll whose elegant gown had been torn, revealing a missing leg underneath. In the other hand she clutched the severed limb. "Charlie did it," the child said with a quivering lip.

"Oh, that was too bad of Charlie, I'm sure," Evalyn said, taking the doll and the leg and looking them over carefully. "But we can make her well again."

"Can we?" the child asked dubiously.

Evalyn took her hand and led her to the table. She seated herself and lifted the child to her lap. She placed the wounded doll on the table, and the two of them examined it carefully. "If you ask your Mamma to put some glue here and here," Evalyn explained, "this lovely lady will be good as new."

"Not her dress," the girl said knowingly.

"Yes, of course, you're right. The dress must be mended with a needle and thread."

"Needle and thread," the child repeated, nodding wisely. She leaned back against Evalyn, gave a shivering sigh to indicate that her crying was over, put her thumb in her mouth and sucked contentedly. Evalyn was about to distract her with the offer of a piece of biscuit, when she looked up and saw that she was being regarded by a woman in the doorway. The woman was full-formed, her buxom figure emphasized by the high-necked swansdown gown she wore. It fit her a bit too tightly and was badly rumpled and stained. Her head was swathed in a rose-colored turban which clashed with the ringlets of bright red hair that escaped from beneath it in youthful disarray. Her complexion was ruddy and marked with fine lines about the eyes and mouth, but despite the rather tasteless clothing and general untidiness, her eyes were merry and the smile that brightened her face gave Evalyn a distinct impression of beauty. "You must be thinking I've kidnapped your daughter, ma'am," Evalyn said.

"Not at all," the lady said in her soft Irish burr. "I was thinkin' that ye must have a gift of magic to have persuaded our little Meggie to go to ye like that. 'Tis a shy one, our Meggie. I've never seen her go to a stranger in all her born days."

"There was no magic, I assure you, ma'am. Just a little bit of biscuit and some sympathy," Evalyn said with a smile. She shifted the child to her shoulder, rose from her chair and brought the little girl to her mother. The lady put out her arms, but Meggie clung to Evalyn's neck.

"Will ye look at that, now!" exclaimed the lady. "She's taken a real fancy to ye, that's certain. Come here to me, Meggie. 'Tis enough time ye've disturbed this kind lady. Come to y'r mother, like the good girl ye are."

But Meggie still clung to Evalyn. She took her thumb from her mouth and whispered, "Tell Mamma about Dolly."

"Oh, yes, indeed, Meggie," Evalyn said. "I'll tell her as soon as you go to her, and my hands are free to show her what to do."

Meggie held her arms to her mother, and Evalyn picked up the doll from the table. "There seems to have been an accident," she said, smiling at the red-headed Irishwoman. "Dolly needs a little glue here at the joint."

The woman thanked her and turned to go. At the door, she looked back. "I suppose ye have children of y'r own, to have such a way with 'em," she remarked.

"No, but children are my profession. I'm a governess."

"Are ye now? Well, ye must be a mighty good one. I wish I—"

At that moment, the parlor door slammed and a grey-haired gentleman appeared in the passageway, bearing a crying infant. He was tall and quite thin except for a rounded stomach which made a surprising protrusion in his otherwise lanky frame. "Oh, there you are, Mavis," he said irritably. "Why do you stand there dawdling, while I'm left alone to contend with the baby and the rest of this disreputable brood? Oh,

I beg your pardon, ma'am. I didn't see you there."
And he nodded embarrassedly to Evalyn.

"This lady was mindin' our Meggie. She's a governess, and a good one, too, if I'm a judge. Only
thankin' her I was. Is the wee one still cryin'?" Mavis
exchanged children with the gentleman and looked
at the baby in concern. "He feels feverish to me, my
dear," she said worriedly. "I'm thinkin' we'd best be
on our way. The sooner I get him home, the better."

"It's folly to be setting out in this snow, Mavis. Let's
put up here for the night and have done. We never
should have left my mother's, as I warned you."

"Have done y'rself! 'Tis enough I've heard on that
score. I'll not rest content until we're in our own home
with our own nurse to tend to this sick babe. There's
no one in y'r mother's house knows a thing about
babies."

"But what if we're stuck in the ditch? Do you want
to spend the night in a drafty coach?"

"Stuck in a ditch?" Mavis exclaimed. "Never've I
known ye to do such a thing. Ye'll not let that happen." She smiled up at her husband with a flirtatious
glimmer. "Not such a skillful, artful, talented driver
as y'rself."

Evalyn could see the warmth of his eyes, though he
pretended to be angry. "Serves me right," he growled,
"for marrying a red-headed, stubborn, willful Irish
puss! All right then, let's get the children dressed
again."

"If you wish," ventured Evalyn, "I'd be happy to
help you get them ready."

"I must say, that's deuced kind of you, ma'am," said
the gentleman with enthusiasm. "With six spoiled brats
plaguing us, a bit of help would be much appre-
ciated."

"Six? That's an impressive number," Evalyn said
smiling.

"Impressive is not a word I'd use," Mavis laughed.

"We must seem utterly without manners," said the

gentleman. "I am Hugh Caldwell, and this is my wife, Mavis."

"How do you do? I'm Evalyn Pennington. And I think we should get the children ready without further ado. The wind seems to have come up stronger than ever, so, if you are determined to set out tonight, you had better waste no more time."

Half an hour later, the children had been cleaned up and dressed, the baby fed and bundled up warmly, and the entire Caldwell clan stood ready to depart. Mavis, the baby in her arms, turned to Evalyn in gratitude. "Oh, my dear" she said earnestly, "I don't know how to thank ye. 'Tis a gem ye are, truly."

Mr. Caldwell nodded in agreement. "I would appreciate the direction of your employer, Miss Pennington. It would give me great pleasure to write to him and tell how helpful you've been."

Evalyn blushed in embarrassment. "Thank you, but you see I . . . I mean, that will not be necessary."

"But why not?" cried Mavis. "Sure and there's no harm in makin' sure your employers appreciate ye as ye deserve."

Evalyn lowered her eyes and shook her head. Mavis looked at her shrewdly. "Charlie," she said to the oldest boy, "take the children to the carriage and get them in." Then she handed the baby to her puzzled husband and took Evalyn's hand. "Something is not right with ye, I'm thinkin'," she said, looking at the governess's face. "I've been wonderin' why a governess is all by herself at an inn on Christmas eve. Ye've been kind to us. If there's some trouble ye're in, it would surely be a joy to us to do something for ye in return."

"Thank you, Mrs. Caldwell, but I'm in no trouble. I'm on my way to London to seek a post, that is all."

"To seek a post?" asked Mr. Caldwell. "Do you mean to say that you are not now employed?"

Evalyn nodded. Marvis stared. "I'll not believe it! What a bit o' luck for us! Ye'll come and work for us, then, if the size of our brood doesn't frighten ye. Right, Hugh?"

"By all means," said Hugh Caldwell firmly. "How long will it take you to get your things?"

"Oh, no," Evalyn objected breathlessly. "You cannot mean it. You don't know me well enough. I have not even . . ."

"What haven't you, Miss Pennington?" asked Mr. Caldwell.

"A . . . a letter of commendation. You see, my last employer discharged me without giving me one."

"More fool, he," laughed Mavis, embracing her like a long-lost sister. "I had y'r measure the first moment I clapped eyes on ye. There's no letter I'll be needin'."

"Nor I," smiled her husband. "So get your things, before the children upset the carriage. Unless, of course, you think you'll not relish six charges."

"On the contrary, it sounds like just what I'd relish. But did you not mention a nurse you have at home?"

"Yes, indeed," Mavis explained. "She's a dear old thing, and I'd be lost without her, but six are much too much for her. Sure, y're a Christmas miracle, my dear, so let's hear no more. Now, will ye get y're things?"

She embraced Evalyn fondly and pushed her toward the taproom. Evalyn picked up her cloak and portmanteau quickly. She looked around for the innkeeper and his wife, but they were not there. Old Sam'l still sat at the corner table sipping his ale. "Excuse me," Evalyn said to him. "Have you seen Mr. or Mrs. Fern?" He shook his head. "Will you tell them goodbye for me? I'm sorry I'll not be using the room, but I've left the money I owe them here on the table."

Sam'l nodded. Evalyn thanked him and ran out to the waiting coach.

CHAPTER SEVENTEEN

Before breakfast on Christmas morning, Clarissa knocked on Philip's door. She had spent a sleepless night worrying about Sally's missing earrings and had decided that Philip should be told without further delay. Wellstock opened the door. "Is his lordship dressed, Wellstock?" she asked.

Philip's voice answered her from the dressing room. "I'm in proper enough attire to receive my sister," he said, coming in from the dressing room in his shirtsleeves. "You may go to Jamie, Wellstock. I can manage the rest myself."

Wellstock bowed and withdrew. Clarissa looked at her brother with concern. "You must have had a difficult night, too," she said with solicitude. "You look quite knocked up."

"A difficult night, *too*? If *you've* had trouble sleeping, it certainly doesn't show, my dear. You look as bewitching as always."

Clarissa snorted. "Don't try to flummer me, my lord. I have a mirror or two in my room. This wretched house party is making an old hag of me."

"What's wrong? I thought everything was proceeding famously."

"On the contrary. It's been a week full of major and minor crises—the sort of domestic contretemps that you never notice. But this one, I'm afraid, is too serious for me to handle on my own."

Philip felt a stab of alarm. "It's not—? There's no one seriously ill, is there?"

"No, no. Thank goodness, it's not quite as bad as that. I suppose I'm being overly dramatic to have made you think that. It's Sally. She reported to me last evening that her diamond earrings have been stolen."

With a relieved sigh, Philip took Clarissa's hand and led her to a chair near the fire. "Stolen? Rubbish! She's probably only misplaced them."

"That's what I thought at first," Clarissa said, sinking into the chair with a feeling of relief to be able to share this burden, "but I'm afraid Sally is right. She remembers quite clearly putting her earrings away in her jewel box, with her abigail looking on. It seems that this procedure is their way of making sure that Sally doesn't leave her jewels lying about carelessly, as she had been used to do. So the other day, as usual, Annette watched her lock her things away. And then, the next time they opened the box, the earrings were gone. I hate to admit it, my dear, but it does seem as though we have a thief in our midst."

"Unlikely. Most of the servants have been with us for years, and our guests are certainly above suspicion. Take my word, Clarissa, the blasted baubles will turn up before another day goes by."

Clarissa gave a hopeful sigh. "Do you really think so? I pray you may be right, but what if they don't?"

Philip gestured impatiently. "Then we'll buy Sally another pair and be done with the matter."

"But, Philip, we couldn't do that! We can't let a thief go undiscovered, can we?"

"I suppose not," Philip said with a sigh of resignation. The pair remained silent for a moment. Then Philip made a grimace of annoyance. "Blast that Trevelyan woman!" he growled. "She does have a way of cutting up one's peace."

"Yes, I'm afraid she does. Though watching you last night, I was almost convinced you had suddenly developed a *tendre* for her," Clarissa ventured with a coy glance at her brother from the corner of her eye.

"Don't be jingle-brained," her brother retorted curtly.

"Jingle-brained! Very pretty talking, I must say. I suppose you'll be telling me next that it was some-one else who dangled at her shoe strings all evening!"

Philip darted a quick glance at his sister and grinned guiltily. "Only trying to be a good host, that's all," he said with obvious insincerity.

"What a whisker!" Clarissa declared roundly. "I didn't cut my eyeteeth yesterday, you know. You can't ignore the girl all week and then suddenly sit in her pocket all evening and explain your behavior away on the grounds of your obligations as a good host! You needn't explain yourself if you don't wish to, but I don't for a moment believe that this ex-planation is anything but a hum."

"You're right, of course," Philip admitted, "but since I don't wish to explain, let's get back to the subject of Sally's earrings. I agree that we'll have to investi-gate the matter, but can we wait until after Boxing Day? The household staff has been looking forward to the celebration, and I don't like to have them dis-turbed at this time of year."

"Neither do I. Rumors of a theft would be bound to spread, and everyone would be nervous and upset. I'm sure we can wait two or three days. And perhaps you are right," she added, rising, "that the earrings will turn up before we're forced to take action. Well, hurry and finish dressing. It's almost time for break-fast. I think we should all take Christmas break-fast together."

"Of course. I'll be ready in a few minutes." He took her arm and walked with her to the door.

She hesitated at the doorway. "I was only joking before, about you and Sally, you know. But Philip, is something troubling you?"

"Nothing at all. Why?"

"I don't know. I have the feeling that you're in the dismals and you're trying to cover up. . . ."

Philip leaned down and kissed her cheek. "Silly widgeon. Haven't you enough to worry you? If you must have something else to brood about, try to find signs of affliction in Gervaise. Truly, my dear, there's no need to trouble about me."

"Very well," she said, giving him a tired smile and patting his cheek. She was not at all convinced that all was well with him, for the dark shadows under his eyes belied his smile. But, realizing that he didn't want to discuss his private thoughts with her, she let the matter drop.

Philip, returning to his dressing room, turned back to her just before the door closed behind her. "Clarissa," he asked, "have you seen Miss Pennington this morning? Is she feeling any better today?"

"No, I haven't seen her. She hasn't yet come out of her room. She must still be asleep."

"Don't you think you should inquire?"

"Not yet. If she wishes to sleep late, I don't want to disturb her. I'll look in on her after breakfast, if she still hasn't put in an appearance."

Philip was about to remonstrate but changed his mind. "Well, do as you think best," he said with a shrug. "I'll see you at breakfast."

To Clarissa's delight, almost everyone had assembled in the breakfast room by ten for a repast that bid fair to rival her Christmas dinner. She had provided for her guests a buffet that included eggs cooked in an assortment of styles, pickled salmon, a round of beef, two hams, an assortment of breads, biscuits and jellies, steaming pots of tea, coffee and chocolate, Hyland cream, gooseberry tarts, and even a dish of orange peel. This last was provided specially for Martha who forced herself every morning, Christmas or no, to drop the peel into a cup of boiling water and drink it, being convinced that this unappetizing brew had

the power to dissolve what she called her "flegm."
Since Christmas morning was made especially joyous
by sharing with children the bounty of the day, the
twins had been brought down by Mrs. Noakes and
were seated at the head of the table, still in their
nightshirts and tasselled caps. Piled before them were
a number of parcels Father Christmas had brought
and which they were excitedly opening in full view
of the whole party.

While this was in progress, Hutton quietly came
into the room and bent over Lady Steele, whispering
that Miss Pennington's abigail was waiting outside to
have a word with her. Clarissa nodded calmly but
was struck with a feeling of apprehension. She got up
as inconspicuously as she could and went out.

Nancy stood in the hall holding a letter and three
small parcels, her face revealing her trepidation. She
bobbed a quick curtsey and held out Evalyn's note.
"What is this, Nancy?" Clarissa asked in surprise. "Is
Miss Pennington still unwell?"

"Can't say, ma'am. She asked would you read this
here note."

Clarissa took the note and tore it open. *My dear
Clarissa,* Evalyn had written, *It gives much pain and
embarrassment to have to say my goodbyes in this
fashion. A personal matter has made it necessary for
me to cut short this wonderful holiday and return immediately to my original plan for finding employment,
which I had postponed when I accepted your kind invitation. Since I was convinced that you would use
your persuasive powers to urge me against this course
of action, and that this would probably cause some
disturbance to the household at a time when nothing
but merriment and joviality should prevail, I determined to leave quietly and without ceremony. The
thought that most oppresses me is that you will think
me rude and ungrateful because I left without a word
to you. Please believe, most dear friend, that this is not
the case. I shall never forget the many kindnesses you*

*and your family have so generously bestowed on me,
and the many happy hours I have spent at Gyllford
Manor. Please convey to your family and your guests
my thanks and warmest regards, and to Lord Reginald
and Jamie my deep appreciation for their gallant attempt to rescue me from my difficulties at Carbery
Hall. I would like to ask one last favor of you. Nancy,
my abigail, has been a loyal, generous and hard-work-
ing girl, and it would make her very happy to continue in Lord Gyllford's employ. If a place can be
found her here, I will be, more than ever, your most
grateful and devoted—Evalyn.*

Clarissa looked up from her letter with eyes filled
with shock and concern. "I don't understand a word of
this, Nancy. Is Miss Pennington really gone?"

Nancy bit her lip and nodded wordlessly.

"She left last night? In all this snow?"

"Yes'm."

"But why? I can't understand. What personal matter
could have come to her attention at such a time? Had
she received a letter or message from anyone?"

"Don't know, ma'am."

Clarissa perused the letter again, but it gave no
clue. But her suspicion grew that whatever had happened to send Evalyn fleeing from the house had happened here. She looked at Nancy closely. "Did she
quarrel with my nephew, Nancy? Don't be afraid to
tell me the truth."

"With Mr. Everard?" asked Nancy in surprise at
the question. "Not that I know of, my lady. But someone upset her, that's certain."

"Someone here, in this house?"

"I don't know, ma'am. She wouldn't tell me."

Clarissa sighed deeply. "Oh, dear, I'm at a complete
loss as to what to do. Please sit down over there on
that bench, Nancy. Lord Gyllford or I may want to
speak to you in a moment or two." And she turned to
go back to the breakfast room.

"Don't you want these?" Nancy asked, holding out the parcels.

"What are they?"

"These are for the twins, Miss Evalyn said. From Father Christmas, you know. And this one is for you. She made it for you, all by herself. I'd find her working on it every spare minute."

Clarissa's eyes misted over, and the tears spilled over and rolled down her cheeks. "How like her to do such a thing," she said, brushing away the tears with the back of her hand. She took the parcels tenderly. "I can't bear to think she's gone."

She did not know precisely what, but it was clear to Clarissa that something had to be done. Where could Evalyn have gone in such a storm? And why? She returned to the breakfast room in a turmoil. The only explanation that had presented itself to her agitated mind had been the possibility that Evalyn and Jamie had quarrelled. Had Jamie changed his mind about marrying her? But no gentleman could cry off once a promise had been made! Had Evalyn realized (as Clarissa herself had already sensed and not let herself face) that she and Jamie were not suited? Or had Jamie's obvious neglect caused her to run away? Clarissa clutched the letter in her hand, wondering if she should take some time to reflect before coming to any decision about a course of action. She forced a smile and walked to the head of the table. "Here are two more presents," she said to the twins as she deposited the parcels before them.

"More gifts? These sons of mine shall be quite spoiled. Who sent them?" Martha asked.

"They are from Miss Pennington," Clarissa answered, sitting down at her place wearily.

Philip looked up from his plate. "Why didn't she bring them in herself? Is she still ill?" he asked tensely.

Clarissa glanced at Philip, then over at Jamie, who was wolfing down a mouthful of salmon, completely unconcerned. Her moment of hesitation, however, caught the attention of the others at the table, and she found herself being regarded curiously by seven pairs of eyes. "Well, I suppose I may as well tell you all now as later," she said with a sigh. "Evalyn's gone."

"Gone?" Philip echoed, getting to his feet so precipitously that his chair fell over. "What are you talking about?"

"Here, read this," she said and held out the letter. Philip reached across the table, snatched the letter, and strode to the window, while the unobtrusive Hutton stepped forward from his station behind the buffet and replaced his lordship's chair. Philip turned his back to the room, ignoring the faces staring at him curiously, and read the letter hastily. Then he shook his head in a puzzled manner and read it through more slowly and carefully.

Meanwhile, a babble of voices rose. Everyone in the room demanded of Clarissa some information. Had Evalyn left the house? When? How could she have departed in a snowstorm? Where or to whom had she gone?

"Please," said Clarissa, holding up her hands, "wait until Philip has finished reading her note. Perhaps he— or *someone* in this room"—and she glared at Jamie pointedly—"can make more sense of this than I can."

Jamie, completely puzzled by his aunt's look, asked in sincere confusion, "Why do you look at me so? *I* don't know where she's gone."

Clarissa blinked. Could her nephew be as innocent as he looked? She had been like a mother to the boy since his childhood. He had never lied to her. More confused than ever, she glanced at Philip, but he was still perusing the letter. "Well," she said, avoiding Jamie's eyes, "let's wait until Philip can join the discussion. Meanwhile, shall I open this package? It's a gift from Evalyn. The dear girl evidently fashioned it herself in her spare moments."

Edward stood up and bent over his wife's chair.

"Don't you think we might excuse the twins, my dear? I'm sure they would rather be playing with their new toys in the schoolroom than listening to our discussion," he suggested discreetly.

"Oh, yes," agreed his wife. "Would you take them upstairs, Mrs. Noakes?"

"But we would like to hear what happened to Miss Evalyn," Freddie objected promptly, well aware that his father feared that the ensuing discussion might not be suitable for their little ears. Edward frowned at his outspoken son with severity, and the boy lowered his eyes. Mrs. Noakes quickly thrust a load of parcels into his arms and, after a smile and curtsey for the guests, hastily shepherded the boys from the room.

Clarissa opened the parcel and took out the little lacquered box. "Oh, how lovely," she exclaimed, holding it up for the others to see.

"Yes, it is," Martha said admiringly. "May I hold it?" She took the box and turned it lovingly in her hand. "It's so light. I think it's made of *papier-mâché*. I wish she had told me about it. I would have loved to learn the way of making it."

Sally, to whom this latest turn of events was quite a shock, shifted uncomfortably in her chair. Her plans were going all awry. Why had she not considered the possibility that Evalyn's enamelled box might be a gift for someone else?

"Open it," Gervaise urged. "Let's see what it looks like on the inside. I'm fascinated by all the things one can fashion from this interesting material. I hear that Prinny has a coat with *papier-mâché* buttons!"

Clarissa lifted the lid. "It's beautiful," she said, running her fingers over the satin. "She's lined it complete—why, what's this?" Her fingers had felt something hard and sharp beneath the lining. In another second the diamonds were in her hand. She stared at her hand in horror. "Good God!" she breathed. "Sally's diamonds!"

"How on earth did your diamonds get *there?*" Martha asked curiously.

"I have no idea," said Sally cautiously. "I'm as surprised as you are." She glanced at Philip, to see what his reaction was to this latest revelation, but he was staring out of the window, his face pale and his mouth set in a rigid line. He had obviously not heard a word of their conversation.

"Are you sure they are Sally's earrings?" Gervaise was asking. "Why would they be? Have Sally's been missing?"

Clarissa gave Gervaise a nervous glance. "They must be Sally's. Are they, my dear?" she asked. Sally nodded. Clarissa's hand began to tremble, and she set the diamonds down on the table before her as if they burned her palm.

"Yes, they're mine," Sally said. "I reported to Clarissa yesterday that they had disappeared."

"Disappeared? You don't mean *stolen?*" asked Gervaise, shocked.

"What else?" Sally said shortly.

"You can't mean it," Reggie said with disapproval.

"I don't see what else it could have been. My maid saw me put them in my jewel case, and I haven't seen them since. Until this moment, that is."

Clarissa gasped. "You're not thinking . . . suggesting . . . that *Evalyn* stole them?"

"I'm not suggesting anything," Sally shrugged. "I'm as much in the dark as everyone else."

The entire assemblage was struck dumb. They stared at the diamonds in dismay. Philip, who had turned to hear Clarissa's outcry, glared at them all and bit back a retort. He must try to remain calm. He was too upset by Evalyn's letter to express his feelings now without giving himself away.

Edward was the first to speak. "The girl *has* run away," he suggested tentatively.

"I see what you mean," Sally said coolly. "The fact

that she has run off seems to add substance to the suspicion that she *did* steal them."

A sound came from Philip's throat but went unnoticed in the hubbub Sally's words had aroused. "I don't believe it," Martha declared roundly.

"It'th a ridiculouth idea!" Reggie said firmly.

"If she were the thief," Gervaise asked reasonably, "why would she put the diamonds in Clarissa's gift box, only to give them—and herself—away?"

"Exactly what I was about to point out," Jamie said.

Edward cleared his throat. "I do not for a moment suggest that Sally is right in her suspicions, but she does have a point. It is possible that Miss Pennington did indeed steal the gems and secrete them in the lining of the box. Then in her haste to leave, she simply forgot to remove them from their hiding place."

Clarissa groaned. "Oh, Edward, no!"

"Edward, that was dreadful of you," his wife snapped.

"There must be many other more plausible explanations than that!" Jamie said staunchly.

"That'th right!" Reggie said loudly, then muttered under his breath, "I wish I could think of one."

Philip, listening from the window in white-lipped fury, could restrain himself no longer. "I cannot believe," he said angrily, "that you can persist in discussing such an impossibility! How can anyone who has been more than five minutes in Miss Pennington's company doubt for a moment her honesty, her sincerity, her forthrightness? You, Edward, do you already forget how she cared for your son during his sickness? And Gervaise, did you not remark to me how impressed you were by her straightforwardness that night we discussed the enfranchisement of the working classes? There's not one of you to whom she has not been generous and helpful. Yet at the first wild, unsubstantiated and quite illogical theory that she may have been guilty of thievery—a thievery we don't even know took place!—you are, none of you, ready to stand up for her character!"

The room was silent. Everyone looked down at his hands. Then Gervaise looked up at his friend. "We all think the world of Miss Pennington, my boy. Yet in our defense, you must admit that she did run away."

"And a thievery *did* take place, did it not?" Sally put in, emboldened by Gervaise's remark to see what she could rescue of her original plan.

"Perhaps it did," Philip retorted curtly. "All we know is that the diamonds were removed from your box and reappeared in this one. The circumstances, I grant, are strange, but they do not necessarily point to thievery. And at least you have your baubles back." He picked up the diamonds from the table, walked around to Sally and dropped them in her lap. "I shall do what I can to investigate the matter and solve this mystery, but I tell you all here and now that were I to find a witness who claimed to have seen Evalyn *with her hand in Sally's jewel box,* I would not believe she had stolen them! Nor, I think, should anyone with eyes in his head!"

"Hear, hear, Philip!" Clarissa cheered warmly. "I think you're absolutely right!"

"And so do I," Jamie said, smiling proudly at his father.

"Oh, you do, do you?" Philip growled at his son. "It's more than time to have heard something of the sort from you!"

Jamie looked at him in surprise. "What do you mean by that, sir? I don't understand you."

"Then I'll make myself plainer. Accompany me to the study, if you please, if our guests will excuse us."

"No, we won't," said Gervaise with asperity. "We want to know what is in that letter, dashed if we don't. I'm not cowed by your grand manner, my lord, even if everyone else is. Known you too long and too well, so it won't do you any good to get on your high ropes with me. If it weren't to make off with the gems, why *did* the girl take to her heels in weather like this?"

"I wish I could answer that, Gervaise, but I'm as perplexed as you. Perhaps my son will be able to cast some light on the matter. In the meantime, I hope you will all forgive me for getting on my 'high ropes,' as Gervaise puts it. This has been a sorry interruption of our holiday activities. Please try to continue them cheerfully and leave me to deal with these matters." And with an affectionate clap on Gervaise's shoulder, he quickly left the room. Jamie exchanged a puzzled shrug with his friend and followed his father out.

In the hallway, a tense and nervous Nancy stood waiting. "What is it, Nancy?" Philip asked her. "Did you want to see me about something?"

"No, me lord, but Lady Steele said I was to wait. She said you might be wanting to ask me some questions."

"As a matter of fact, I do. Did you see the box that Miss Pennington made for Lady Steele?"

"Yes, sir. I saw it lots of times."

"Did you see what Miss Pennington put inside it?"

"Inside it? You mean the lining?"

"No. Something else."

"I didn't know there *was* anything inside it, except the lining."

"Well, there was," Philip said, his eyes fixed on her face. "Miss Trevelyan's diamond earrings were inside it."

Nancy gaped at him. "No, sir, that can't be. How could they be in Miss *Pennington's* box?"

"That's what we'd like to ascertain," Jamie put in drily.

"What my son means," Philip said, "is that we don't understand either, but they surely were there."

"This ain't making any sense, sir. I helped to wrap the box meself, and there wasn't anything inside it. And no one's touched that box but me, ever since

Miss Pennington left. Until I give it to Lady Steele, that is."

"It certainly seems strange. Have you ever seen Miss Trevelyan's diamond earrings?"

"No, sir, I ain't. Unless she was wearing 'em, o' course, but even then I wouldn't reco'nize 'em, not knowing the difference between a diamond and a piece of glass from that there chandelier."

"Have any of the servants ever spoken to you about diamonds, or seemed particularly interested in them?"

"No, sir. Why would they? None of us'll live long enough to get to own one. And even if we did, what'd be the good? If we wore one, nobody'd believe it was real."

"That may be," said Jamie, "but diamonds can be sold for a good price, and money can be used by anybody."

Nancy looked at him shrewdly. "Are you saying that Miss Trevelyan's diamonds was copped?"

"She thinks they were stolen, yes," Philip said.

"And then they showed up in Miss Pennington's box?" she asked incredulously.

"So it appears."

"Lord, love me! Miss Trevelyan ain't thinking it was *me* that copped 'em, is she?"

"Your name wasn't mentioned," Philip assured her.

"Praise be for that!" she said, relieved. Then her eyes opened wide and she grew pale. "She surely wouldn't suspicion Miss *Evalyn!*" she asked, horrified. The two men didn't answer but just stood watching her. "Oh, me lord, not *you!* Miss Trevelyan, she ain't got eyes for anyone but her own self, but you . . . well, everyone below is always saying how you're up to the mark and nobody could tip you a rise. You can't believe such a thing! Why, anyone knowing Miss Evalyn would swear she could no more do such a thing than cut her hand off!"

Philip's tense face relaxed a trifle, and he patted the girl's shoulder. "Good girl, Nancy. I'm quite of the same mind. We'll talk no more of this diamond business now. But what I can't understand is how a plucky girl like you could have let your mistress go away in a snowstorm, without a word to us."

Nancy hung her head. "There wasn't nothing I could do. She was plumb set on it. She was so heart broke, I couldn't argue."

"Heart broke? What do you mean?"

"Someone must've hurt her some way. She wouldn't say how, or who."

Philip glared at his son, but the boy was looking at Nancy with completely innocent interest. He showed not a sign of guilt or misgiving.

"But how did she go, Nancy?" Jamie was asking. "She couldn't have *walked* in such weather."

"I can't say, sir."

"Can't say, or won't?" Philip asked sternly.

Nancy kept her face lowered and her eyes on her shoes.

"Listen to me, girl, and listen carefully," Philip said to her warningly. "I know you think you're being loyal to Miss Pennington, but if she's lost or without shelter somewhere out there in that storm, you won't help her by keeping secrets. Now you sit down over there and think it over, while I have a little talk with my son. Come, Jamie."

With those grim words, he stalked off to the study, Jamie following at his heels. "Close the door and sit down," he said, between clenched teeth. Jamie looked at him perplexed. He had never seen his father so agitated. He was pacing in front of the fire in angry strides, his mouth set in a hard line.

"I don't think you need worry so about Miss Pennington," Jamie offered, sitting down gingerly on the edge of a wing chair. "She's quite able to take care of herself. She's really a redoubtable girl, you know."

"So you've told me repeatedly," his father said curtly. "You amaze me, Jamie. I find your lack of concern completely baffling."

"I'm not lacking in concern, sir. I'll feel much more comfortable about Evalyn when I hear she's safe and sound."

"Safe and sound?" Philip asked in a voice heavy with sarcasm. "And how do you propose to get that news? By post, next spring, if the lady should honor you with a letter?"

"Well, I suppose that's one way," Jamie said, nonplussed. "Or I may hear about her from friends, or one way or another."

Philip groaned. "Does it occur to you that perhaps you should go to look for her, to make *sure* she's safe and sound?"

"Go to look for her?" asked Jamie, standing up in surprise. "In this snow? But why? If she chose to leave, I don't see what I can do about it."

"Confound it! What sort of a man are you?" Philip shouted, pushing Jamie back into the chair. "I never thought to hear my own son talk like a loose screw, and a cowardly one at that! Don't you feel any responsibility for her at all?"

"Responsibility? But why?"

"Why? *Why?* Need I tell you why? You brought her here, filled her with high expectations, and then you proceeded to ignore and humilitate her in every possible way! Finally, the poor girl could bear it no longer and ran away. And you have the effrontery to stand there and ask why you should feel responsible?"

"Hang it, sir, you're talking utter balderdash!" said Jamie, jumping up from his seat again. "I don't mean to be disrespectful, but your notions sound positively gothic! I know I brought her here, but I didn't think you'd expect me to dance attendance upon her, or entertain her! Nor do I think she expected any such thing!"

Philip stared at his son in amazement. "Gothic?" he exclaimed. "Sit down, you fool! You think I'm behaving like a gothic father when I expect my son to treat the woman he is going to marry with some affection?"

Jamie gaped at his father stupidly. "Marry? *Me?*"

"Yes, you! How can you ask a girl to marry you when you haven't the least notion how to go on in such circumstances?" Philip ranted, too preoccupied with his outrage to comprehend his son's reactions.

"I think you must be foxed!" Jamie gasped. "What on earth made you think that Miss Pennington and I were to be *married?*"

Philip stopped his pacing and fixed his eyes on his son's bewildered face. "You told me so yourself," he said sharply. "You told me so the evening of the day you arrived home."

"One of us must be touched in his upper works!" Jamie exclaimed angrily, jumping to his feet a third time. "I never could have told you anything so preposterous!"

"I see nothing preposterous about it! I couldn't have misunderstood you. I remember it distinctly. You said . . . you said that you and Miss Pennington had an understanding . . . or some such phrase. Didn't you?"

Jamie shrugged. "I may have said something of the sort. Evalyn and I did have a kind of understanding. . . ."

"Aha! Then I didn't misunderstand." He glared at his son impatiently. "I told you to sit down!" he growled.

"I won't sit down! Not until we have this thing cleared up. If you think our understanding—Evalyn's and mine—had to do with marriage, you're out in your reckoning!"

"Well, what sort of understanding did you have?"

"It had to do with helping her to find a new post."

"A new *post?* What can you mean . . . ?" His breath caught in his throat. "You mean you never had any plans to *marry?*"

"Marry? Of course not! How could you think such a thing?"

Philip had the distinct sensation that the floor lurched under his feet. He put his hand to his forehead. "Pardon me, Jamie, but I'm beginning to feel too old for all this. Let's both sit down."

"I'm sorry about all this, father. If I'd known what trouble she would cause, I'd have left her on the Carberys' doorstep," Jamie said, returning to his chair.

"No, no," said Philip, sitting down opposite Jamie and leaning back wearily. "You could not have left her there. You've behaved quite well. I see that now. It's *I* who—Good Lord, what have I done?"

"Done?" Jamie asked bewildered. "I don't see how you can blame yourself for Evalyn's behavior."

But Philip understood at last. He had taken her in his arms and had seen her look up at him with that innocent face full of warmth and joy and trust, and he had thrust her aside. The recollection made him wince in pain.

"What is it, sir? What have *you* to do with this coil?" Jamie asked.

Philip shook his head. "I've been unbelievably stupid," he said in a constricted voice, "and caused all this hobble myself."

"Does it have something to do with the diamonds?" asked Jamie, utterly confused.

"Hang the diamonds! Of course not! I'll wager anything you like that Evalyn doesn't know a thing about them."

"Then what hobble are you speaking of?"

"The only hobble that concerns me—that she's run away." He got up and paced the room again. "Tell me, Jamie," he asked more quietly, "did Evalyn—Miss Pennington—understand why she was brought here? She could not have misinterpreted your intentions as I did, could she?"

"No, not possibly. I explained the whole plan to her quite carefully."

"Plan? Just what was this plan?"

"I asked you to invite her here so that she could

spend the holidays with us, to permit Aunt Clarissa to get properly acquainted with her. . . ."

"But why? Doesn't that in itself sound like the plans of a bridegroom—to permit his family to become acquainted with his prospective bride?"

"I assure you that *that* aspect never occurred to either of us. Evelyn knew why I wanted Aunt Clarissa to know her. She had been discharged without a letter of commendation, and I wanted my aunt to write one for her. In fact, we hoped that Clarissa would know of a household where Evelyn's services might be needed."

"I see. And that was *all* that was between you?"

"That was the whole of it."

"I . . . er . . . dislike to pry into your private affairs, Jamie, but I must know. Are you quite sure . . . without any doubt at all . . . that you are not . . . in love with Miss Pennington?"

Jamie laughed. "I'm dashed if you don't sound exactly like Reggie!"

"Like Reggie? What on earth do you mean?"

"Not two days past, he asked me the very same question about Marianne!"

"Marianne? How ridiculous! She's only a child. You couldn't be in love with her."

"Yes, so I told him. But he's in love with her himself, you see, so he . . . " His voice trailed off as an idea hit him with a shock. Could his father, who had seemed so impervious to women all these years, possibly have fallen in love with Evelyn? No, it wasn't possible. Not his father!

"Reggie?" Philip was asking. "In love with Marianne? You can't mean it!"

"Why not? You didn't think it strange for me to be in love with Evelyn, and she's a far less likely girl for either Reggie or me to be taken with."

"I don't see that at all. Marianne is only seventeen, a mere child. Whereas Evelyn—"

"Evelyn must be *years* older than I," Jamie declared,

his eyes fixed on his father's face with a penetrating gleam.

"She's twenty-two," his father said with some asperity. "Exactly your age."

"Oh, *is* she?" Jamie asked innocently. "Well, perhaps she's not old, exactly, but she seems so to me. As I assured Reggie, I'm not in the petticoat line, but even if I were, Miss Pennington wouldn't be at all my style. Too serious by half."

"Rubbish! She has an irrepressible sense of humor."

"Does she, sir?" asked Jamie with a mischievous twinkle. "How clever of you to have observed it."

Philip shot a glance at his son, caught the look and reddened to his ears. "Never mind, jackanapes," he said with a rueful grin. "I'll brook no disrespectful quips about Miss Pennington or myself. A whisky-frisky, greenheaded, rope-ripe court-card like you cannot be expected to appreciate the qualities of a lady like Evalyn. I dread to think of the platter-faced, addle-brained fidget you'll eventually bring home to marry."

Jamie grinned broadly and jumped to his feet. "Well, whoever she is, sir, she couldn't be half the woman you've chosen," he said, wringing his father's hand with enthusiasm. "I must be a greenhead not to have noticed before that you and Miss Pennington are perfectly suited."

"Don't fly into the boughs too soon," Philip said, getting up from his chair and crossing to the wide window behind the desk. "Now that I understand the circumstances, I am painfully aware that it was my own stupidity that drove her from this house. She must be found! There will be time later to determine whether *she* thinks we're suited."

"You're right, of course," Jamie agreed, his smile fading. "I'll ride out immediately. If we're lucky, she'll not have got beyond Ashwater."

"Take a damper, boy!" said his father firmly. "Who asked you to go?"

"You did, not five minutes ago. The flattering names you called me are still ringing in my ears. A cowardly loose-screw, I think you said. And quite right, too."

Philip came quickly to Jamie and put his hands on the boy's shoulders. "Forgive me for that, Jamie. It's been bellows to mend with me ever since I laid eyes on the girl. I thought it was you who had driven her away, but of course, that isn't the case. So go back to our guests and forget what I said. I'd be much obliged if you would."

"Would you indeed?" said Jamie mockingly. "And what's to become of Miss Pennington, out there in God knows what kind of scrape? I refused to go before, because I thought it was none of my business, but that's not true any more. So I think I should set out at once, don't you?"

"Am I to understand by those remarks that you think your father too old and doddering to ride out in the snow?"

"Cut line! You did ask me before, did you not?"

"Only because I thought it was your responsibility. Now, I am happy to say, it is mine, and I intend to see to it. So if you'll excuse me, I'll get started." And he walked swiftly to the door. With his hand on the knob, he hesitated. Slowly, he turned back to his son. "Jamie," he said soberly, "this matter is too serious for hoaxing. Please be straight with me. Are you absolutely *sure* you're not in love with Evalyn yourself?"

"Oh, I love her!" Jamie replied with a wide grin. "I truly do. But only as a mother, I assure you, sir. Only as a mother!"

CHAPTER EIGHTEEN

Nancy had taken to biting her nails again. She had not done it since she was a child, but sitting here in the hall waiting for his lordship to reappear had made her so nervous that she found herself chewing them. Three nails had already been badly reduced, and she was starting on a fourth when the study door opened and Lord Gyllford emerged. She jumped to her feet and made an awkward curtsey.

"Well, girl, have you thought it over? Who took Miss Pennington from the house last evening?" Philip asked curtly.

Nancy hung her head in misery. "Can't say, sir. I promised," she mumbled.

"It's a bad promise, Nancy, but I'll not press you further. I think I can guess the answer to that question. I want you to get Joseph and that other girl— what's her name?—Miss Trevelyan's maid."

"Annette?"

"Yes. All three of you are to be in my study in half an hour. Meanwhile, where is Lady Steele? Is she still in the breakfast room?"

"No, sir. She went to her room. I heard her say she had the headache and wanted to lie down."

Philip nodded and strode quickly to the stairs. "Remember, Nancy, all three of you in half an hour," he called over his shoulder and took the stairs two at a time.

Clarissa answered his knock in a feeble voice. He found her stretched out on her bed, a cold cloth across her eyes. "I told you I don't need you, Mathilda," she said querulously, without looking up. "I'll do very well if I'm left alone."

"If you mean that, my dear," Phiilp said teasingly, "I'll take my leave and disturb you no further."

"Philip!" Clarissa cried eagerly, sitting up and pulling the cloth from her eyes. She snatched at his sleeve and pulled him down beside her. "Don't you *dare* to leave! You know I didn't mean you! It's my wretched abigail. Mathilda insists on hovering over me whenever she suspects I'm in the least indisposed. It's enough to give one a fit of the dismals. But never mind that. I've been beside myself waiting for you to finish talking with Jamie. What did he say? Has he quarrelled with Evalyn? Did he give you any information at all? Tell me quickly."

Philip patted her soothingly on her shoulder. "He gave me all the information I needed. Prepare yourself for a shock, my dear. Jamie hasn't engaged to marry Evalyn at all."

Clarissa gaped at him. "What are you saying? They broke it off?"

"No, there never has been anything between them. It was all my fault, I'm afraid. I leapt to the wrong conclusion when he and I had that talk the night he arrived. I simply misunderstood what he told me."

Clarissa could not grasp his words. "You couldn't have misunderstood! Not on such a matter as that," she said, bewildered. "Besides, he wrote to me about it himself, before they arrived!"

"I remember the letter you speak of. Think back carefully, Clarissa. He only wrote to ask us to invite a young lady to spend the holidays with us, isn't that so?"

Clarissa frowned, trying to remember. "Yes, I suppose that's true. But even so—"

"There really was nothing in that letter to make us assume he wanted to marry her," Philip pointed out.

"I disagree completely!" Clarissa declared roundly.

"How can you say so? A man can't bring a girl home for no purpose! Why else would he want her here?"

"As it turns out, his reason was quite altruistic and impersonal. He wanted you to become acquainted with her so that you would think well enough of her to find her a post."

"A post? What can you mean?"

Philip had to grin at his sister's utter confusion. "Our dear Jamie was being gallant," he explained. "Evalyn had been discharged without a notice, and Jamie and Reg wanted to help her. You were to be the instrument of that help."

"I?"

"Of course. It's quite logical, really. You could not have recommended a *stranger* to one of your friends, but they felt sure that once you grew to know Evalyn, you would have no qualms about recommending her."

"I was to help her find a post as governess? Is that why they brought her here? Then why didn't the idiots *tell* us?"

"They did. But we had our minds so set on marriage plans and grandchildren and such, we didn't hear them."

"Oh, Philip," Clarissa moaned, putting her face in her hands, "it's all my fault. I was the one who put that nonsense into your head."

"I'm the one who interviewed Jamie when he arrived. And I'm the one who didn't listen to what he tried to tell me. Not that it signifies. There's no point in attaching blame."

Clarissa stood up and began to pace about the room, trying to adjust her mind to this new surprise. "Poor Evalyn," she sighed. "She must have thought me completely buffleheaded. I never once discussed finding her a post." She stopped in front of Philip and put her hand to her forehead in confusion. "Philip, nothing as yet makes sense to me. If Jamie didn't drive her away, why did she leave?"

Philip looked down at his hands. "That's the most

difficult part I have to tell you. Sit down here with me, will you?"

She looked at him worriedly and dropped down beside him on the edge of the bed. "Is it very awful? Oh, Philip, I don't think I can *bear* it if you're going to tell me she took the diamonds—or something equally dreadful."

Philip made an impatient gesture. "Can't anyone forget those blasted diamonds? I tell you Evalyn had nothing to do with them!"

"Then what is it you have to tell me?"

"Clarissa," he said hesitantly, "I'm very much afraid that it was I who drove her away."

"You? Rubbish! I'll never believe that. What could you have done?"

"You'll think me a sorry specimen, I'm afraid," he said, getting up and going to the window. He stared out, unseeing, at the snow and the leaden sky. "My behavior has been utterly reprehensible," he went on in a lowered voice. "I convinced myself that she was playing some sort of deep game—I scarcely know how to explain it to you. But I offended her—hurt her badly, I'm afraid, and I think that's why she left."

Clarissa looked at her brother, a puzzled crease between her brows. He was speaking so strangely— so unlike himself. "My dear," she suggested gently, "perhaps you had better start at the very beginning. This isn't making any sense to me at all."

He turned, a strange, self-mocking smile curling his mouth. "It will all become clear when I tell you that I fell head-over-heels in love with her like the veriest schoolboy."

"In love—! Philip!"

"Shocking, isn't it? At my age? And with a girl who I thought was to become my son's wife! You can imagine my sense of guilt, and the self-torture I endured. I was furious with myself. The more I grew to know her, the less able I was to control my feelings. But more disturbing to me than anything else was *her* attitude. You know, I've never thought of myself as a coxcomb, Clarissa, yet I was convinced that she responded to my feelings."

Clarissa drew in her breath. She could hardly believe what she was hearing. Philip looked at her in quick understanding. "No, no, you must not think that anything passed between us that was not within the bounds of the strictest propriety. It was just . . . the warmth she seemed to exude when we spoke . . . or the way her mind and mine seemed attuned. I would have been a fool not to have noticed. Yet she had accepted *Jamie's* offer—or so I thought! I could not understand what her motives were. I even suspected her of playing a double game—like an adventuress—holding out for the biggest matrimonial prize!"

"An adventuress! Oh, Philip, no!"

"Was there ever a greater, more puffed-up coxcomb than I?" he asked, the self-mocking sneer more pronounced. "Can you bear to hear the rest?"

"I couldn't bear *not* to. Please go on."

He turned back to the window. "The day before yesterday—well, I cannot tell you what passed between us, but I suddenly realized that I had gone too far, and . . . let me just say that I hurt her. I had determined to ignore her—to cut her if necessary—so that I wouldn't be tempted to any disloyalty to my son. I assumed, of course, that she would understand why I had done it. But how could she have understood, knowing nothing of the misconception that had misled me? I wonder what the poor girl thought of my behavior. Good God! What else can she have thought but that I had found her beneath my touch?"

Philip fell silent. Clarissa, too moved to say a word, watched him wide-eyed. Finally, Philip turned from the window. "Have I shocked you beyond words?" he asked with a rueful grimace.

Clarissa shook her head. "Do you care for her enough to . . . to think of *marriage*?"

"I daren't think of it. But I *dream* of nothing else," Philip answered in his tone of self-derision.

"Oh, my dear, how blind I've been," she sighed, her ready tears spilling over.

Philip came quickly to sit beside her. "I was afraid this would upset you," he said, taking out his handkerchief and wiping her eyes.

"I'm sorry to be such a watering-pot, but to think of you in love at last is quite overwhelming. How could it have happened without my noticing?" She smiled up at him, amusement shining through the tearful eyes. "When I think of how I've contrived, arranged and schemed! How I've trotted out every girl I could find to parade before your eyes! And then you, without any help from anyone, find for yourself the *perfect* girl!"

"But, Clarissa, I've made such a mull of it!"

"Yes, you have. So you must find her and make it right."

"I must find her, of course. I couldn't rest without knowing that she's somewhere safe and well. That's why I've told you all this, my dear. I mean to leave right away, if you think you can spare me from your Christmas dinner. And Boxing Day tomorrow, if need be."

"Heavens! For a moment I'd forgotten all about Christmas and our guests and everything. Well, I can muddle through the festivities without you, I expect, though your absence will be awkward to explain."

"Just tell them the truth—that I've gone to find Evalyn."

"Very well, I suppose that will be best. But I cannot like your going out in this storm. Do you think it wise?"

"I must go, Clarissa. I think I'd go mad if I had to sit about here at home, worrying about her out there in this storm—alone, perhaps without funds, in who knows what sort of fix. . . ."

"Yes, of course you must go," she agreed, slipping an arm about his waist and leaning her head on his shoulder. "Oh, how happy we all shall be when you come back with her! She'll make a wonderful wife for you, Philip. I won't have a care left in the world!"

"Silly widgeon," Philip said fondly, "ten to one she won't have me. After all, she's half my age!"

"Well, you're out there!" she assured him with a tremulous, sparkling smile. "You're the *perfect* age for a husband—Evalyn told me *that* herself! Go and find her quickly, and bring her back to us!"

Joseph, Annette, and Nancy waited in the study nervously, not speaking. Each was reluctant to voice to the others the fear that they would all find themselves without employment before the day was out. None of them could face with equanimity this dire prospect. None of them had the faintest idea of where to go or what to do if present employment were to cease. Joseph had of course told Annette that he had driven Miss Pennington into Ashwater. Annette's feeling of loyalty toward the lady who had saved Joseph's life was as strong as his, and she fully supported him in his action in Miss Pennington's behalf. There was nothing any of them would not have done for Miss Pennington. Whatever the consequences, they, all of them, were agreed that they had done the right thing, and they would face whatever punishment was meted out. But they were far from joyful at the prospect.

Philip entered the room purposefully. Although he noticed the frightened expressions, he did not permit himself to soften his glare as he looked at each one of them in turn. "Well, which one of you is going to tell me what happened?" he asked sternly. "I want a complete and honest account, with no roundaboutation, if you please."

Nancy resorted to gazing at her feet. Annette made a movement of her hands indicating that she meant to make a complete denial of any wrongdoing. Joseph stayed her with a gesture. "Might as well make a clean breast of it, my lord," he shrugged. "You must've guessed it anyway, or you wouldn't have us here."

"I surmised that it was you who conveyed Miss Pennington to her destination. But I want to know the how and the where."

"I . . . er . . . borrowed the curricule, my lord. At the lady's request, it was. About six in the evening, yesterday. She asked me to take her to Ashwater."

"Ashwater? Why Ashwater? Did she tell you her plans?"

Nancy looked up and stuck out her jaw belligerently. "Don't tell 'im, Joseph. Miss Evalyn didn't want him to know, or she would've told 'im herself. You can sack us, me lord, but we ain't going to tell you anything more. We ain't going to help you find her and turn her over to the magistrates."

Joseph and Annette turned to her in surprise. "What's this about magistrates?" Joseph asked, looking from Nancy to Lord Gyllford in perplexity.

"I don't know what you're talking about, girl," Philip said impatiently.

"Don't think you can pull wool over me eyes so easy," Nancy declared bravely. "Why else would you be looking for her, if not to turn her over? You're thinking she took them diamonds, ain't you!"

"Diamonds?" asked Joseph, completely confused. "What diamonds?"

"Damn it, I wish I had never heard the word diamonds!" Philip said in disgust. "Will you forget about the trumpery things? They have absolutely nothing to do with my desire to find Miss Pennington."

"Well, then, what do you want to find her for?" Nancy asked challengingly. Annette and Joseph listened to her with openmouthed dismay. Philip merely frowned.

"I'll overlook your impertinence, young woman, because of your loyalty to Miss Pennington, which I cannot help but admire. As for the answer to your question, I've already given you all the answer you're going to get. Must I explain again that Miss Pennington may be stranded somewhere in this storm, destitute and friendless? Don't you want her to have help if she needs it?"

Nancy's eyes wavered, and she twisted her fingers in indecision.

"There ain't any need to worry about her, my lord," Joseph put in. "She can't have left the Bull, not in weather like this."

"Is that where she went? To the Bull? What did she intend to do then?" Philip asked quickly.

Joseph looked at Nancy for guidance, but the girl was no longer so sure she should restrain Joseph from answering. She gave a helpless shrug. Joseph faced his employer squarely. "She was going to hire a hack for Launceston."

"Launceston? Whatever for?"

"The Exeter stage leaves from there," Joseph explained.

"Oh, I see. And the London stage from Exeter, I presume. I think that's all I need now. Unless, of course, there's anything else you can think of that will help me find her."

"No, no, my lord. There's nothing else I know," Joseph said.

Philip turned to Nancy. "Come here to me, girl," he said, a little more kindly. "Look at me closely—not at the floor. There. Now, Nancy, I want you to believe that I mean no harm to your mistress. You have my word. Do you believe me?"

Nancy glanced up at him, looked down quickly and nodded.

"Good, then. Now, I want you to think carefully. Did Miss Pennington tell you anything about her ultimate destination? Did she tell you where, or to whom, she was going?"

"No, sir, nothing. She never said nothing about anyone she knew away from here."

"She never mentioned any relatives? Or anyone she might be acquainted with in London?"

"No, sir."

"Very well then, I'll be off." He crossed to the door quickly, and then looked back at them. "I needn't remind you, I suppose, that this matter is not to be talked of among the staff."

"You can trust us, my lord," Joseph assured him. "We won't say a word."

"Good. Then you may go back to your duties," his lordship said abruptly.

"Our . . . duties . . . ?" Joseph asked in surprise. But his lordship was gone.

Annette threw her arms about Joseph's neck. "He didn't give us . . . how you say? . . . the sack!"

"It's a bloomin' miracle," Joseph said, staring at the door. "Twice, now, he's had cause to send us packing, and twice he's let the matter pass." He looked at the door and shook his head. "But I feel in my bones we'd best not try him a third time."

"I only hope," sighed Nancy worriedly, "that we ain't served Miss Evalyn a back-handed turn."

Annette's brow puckered. "The diamonds you are thinking of, *non?* I too am not—how you say?—easy in my mind. There is something about the business I cannot like."

"What are you talking about? What is all this about diamonds?" Joseph demanded.

"Oh, *chérie,* I have not related to you the events. Ma'm'selle's earrings, they have disappeared."

"That's not all," Nancy added. "They showed up again—"

"This I did not know," said Annette, surprised. "Where?"

"In the box Miss Evalyn made for Lady Steele!"

Annette gaped. "How can this be?"

"The whole thing has me fair bamboozled. I was with Miss Evalyn when she wrapped the box, and there was no diamonds in it. The box stayed with me 'til I give it to Lady Steele. Next thing I know, his lordship is asking me how the diamonds got there!"

"It is of all things the most perplexing," said Annette thoughtfully. "I remember thinking that Ma'm-'selle was up to something when she told me to watch her put those earrings away. She was most strange. But I cannot think what she intended."

Joseph looked at Annette intently. "Who discovered that the diamonds was copped?"

"Me, myself," Annette said.

"Did Miss Trevelyan accuse you?" he asked.

"No, she did not. I was much surprised. But she said it would be stupid of me to do it."

Joseph rubbed his chin speculatively. "When was it you discovered they were gone?"

"*Hier* . . . yesterday. When she came up to dress for dinner."

"Yesterday, eh? Did she have 'em the night before?"

"I did not think to look. She said she did not want to wear any jewels. This in itself is most strange."

"But why are you asking these questions?" Nancy asked. "Do you know something o' this?"

"I do recollect something that might—" He turned to Annette and said reproachfully, "I wish you'd told me about the diamonds before."

"I did not think of it. As long as I was not—how you say *soupçonné?*—in suspicion, the matter went from my head."

"But tell us quick," Nancy urged Joseph impatiently. "What is it that you know?"

"I don't know if what I saw is important or not. But I was in Miss Trevelyan's dressing room. Day before yesterday, it was. She'd gone out riding—remember, Annette, when you told me to come up to her room?"

Annette clapped her hands to her cheeks. "Oh, but yes! And she returned early and I had to go to her and left you in the dressing room. . . ."

Nancy looked from one to the other in disgust. "Don't tell me you got yourselves in that same fix! What'd you do? Climb out the window again?"

"Not me!" Joseph said with a snort. "You'll not catch

me like that again! I crawled into the commode!"

"The commode?"

"It was the only place I could find to hide in! A tight squeeze it was, too. I couldn't even get the door closed. I was shaking so much I thought the bowl and pitcher on top would begin to rattle. Well, to get on with it, Miss Trevelyan comes in and goes to the dressing table, takes out the diamonds and looks at 'em in the light. Then she hides the key—I couldn't see proper where—and goes out. But I see before she goes out the door, that she drops 'em down her bosom. I thought it was a bit peculiar, but then she went out and I was so happy to make me escape, I didn't think no more on it . . . 'til now, that is."

"*Mon dieu*, I see it all! From the first Ma'm'selle takes a dislike to Miss Evalyn. She put the earrings in Miss Evalyn's box. She sent me away that day, telling me she was tired. Tired, pooh! She hides the diamonds in her bosom, steals into Miss Evalyn's room and hides them there."

Nancy chewed an already well-bitten nail thoughtfully. "I would say you've gotten to the bottom of it, except . . ."

"Except?"

"Except that something ain't right. If, as Joseph says, Miss Trevelyan took the diamonds in the afternoon, how is it that there was no diamonds in the box that night when Miss Evalyn and I wrapped it up?"

"You make too much the *logique* for me. I do not care for so much reasoning. I know Ma'm'selle has made this trouble, because I feel it here!" And she pointed to her heart with a passionate gesture.

"I ain't disagreeing with you," Nancy assured her. "It's the only thing what makes any sense at all."

Joseph sank into the nearest chair. "If you both feel that way, we're back in the soup again," he groaned.

"In the soup? *Je ne comprends pas.* Why?"

"Because I'll have to tell his lordship what I saw.

And when he hears how I came to see it, well—" Joseph shrugged hopelessly.

"We should say nothing perhaps?" Annette suggested in a tone that plainly indicated she hoped her suggestion would not be taken.

"I think we should tell him. If we could clear Miss Evalyn's name, it would surely be a satisfaction to me."

"And if Ma'm'selle had to pay for some of her mischief, it would be a satisfaction to me of the most enormous," Annette agreed with a wicked grin.

"I hope that satisfaction will keep you both warm when we're out in the snow," Joseph sighed and pushed himself to his feet. "Well, then, let's try to catch his lordship before he leaves the house."

Philip, dressed in his riding clothes, was almost out the door when they stopped him. "I'm sure that whatever it is you have to tell me can wait," he said to them, impatient to be off.

"I think you'll find it important, my lord," Joseph said. "I remembered something I think you'll want to know."

Philip stopped. "About Miss Pennington?" he asked.

"Well, not exactly." And Joseph hastily recounted what he had seen in Miss Trevelyan's dressing room. "And Nancy and Annette, here, is convinced that Miss Trevelyan, not being overly fond o' Miss Evalyn, did it herself, to get Miss Evalyn in a mess o' trouble."

"There's only one thing that don't fit," Nancy said in her unquenchably honest way. "I still don't see how the diamonds got into the box when they wasn't there when Miss Evalyn and me wrapped it."

Philip clenched his teeth and his eyes grew hard. "They were there, Nancy. You and Miss Pennington just didn't know it. They had been slipped into the lining."

The three exchanged glances while Philip sought to control the furious anger welling inside him. His instincts urged him to burst in on Sally and give her the tongue lashing she richly deserved. But she wasn't worth the time—precious time which would keep him even longer from finding Evalyn. No, he'd leave the handling of Sally to his sister. He turned to Joseph. "I want you to tell the whole story to Lady Steele right away. She will know what to do."

"The whole story . . . ?" Joseph gasped.

"Yes, of course. Why not?" Philip asked impatiently.

"Well . . . you see, sir . . . she's bound to ask how I came to be hiding in the commode. . . ."

Philip's lips twitched. "Indeed she will. And when she learns of your behavior, she may well be much less lenient than I've been, is that it?"

Joseph nodded glumly.

"If she gave you the sack, it would be no more than you deserve. We cannot have our household staff carrying on in such a maner. And you had been warned before, after all." He looked at the three of them, miserably staring at the floor, and a laugh broke out of him. "Come now, cheer up. After all, Lady Steele doesn't know that you've been in this fix before. Besides, I think I've a solution to this hank. Annette, you give notice to Miss Treveylan right away, and tell Lady Steele to see that you and Joseph are married as soon as possible. Maybe that will restore some respectability to this disreputable household."

' And with that he was out the door, leaving the three rascals dancing about the hallway in joyous abandon.

CHAPTER NINETEEN

Philip found the trip to Ashwater more than he bar-
gained for. The northerly wind blew in his face with
biting force, the swirling snowflakes almost blinding
him. His horse could only pick his way slowly through
the more than three feet of snow that had accumu-
lated during the storm. Sometimes the drifts were so
high that Philip had to guide the beast completely
around them. The only comfort he could derive
from the dreadful action of the elements was the
certainty that Evalyn could not have left the inn at
Ashwater in such weather. As the few miles separating
them slowly lessened, his spirits rose despite the irritation caused by freezing ears and shivering limbs.

It had grown dark by the time he arrived at Ashwater. The lights of the Bull showed through the swirling snow like a welcoming beacon. He was overwhelmed with a boyish eagerness to dash into the inn
and seize her in his arms without a moment's delay.
But there was no sign of an ostler to care for his horse,
and no answer to his call. He led the horse to the
stable himself and reined in his impatience while he
tended to the animal's needs. It was an endless half-
hour later that he at last entered the taproom of the
Bull.

The room was deserted. The fire was dying in the
fireplace and no candles burned on the tables or the
bar. "Hello?" he called, somewhat dismayed. "Ho,
innkeeper!"

A light appeared at the back of the room as a door

opened and Mr. Fern emerged, blinking his eyes in surprise. "Who's there?" he asked, peering into the darkness.

"I'm here to see Miss Pennington," said Philip impatiently. "Please go up to her room and ask her to step down here to see me."

Mr. Fern had by this time come close enough to recognize who the unexpected traveler was. "Blimey, it's Lord Gyllford! Please, yer lordship, won't you sit down? It's been mor'n six years since you last honored us like this! Please, sir, take this chair. I'll have the fire going in a trice. I never expected to see a soul tonight, I can tell you."

"Thank you," Philip said with forced politeness, "but I am most eager to see Miss Pennington. I'd be much obliged if you'd forego the amenities and take my message to her right away."

"I'd be glad to oblige, me lord, but there ain't nobody here by that name. I ain't seen a living soul this day, except for Mrs. Fern, o'course."

Philip couldn't believe his ears. "There must be some mistake. She arrived yesterday. Perhaps she kept to her room all day today."

"No, me lord, I mislike to contradict you, but there ain't a single guest in the house."

"Are you sure, man? I was told she was put down here last evening. Surely she can't have gone away from here in this storm."

"If you're meaning the young lady what had dinner here last night, she's gone."

"Gone! How can that be?"

A sudden flood of light turned both their heads to the source. Mrs. Fern entered with a large branch of lighted candles. "What're you doing, talking in the dark?" she asked, coming toward them. At the sight of Philip, she stopped and stared.

"Good evening, ma'am," Philip said absently. Mrs.

Fern made an eager curtsey, her face growing pink at the honor of welcoming the greatest nobleman of the district.

"A most happy Christmas to you, me lord," she said in an awed whisper.

"His lordship's asking for the young lady what came here last night," the innkeeper told her. "I was just explaining that she up and left without a word."

"It's true, me lord," nodded the woman. "I was that surprised, I can tell you, when I'd found she'd gone. Though who she could've found to take her to Launceston through all that snow I can't imagine."

"She went to Launceston?" Philip asked tensely. "Are you sure?"

"Well, we couldn't say for sure where she went. I told her there was no one we knowed who'd be fool enough to go off on an errand like that," Mrs. Fern explained.

Philip sank into the chair the innkeeper still held for him. The sense of anticipation which had buoyed up his spirits on the ride now evaporated, and he was left benumbed in mind and body. He shook his head and tried to think purposefully. "Are you sure it is Miss Pennington of whom you speak?" he asked.

"There was only one young lady came here last night. Must've been her."

"A slim, dark-haired lady with grey eyes?"

"That's the one," the innkeeper said with assurance.

"And you have no idea whom she may have hired to drive her to Launceston?"

"No, me lord, none. Why, if Sam'l wouldn't take her, there's no one within miles who would!"

"Samuel?" asked his lordship. "Who is he? Was he here last evening?"

"Comes in every evening, does Sam'l. Wouldn't surprise me none if he come in tonight! A bang-up driver is Sam'l, old as he is, and knows all the roads hereabouts."

"Did he talk to Miss Pennington? Are you sure he didn't take her to Launceston after all? Perhaps she persuaded him."

"Couldn't have. He was still here after the lady was gone. And as for talking, it ain't likely. It's hard to get a word out o' him. Just sits and drinks his brew, with hardly a word to anyone."

"I see. Nevertheless, I should like to question him. You say he may come in tonight?"

"Wouldn't surprise me a bit, me lord."

"Even in this weather?"

"He only lives a few steps down the lane. If you're wishful to see him, I'll bundle up and get him for you."

"Thank you, but if you give me his direction, I'll go myself," Philip said rising.

"I'll not hear of it, me lord," said Mrs. Fern in motherly solicitude. "Your coat is damp, your hair is wet, and look at those boots—soaked through they are! You'll not stir from this inn, if I've anything to say. You'll sit here while I get the fire going. A rum toddy and a bit o' food's what you need now."

"Be still, woman," muttered her husband. "Watch how you talk to his lordship! But there's good sense in what she says, me lord."

"Yes, there is. Thank you, ma'am. Well, then, Mr. Fern, if you'll bring your friend Samuel to me, I shall be most grateful."

At Gyllford, the Christmas dinner was promising to be an awkward occasion. The snow would keep the neighbors who usually gathered for the occasion close to their own firesides, making the meal almost a family affair. Clarissa knew that Philip's absence would be sorely felt, and the mystery of the diamonds and Evalyn's disappearance would hang like a cloud over the evening's proceedings. But one shining bit of joyous news would help her to face the dinner with a light heart—Philip was in love and, with any luck, would be married soon. She knew she should not mention the business to a soul, but she longed to share the news with Gervaise. As Christmas afternoon wore on, she felt she must find him and tell him, or she would burst. Edward and Martha had gone to the nursery to play with the twins and their new Christmas toys; Reggie and Marianne were playing billiards with Sally and Jamie. Clarissa had a good idea where Gervaise was to be found.

She peeped into the library. There he was in a wing chair before the fire, a handkerchief spread over his face, fast asleep. With a sigh of frustration, she turned to let herself quietly out of the room, too shy to wake him up with such news. But just as she put her hand on the knob, he stirred.

"Hmm? Wha'? Who is it?" he mumbled, pulling his handkerchief from his face and blinking.

"I'm sorry to have disturbed you, Gervaise dear. But I'm glad you woke up. I . . . I've been dying to tell you something that I think will please you enormously."

Gervaise had been about to yawn, but the expression on her face caught his interest completely and brought him fully awake. "Well, then, no need to apologize. Sit here and tell me at once."

"I know I shouldn't be telling you about it as yet. It's all so indefinite. Besides, I'm sure Philip would not want me to reveal . . ." And her voice trailed off guiltily.

Gervaise looked at her askance. "If it is something which Philip would not want you to tell me, then by all means don't. It's not like you, Clarissa, to want to betray a confidence."

"Oh, pooh. Don't moralize at me, Gervaise. I've always confided in you, as you well know. It wouldn't be the first time I've told you something I shouldn't. It's probably very wrong of me to talk about this, but it is such good news, and you deserve to know it, if anyone does."

"Well, you've thoroughly aroused my curiosity. I

would no more stop you now than I would forego the plum pudding tonight, though both indulgences will weigh heavily on my conscience. So proceed with your news, my girl, and don't keep me waiting any longer."

"Oh, Gervaise," Clarissa cried, released by his words from her guilt and flinging her arms about his neck, "Philip is in love! With any luck at all, he will soon be married!"

Gervaise, who had never, in the many years he had known her, taken Clarissa in his arms, was for a moment so stupefied that he let his arms remain limply in his lap. Then, as the awareness slowly came over him that his dream of many years was coming true—that it was truly Clarissa who had embraced him so impetuously—he put his arms around her and held her close. "Oh, my dear," he whispered, "is it really happening? Are you to be mine at last?"

Clarissa, suddenly becoming aware of the impropriety of her behavior, reluctantly withdrew from his embrace. Smiling shyly, she said, "I think so, Gervaise. If all goes well with Philip's romance, I see no reason why we can't be married. . ." She flicked a glance at his face, the color rising in her own, as she added, ". . . soon."

Before she could resist, she was swept into another embrace, and it was some minutes before a sense of the proprieties was awakened in either of them. Finally, Clarissa murmured, "Oh, Gervaise, no. Someone may come in. We must be careful not to set tongues wagging yet awhile. Philip is not yet able to give us any assurances. . . ."

Gervaise chuckled. "Miss Pennington is leading him a merry dance, eh?"

Clarissa stared. "Gervaise! How did you guess—?"

"I have eyes, m'dear, I have eyes. There's not much I miss. I've known for days that he was taken with her tail-over-top. And she with him, if I'm any judge of women. I hope you're pleased with his choice, for two people more suited to each other I never did see, despite the fact that she's so young."

"I'm more than pleased. I quite loved her like a sister before I ever dreamed she might turn out to be one."

"Then we've nothing to worry about," Gervaise chortled.

"Don't fly into the boughs too soon," Clarissa cautioned. "He's mishandled the whole matter—my fault, I'm afraid. I'll tell you the whole silly story one day. Now we must hope that he can find her and persuade her to forgive him."

"I refuse to be damped. Didn't Shakespeare say that love will find a way? Well, if he didn't he should have, for it will, nine times out of ten."

They left the library soon after, to find Nancy, Annette, and an under-footman waiting for Clarissa in the hallway. "Could we see you alone, ma'am?" Nancy asked, with a sidelong glance at Gervaise.

Gervaise bowed to Clarissa. "I'm off to dress for dinner, my dear. Can't tell you how I'm looking forward to the Christmas goose. Your cook has a way with them that is positively mouthwatering." And off he went with a little dance in his step that brought a sparkle to Clarissa's eyes as she watched him go.

The tale unfolded by the servants needed much repetition and amplification before its full import was clear to Clarissa. So overjoyed was she at the solution to the mystery of the diamonds and the realization that no one she cared for was involved in a theft that her disapproval of Joseph's and Annette's transgression in using a guest room as a rendezvous was softened.

"You've all behaved in a most irregular and reprehensible manner," she told them at the end of the interview, "and I fully expect that I shall never find you involved in such goings-on again! However, you have been a help to us in the end, so I shall let bygones be bygones."

It was clear to Clarissa that something would have to be done about Sally, and that the others would have to be told the truth, if only to clear the cloud of suspicion that hung over Evalyn. She looked at the trio standing ill at ease before her and said sternly, "I've been thinking that this is not quite the time to do anything about this matter. It is Christmas Day, after all. And tomorrow is Boxing Day, which I know you and the other servants have so been looking forward to. Nothing should disturb that day. Therefore, I would be obliged if nothing of this is said. I will take no action until the day after. In the meantime, I trust that I can rely on your discretion."

"Lord Gyllford already cautioned us, ma'am," Joseph said. "You can count on us to keep our lips shut."

The Christmas dinner turned out to be more delightful than Clarissa dared to expect. The evening started with Jamie's arrival at her bedroom door, stating his intention to escort his aunt to the drawing room. As they walked down the hallway, he asked if Philip had told her about their interview. She nodded and gave him an embarrassed apology. He teased her for being "goosish" and for thinking that he was ready to get himself "buckled" to any female. They laughed heartily over the whole silly pass. "But it shall all end well, when Father marries Miss Pennington in my place," Jamie said, expecting to give his aunt a pleasant shock. Her surprise, however, was only caused by his having guessed.

"How did you know?" she squeaked. "Did Philip tell you?"

"I guessed it, finally. I must have been a complete cawker not to have seen it before."

"I was worse!" Clarissa admitted. "I never guessed at all. Philip had to tell me himself!"

Their high spirits were evident from the moment they entered the drawing room, and Clarissa beamed at everyone so joyously and laughed at all the pleasantries so merrily that good will soon spread to everyone in the room. Only Sally felt uncomfortable. Not only was she bored to death with Philip absent, but Clarissa, who was spreading Christmas warmth everywhere in the room, seemed to turn cold every time she looked at Sally's face.

At the Bull, the fire was crackling in the grate, Philip had surrendered his coat to the ministrations of Mrs. Fern, and sat sipping his second toddy when Mr. Fern returned with Samuel. The taciturn old man stood before Philip and surveyed him with a complete lack of concern for Philip's elevated rank. Philip felt that the old, bird-like eyes were taking his measure, and he rose and shook Samuel's hand and thanked him for coming out on such a night.

"Tain't nothing," Sam'l said.

Philip urged him into a chair and the innkeeper gave him a tankard of ale. "I understand that a young lady asked you last night to drive her to Launceston," Philip began.

The old man nodded.

"Did she find someone else to take her?"

"No, sir," Sam'l said.

"Can you be sure?" Philip asked him urgently. "How else could she have left here?"

"In a carriage. A private carriage."

"Come on, Sam'l," the innkeeper said in annoyance, "where would she find a private carriage?"

"Came here last night, full o' little tykes. You gave 'em dinner, remember?" Sam'l said to the innkeeper in a tone of superiority. The old man's eyes gleamed with pleasure at having shown a better memory than the younger Mr. Fern.

"What's this?" asked Philip, leaning forward. "There was another party here last evening?"

"Well, yes," said Mrs. Fern. "A very big family, it was. They stopped here for a bite o' supper."

"But they bespoke the private parlor," Mr. Fern objected. "I don't think the young lady even saw 'em."

"She did, too," Sam'l said decisively. "Played with their little girl."

"Sam'l, you're an old fool. So what if she played with their brat," said the innkeeper. "She wouldn't go off with 'em. They was strangers. She was a lady. A lady wouldn't go off with strangers."

"Don't know if she was a lady," Sam'l said. "Don't know if they was strangers. She went off with them. Saw her."

"She went off in the carriage with this family?" Philip asked urgently. "Are you sure, man?"

Sam'l merely nodded. Philip turned to the innkeeper. "Did you get their name?"

"No, me lord, I never did. Did you, Mrs. Fern?"

"No. All I did was bring in a couple o' trays to 'em."

"But *you* know it, don't you, old man?" Philip said to Sam'l with a smile. "You don't miss very much, do you?"

"Didn't get their name, but I could find 'em, right enough," the old man said to Philip with a twinkle.

"How?"

"Can't live too far from here, or they wouldn't 've left so late in all that snow. The mother had red hair. The father called 'er his Irish puss. Someone around 'ere 'll know a big family like that with a red-headed Irish mother." And he lifted his tankard and took a deep draft, as if to recover from the effort of that long speech.

Philip grinned. "I knew I could count on you, old man. Come then, let's go and find them."

The old man cocked his head and eyed Philip with an expression that mixed amusement with disdain. "You young'uns are all alike," he cackled, "'specially when y're chasing a filly. Makes yer think-box stop working proper."

"Sam'l!" cautioned the innkeeper sharply. "Mind yer tongue."

"Philip ignored the interruption. "Are you saying

you don't want to help me find them?" he asked Sam'l bluntly.

"Not tonight I don't," Sam'l answered with equal bluntness. "Nor should *you* want to neither. We'd have to move about too slow in all this snow, and when you don't know where yer going, 'twould be plumb foolish. We'd never get there. Take the word of an old man, me lad, that y're stuck here 'til the snow stops, and that's a fact."

Philip went to the window and looked out. The lantern burning atop the post at the entrance to the inn showed the snow deepening steadily. In the light of the lantern he could see the large flakes swirling about in thick profusion. The sign of the Bull was completely whitened, and a high drift was already covering the lower half of the window from which he was looking. The old man was right, of course. It would be foolhardy to do anything but wait for the storm to pass. Even the gods seemed to be mocking him, for at that moment the force of the wind strengthened, its howl penetrating clearly through the panes and shaking them with unprecedented fury. When the gust died down, the snowflakes in the light of the lantern appeared to be falling in even greater concentration than they had before. To Philip it seemed that they would never stop.

CHAPTER TWENTY

Mr. Caldwell was the owner of a rambling country house halfway between Ashwater and Hatherleigh which he had inherited, along with a more than modest competency, from a childless uncle. The news of his inheritance came to him in his twenty-fifth year, when he had been living in London, struggling to make ends meet as the owner of a badly situated bookshop and tail-over-top in love with a red-headed young Irishwoman employed as a milliner in a shop down the street. As soon as he learned of his good fortune, he sold the shop, married the redhead and carried her off to a house in Devonshire which neither of them had ever seen.

The house had a good number of bedrooms, and the happy couple promptly proceeded to fill them up. The first-born was Charles, followed in a year by Catherine. Then came Sean, Mary, and Meggie in quick succession. After Meggie was born, there was a three-year hiatus, but at last, to everyone's delight, another little boy was born. He was named Michael, but thus far he was called "baby." Baby was a delight to the entire family and to the cook, the nurse, and the neighbors as well. Only Meggie, her nose out of joint because she had been replaced as the youngest of the household, regarded the infant with growing chagrin. She whined and nagged and wept and pouted, but baby would not go away.

This was only one of the problems encountered by the new governess on her arrival, late on Christmas eve, at the Caldwell home. The house was loosely run and carelessly cleaned. The children were disciplined mainly by pleadings or scoldings from their loving Mamma. Their father withdrew from household crises by riding off to the nearest public house. But the most severe problem facing Evalyn was the elderly woman affectionately called Nurse by everyone in the household. Nurse had taken one look at Evalyn and, contrary to the expectations of Mrs. Caldwell, had become as smitten by jealousy of the new governess as little Meggie was of the baby.

The four days following their arrival had not been easy ones for Evalyn. The baby's fever had risen alarmingly the first night, and Nurse would permit no one near the child but Mavis Caldwell and herself. She rejected out-of-hand any suggestion made by Evalyn for his care. Mavis, however, had instantly felt an affection for Evalyn, and as each day passed grew more and more to respect her good sense and rely on her judgment. By tactfully consulting Evalyn when Nurse was not present, Mavis managed to pull her baby through.

Evalyn was in some ways glad that her position was so difficult and challenging. It left her little time to brood over the pain that hovered like a cloud at the back of her mind. The night of her arrival, after she had helped to put the over-tired, quarrelsome children to bed, she had found herself alone in a tiny bedroom under the eaves. The room was dusty and smelled stale with disuse, and it measured only six paces from the doorway to the opposite wall. She had surveyed the cheerless little window set in a deep dormer, the stained Holland bedcover and the smoking fireplace, and a recollection of the room in which she had slept the night before overwhelmed her. Memories and misgivings attacked her, and the realization that she had buried her tracks, that she had irrevocably turned her back on Gyllford Manor, and that she would never again lay eyes on Philip Everard suddenly became too much for her to bear. For the second time in her life, she gave way to her emotions and wept until sleep finally came. At dawn, she had looked at her face in the little mirror on the wall at the foot of her bed. The worn silvering of the glass had emphasized the look of weariness and pallor of her face. She knew that self-pity, even more than lack of sleep, had given her face that hollow look. Then and there she had made a vow to busy her mind with her work and avoid any situation which would encourage idle reflection. Mavis Caldwell had been a godsend to her, and, in gratitude, Evalyn would give to the Caldwells all her waking thoughts and energies.

Now, four days later, Evalyn was beginning to feel that her efforts in the Caldwell establishment were having an effect. Charlie and Cathy, the oldest children, were starting to take seriously the course of study she had laid out for them. Sean and Mary were becoming less quarrelsome. And Meggie, who had adored Evalyn from the first moment at the inn, followed her about the house contentedly, the mended doll dangling from her left hand and her right thumb in her mouth.

The snow had stopped the day after Christmas, but the sun had not made an appearance until today. Evalyn, lifting her eyes from the history book she was reading to the children, looked out of the schoolroom window to see an unfamiliar brightness in the sky. "Oh, look!" she exclaimed. "The sun's come out!"

The children ran to the window. The sun sparkling on the unmarked snow dazzled their eyes. The sight was overpoweringly inviting. Evalyn did not need much persuasion that an hour or two of play in the snow would be more beneficial to children who had been cooped up in the house for four days than the best of history books. In less than a quarter of an hour, five pairs of galoshes had been donned, five pairs of mittens had been fetched, and five throats had been securely bound with mufflers. The children ran outside with squeals of delight, Evalyn following behind.

They chose the expanse of space at the back of the house as the scene for their play, and their laughter covered the sound of a horse riding up to the front door. It was not until Evalyn heard Mavis calling her name from the kitchen window that she became aware that a visitor had arrived at the house.

"There's someone here to see ye, Evalyn," Mavis called with an air of suppressed excitement.. "Hurry inside! Charlie can take care of the children, can't ye, Charlie boy?"

Mavis shut the window before Evalyn could ask the identity of the visitor. Who it could be she could not imagine. The only possibility was that Mrs. Cald-well wanted to introduce her to a neighbor who had dropped in. Evalyn came in to find Mavis waiting for her. "Be quick, girl," she said breathlessly. "Here, ye'd best give me y'r cloak, I'm thinkin', and brush y'r hair back a bit, m'dear. Ye'll be wantin' to look y'r best." With that, she pushed Evalyn before her into the sitting room.

Mr. Caldwell stood at the fireplace, speaking with considerable deference to a gentleman seated with his back to the doorway. Mavis, entering behind Evalyn, clarioned eagerly, "Here she is!" And the visitor rose from his chair and turned. Evalyn, at the first glimpse of the tousled black hair shot with grey, began to tremble at the knees.

"Philip!" she gasped in unthinking gladness. Then her hand flew to her mouth. "Oh . . . I m-mean, Lord Gyllford," she added awkwardly.

Philip, who had been waiting for this moment with mounting tension, felt a burst of laughter break through the knot of nerves which had been tightening his chest. "How do you do, Miss Pennington?" he asked with an amused gleam in his eye.

Evalyn, searching his face with an eagerness born of four nights of trying to recapture just that look in her mind's eye, felt a surge of emotion, but whether it was joy or dismay she could not tell. In this small room he seemed taller and more imposing than she re-membered, and the look in his eyes was so warm and comforting that she would have liked nothing better than to cast herself in his arms and weep away the loneliness of the past four days on his shoulder. But the unexpectedness of his sudden appearance was quite as disturbing as it was miraculous. Why he had come was as much of a mystery as how he had man-aged it. "I never expected . . . that is, I cannot imagine how you f-found me!" she managed to say.

The smile faded from Philip's eyes. "I don't know why you imagined I would not!" he responded with some acerbity, his momentary amusement giving way to a feeling of resentment. He had waited for two days for the snow to cease, and it had taken two more days to find her. They had been dreadful, agonizing days. He had managed to endure them by dreaming of the moment of their reconciliation. But this scene was not being played at all as he had dreamed. He looked at her sternly. "Did you really think I . . . we . . . would let you run away—and in such a storm!—without attempting to assure ourselves of your safety?"

"I hoped my letter would relieve you of that obligation," Evalyn answered in distress.

"That hope was quite ill-judged," he said curtly. "All of us at Gyllford, the family, the staff, and the guests, have been concerned about your welfare."

"I'm very sorry to have c-caused so much trouble," Evalyn said in a voice which sounded suspiciously close to tears.

"And so you should be," Philip heard himself growl. He had heard the quiver in her voice, and he wanted nothing but to take her in his arms and soothe the hurt he knew they both suffered. But the vexation caused by the presence of two strangers watching them with rapt attention seemed to force him to react with a gruff coldness that was quite unlike him.

Evalyn heard only the bitterness of his tone, and the sound weakened the last of her self-control, already badly undermined by the shock of his presence. She turned her face away so that he might not see the tears which had begun to drip down her cheeks.

Mavis, who until this moment had only felt the excitement of entertaining a real earl in her own sitting room, suddenly realized that her dear Evalyn was under attack. She rushed to the girl's side and put a protective arm around Evalyn's shoulder. "So that's the way ye talk to this darlin' girl, is it? No wonder she ran away from ye!" she accused. "Ye must've treated her like a little slavey, I'm thinkin', to make her run away from a situation in a home such as y'rs. Sure, 'n' a body has a right to leave her employer if she's a mind to. Besides, she's employed by us, now, she is, and I'll not have 'er bullied!"

Philip reddened under the unexpected attack. "Bullied!" he retorted angrily. "Do you think I've scoured this countryside through wind and snow for four agonizing days because I wished to find and berate a recalcitrant *employee*?"

Evalyn lifted her head and stared at Philip dumbfounded. Had he truly been searching for her ever since her absence had been discovered? Mr. Caldwell, observing this unexpected scene from his place at the fire, blinked at Philip in confusion. "Are you saying, Lord Gyllford, that Miss Pennington was *not* in your employ?"

"She certainly was not," Philip answered shortly.

"I see," said Mr. Caldwell, reddening. He crossed the room to his wife. "I think, my dear, that this is something which does not concern us. It seems to be a private matter. We had best leave the room to Miss Pennington and her . . . guest."

Mavis looked at her husband questioningly. Then a glimmer of understanding lit her eyes and she glanced quickly from Evalyn to Philip and back again. Her eyebrows lifted. "Ooooh!" she said in a long breath. "Lord bless me soul! Aye, o' course, m'dear, we'll be goin'. There's . . . er . . . the tea things to see to, anyway." She smiled encouragingly at Evalyn, ignoring her husband's tug on her arm. "Please make y'rself at home, me lord," she said with another quick glance at Philip. She permitted her husband to lead her to the doorway, but there she stopped and turned again to his lordship, resisting Mr. Caldwell's persistent tug. "Sure'n' we hope, Lord Gyllford, that after you and Evalyn have . . . er . . . finished . . . that ye'll stay to tea." And her embarrassed husband pulled her from the room and shut the door.

Philip's eyes had not wavered from Evalyn's downcast face. Mavis's lengthy exit had given him time to regret the testiness which had so upset the usually calm Miss Pennington. For a long moment neither of them moved. Then Philip went to her and lifted her chin. "What a clodpole I am!" he said regretfully, as he wiped her cheeks with his handkerchief. "The last thing I wanted was to make you cry."

Evalyn forced a small smile. "You could not know I would behave so foolishly. Once I told you I never cried."

"So you did," Philip agreed gently and led her to the sofa, drawing her down beside him. "Only an ogre could cause the redoubtable Miss Pennington to cry. I should be horeswhipped for speaking to you so harshly. Please forgive me."

She shook her head. "No, there's nothing to forgive. It's I who . . . I never dreamed you would go to the trouble of finding me. I cannot fathom why you should have done so, or how you managed it."

"I've already explained the why. You underestimate the esteem in which you are held at Gyllford. As to the how, I encountered a very clever and observant old fellow at the Bull by the name of Samuel who had seen you leave in the carriage of a red-headed Irish lady with a large brood of children. Such a personage is bound to be noticed, and it was not long before we were able to ascertain her identity."

Evalyn lowered her head in shame. "I cannot apologize enough for causing you this trouble, my lord. Will you please tell Lady Steele and everyone at Gyllford how sorry I am to have created such a turmoil?"

"You must come back with me and tell them yourself."

She lifted her head and gave him a baffled look. "Why do you ask me to come back, sir? There is no need for it, surely, now that you see me satisfactorily established."

"You're quite wrong," Philip said in a low voice. "There is a great need for it."

"I don't understand. What need?"

"My need," he said simply. Evalyn's pulse, which had quieted somewhat since he'd seated her on the sofa, started to race again. His meaning could not be what it seemed. She waited wordlessly, her eyes fixed on his, for him to explain himself.

He saw the confusion in her eyes and got to his feet. Now that the moment had come—the moment for which he had waited since Jamie's disclosure—his courage failed him. What was he doing, he asked himself, forcing his attentions on this lovely young woman half his age? She had just declared that she was satisfactorily established. She obviously wanted nothing further from him. He had convinced himself that she cared for him, but on what evidence? Merely on a look—the look on her face that day in the snow. On that flimsy foundation he had built his castle of dreams, and now the whole cloudy structure seemed to be evaporating.

He went to the fireplace and leaned on the mantle. What should he say to her now? Could he bring himself to leave her here in this place, to struggle to raise a large brood of children not her own? Even if she would not marry him, he had to find some way to take care of her, to help her to find a better life than she would find buried away here, an outsider in someone else's family. But he could think of no other way. "You say you are satisfactorily established here," he said in a constricted voice, his eyes on the fire in the grate. "Does that mean you find these surroundings more to your liking than at Gyllford?"

"How can you ask such a thing, my lord? The days I spent at Gyllford were the happiest in my life," she answered earnestly.

"Then why won't you come back?"

"You are more than kind to ask me, but you know I can not. My time there was an interlude, a time of . . . unreality. But sooner or later, reality must be faced. In this case sooner than we expected. But it has not turned out so badly. Even Clarissa could not have found me a better mistress than Mrs. Caldwell."

"Clarissa didn't intend to find you a mistress at all!" Philip muttered bitterly.

"Why, what do you mean?"

"We were a pair of fools, my sister and I," Philip said, turning from the fire and giving her a strained smile. "We thought Jamie had brought you home to make you his bride."

"His *bride*?" Evalyn asked in bewilderment. "*Me*? How could you have believed something so ridiculous?"

"Don't ask me to explain the whole silly coil that led us to jump to that conclusion, but the idea is not at all ridiculous. I only hope the girl Jamie eventually does marry is half so suitable."

"What nonsense," Evalyn said, brushing aside the idea with a wave of her hand. "We both know quite well how unsuitable I am."

Philip glowered at her. "If it is the 'difference in your stations' to which you are referring—a subject which I thought we had long since repudiated—I shall wring your neck!"

Evalyn gave a short laugh. "Well, wring away," she said challengingly, "for although *you* may have repudiated it, I never did. Besides, you must have seen that Jamie did not regard me in any light but as a sort of . . . maiden aunt."

"No, you're out there," Philip said with a sudden grin. "He regards you more as a mother."

"A mother? Whatever are you talking about?"

Philip's smile faded and he turned back to stare into the fire. "It was just a silly joke, I suppose. You see, when Jamie told me that you and he had no plans for marriage, I asked him if he'd mind if *I* married you."

Evalyn stared at him. "If *you* m-married me?" Her cheeks paled and her eyes fell to her hands clenched in her lap. "Oh. Yes, I see. It *was* a silly joke."

Philip spun around. "No, no! I didn't mean it that

way! It wasn't a joke then," he said, agonized. How could he explain what he'd meant? How had he gotten himself so hopelessly muddled? He strode over to the sofa, sat down, and grasped her hands. "Oh, Evalyn, I love you so, and I'm saying it so badly!"

Evalyn felt her heart lurch inside her. "Wh-what did you say?" she asked in a breathless whisper.

"My darling, please say you'll marry me. I wouldn't ask it of you if I thought that this course you've embarked upon would lead to a life of fulfillment or contentment. But to remain here, out of the way of society or the chance of change, raising the children of strangers—no matter how kind they are to you—seems to me to be a life of loneliness and drudgery. Surely a life with me—a man who loves you, who offers you the prospect of children of your own, even though he is twice your age—*must* be a more preferable prospect!"

"Philip, you *fool*! How could you think that your *age* has any—? I wouldn't care if—! Oh, I don't know what I'm saying. Surely you must have guessed . . . have seen that I love you!" she said in a voice that wavered between laughter and tears.

For a moment he seemed not to have understood. Then the misery in his face vanished, and he pulled her to him and held her close. She buried her face in his shoulder and gave a shivery sigh. For a long while she held her breath, not wishing to miss a single one of the endearments he was murmuring into her hair. "Oh, my dear," she said at last, "you *know* you cannot marry me."

He released her and held her at arm's length. "I know nothing of the sort," he said with a grin. "You've said you love me, and there is no possible way you can cry off now. I intend to marry you as soon as I can arrange it. But at this moment, there is something else I'm going to do, something I've been wanting to do ever since that terrible day when I so foolishly interrupted myself." And taking her in his arms again, he kissed her with all the fervor which the long post-ponement had built up in him.

Some time later, he reluctantly released her. "And now, my girl, I think we had better face the Cald-wells and tell them that I'm removing you from their midst as soon as you can gather your belongings."

"Oh, Philip, how can I? I have been with them only four days. How can I leave them so abruptly?"

"You can and you must, for I don't intend to be with-out you for another day!"

"But Mavis has begun to rely on me, and the chil-dren—such adorable little things they are—will be upset, and . . ."

Philip eyed her with a wicked gleam. "Surely Mrs. Caldwell cannot expect to have a countess serving as governess to her offspring, no matter how adorable they may be."

Evalyn looked at him aghast. "A countess! Oh, Philip, I couldn't—!"

Philip laughed and took her in his arms again. "I won't hear another one of your objections, my girl. You are going to be the most beautiful countess in all of Britain. You'll find it quite easy—much easier than being a governess—and I promise you shall enjoy it enormously," he said, kissing her so ardently that her objections were swept away with her breath. "Now, go and tell your Mavis that you are leaving within the hour, and that I shall send her the most good-natured and efficient governess I can find to replace you."

"Oh, Philip, what a wonderful idea," Evalyn said in happy breathlessness. "May I indeed tell her that?"

"Yes, my darling, of course. But you must in all honesty admit to her that I cannot promise to find one as redoubtable as the one she is about to lose."

New year's day had come and gone, but the guests, with one exception, still lingered at Gyllford, enjoy-ing lazy days near the fire, brisk walks through the winter landscape, and convivial evenings in the company of beloved friends. The exception was Sally Trevelyan who, upon learning from Clarissa that she had been observed removing the earrings from her jewel case herself, ordered Annette to pack her things immediately. Annette then announced that she was to be wed shortly to the very man who had inadvertently spied on her and would therefore be unable to accompany Ma'm'selle back to London.

Clarissa had made it clear to Sally that in all fairness to Miss Pennington—who she hoped would be returning to Gyllford shortly—she would have to tell the other guests the truth about the earrings. Therefore Sally was forced to take her leave of Gyllford without a single person present to wish her a good journey and no one in attendance except a coachman and footman who had been pressed reluctantly into her temporary service.

Evalyn and Philip returned to the warmest of receptions, and a spirit of rejoicing filled the house. Philip's announcement of their wedding plans was greeted with more delight than surprise. In this small, intimate circle of well-wishers, Evalyn was able to adjust to her new, elevated position with a minimum of awkwardness and embarrassment, and although Philip had to tease her from time to time about her tendency to remain "determinedly poor," she found it quite easy to bear being coddled, admired and adored.

A small family wedding was planned for the middle of January, and the Covingtons decided to remain for the occasion. Gervaise, who intended to follow Philip's example and lead Clarissa to the altar a fortnight thereafter, also stayed fixed at Gyllford. Reggie, who hoped to become so firmly entrenched in Marianne's affections that her come-out in June would have no adverse effect on their romance, seized the opportunity to remain at her side and also declared his intention of being present at both of the wedding ceremonies in the offing.

Thus it was that a bored and frustrated Jamie wandered through the house one January afternoon, looking for some companionship or activity. A look into the library revealed a contented-looking Clarissa bending over her Gervaise, who was showing her some pictures of the proper attire for the groom at a country wedding as illustrated in *The Gentleman's Magazine*. A search on the grounds revealed his father and Evalyn setting off for a walk, their arms encircling each other's waists. Edward and Martha were settled in the drawing room, he with a book and she with some embroidery destined for Marianne's trousseau. Finally, he found Reggie and Marianne sitting across from one another at the table in the breakfast room, gazing fixedly into each other's eyes, their hands stretched out toward each other and meeting in the center of the table in a loving clasp.

Jamie groaned. "Confound it," he said disgustedly, "this is getting worse and worse. Nothing but lovers wherever one looks! What am *I* to do, I ask you, while everyone in the house is behaving in this buffle-headed way? Do you two intend to spend the whole afternoon doing nothing but staring at each other like a couple of moonlings? Honestly, if I didn't have to stay for father's wedding, I'd take off for London this very afternoon! Do you know what I'm beginning to think? I hate to say this about my own home, but I think this place is becoming a worse bore than even the Carberys'!"

Marianne and Reggie had become accustomed to Jamie's tirades and had not really listened to a word he'd said. However, Marianne became aware of the silence that followed Jamie's outcry and felt that some response was expected. She sighed and—her eyes never leaving Reggie's face—offered her usual, all-purpose reply. "Oh, do you really think so?" she murmured softly.

Dell's Delightful
Candlelight Romances

The irresistible love story
with a happy ending.

THE
PROMISE

A novel by
DANIELLE STEEL

Based on a screenplay by
GARRY MICHAEL WHITE

After an automobile accident which left Nancy McAllister's
beautiful face a tragic ruin, she accepted the money for plastic
surgery from her lover's mother on one condition: that she never
contact Michael again. She didn't know Michael would be told
that she was dead.

Four years later, Michael met a lovely woman whose face he
didn't recognize, and wondered why she hated him with such
intensity . . .

A Dell Book $1.95

REMEMBER IT DOESN'T GROW ON TREES

**ENERGY CONSERVATION -
IT'S YOUR CHANCE TO SAVE, AMERICA**

Department of Energy, Washington, D.C.